By A. Lee Martinez

MONSTER

a Novel

CRYPTOBIOLOGICAL CONTAINMENT AND RESCUE SERVICES

Est. 1977

A. LEE MARTINEZ

orbit

www.orbitbooks.net

New York   London

Orbit
Hachette Book Group
237 Park Avenue, New York, NY 10017
Visit our Web site at www.HachetteBookGroup.com

First Edition: May 2009

Orbit is an imprint of Hachette Book Group. The Orbit name and logo are trademarks of Little, Brown Book Group Limited.

Library of Congress Cataloging-in-Publication Data

Martinez, A. Lee.
    Monster / A. Lee Martinez. — 1st ed.
        p. cm.
    ISBN 978-0-316-04126-3
    1. Monsters — Fiction.   I. Title.
    PS3613.A78638M66 2009
        813'.6 — dc22   2008042328

10 9 8 7 6 5 4 3 2 1

RRD-IN

Printed in the United States of America

*Six books. It never stops being weird. How the hell did
I get here? Damned if I know. There are a lot of
people who deserve to be thanked, but I hate long
dedications/acknowledgments. You didn't buy this book to
read about me. So I'll skip the long list of thank-yous and
just get on with it. If you're not on this list, feel free to use a
pen and add a line for yourself. I don't mind. Really.*

*To Mom and the many fine writers of the DFW Writers'
Workshop. I may be smart, talented, incredibly cool,
and surprisingly humble, but I still couldn't have
done this without you.*

*To the people who keep paying good money to read my books.
You keep shelling out the cash, I'll keep writing 'em.*

And to Henchman 24. You will be missed.

The thing was big and white and hairy, and it was eating all the ice cream in the walk-in freezer. Four dozen chewed-up empty cartons testified that it had already devoured half of the inventory and it wasn't full yet.

From the safety of the doorway, Judy watched it stuff an entire carton of Choc-O-Chiptastic Fudge into its mouth with a slurp. The creature turned its head slightly and sniffed. It had vaguely human features, except its face was blue and its nostrils and mouth impossibly huge. It fixed a cobalt eye on her and snorted.

Judy beat a hasty retreat and walked to the produce aisle, where Dave was stocking lettuce.

"I thought I asked you to stock the ice cream," he said.

"No need," she said. "Yeti is eating it all."

He raised his head. "What?"

"Maybe not all of it," she said. "Doesn't seem to like the vanilla."

"What?"

Dave wasn't the brightest of guys, and the staffing shortage at the Food Plus Mart and the extra hours he'd been putting in had taken their toll. The poor guy got maybe three hours of sleep a night, nine dollars an hour, and two days of paid vacation a year, but it was all worth it to work in the glamorous world of supermarket management, she assumed.

"It's a yeti," she said. "Big hairy thing. Belongs in the Himalayas. Except it's in your freezer, and it's eating the ice cream."

"What?"

She sighed. "Just go look for yourself, Dave. I'll handle the lettuce."

Dave trudged toward the freezer and returned.

"There's a yeti in the freezer," he observed.

"Mmm-hmm."

Dave joined her in piling on lettuce. They moved on to bananas, then grapes. He checked the freezer again.

"Is it still there?" she asked.

"Yeah. Now it's eating the frozen chicken dinners." He rubbed his fat chin. "What should we do?"

"Don't ask me," she said. "You're the manager."

Dave scratched his head. He was obviously having trouble forming a coherent thought. Judy took pity on him.

"Isn't there a book of emergency phone numbers, Dave?"

"Yeah." He yawned. "But I don't think it has anything about yetis in it."

"Have you checked?"

"Uh, no."

"It's in the office, right?" she asked.

He nodded.

"Oh, Christ, Dave. Just give me the keys to the office already."

4

On the way to the office, she passed the freezer. The yeti was making a mess, and she'd probably be the one who'd have to clean it up. She didn't mind. She needed the overtime.

The emergency phone number book was a spiral notebook with a picture of a happy snowman on its cover. She sat in the creaky chair, propped her feet on the desk, and thumbed through the book. It wasn't arranged in any particular order, but she wasn't in a hurry. Fifteen minutes later, she decided on the only possibly appropriate number, picked up the phone, and dialed.

The Animal Control line was automated. A pre-recorded voice informed her of the hours of normal operation, and she was unsurprised to discover that three in the morning wasn't among them. She almost hung up, but it was a choice between listening to a recording or starting on the canned goods aisle, so it really wasn't any choice at all.

After two minutes of interminable droning that Judy only half listened to, the voice instructed, "If this is an emergency, please press one now."

She did.

The phone started ringing. She counted twenty-five before she distracted herself with an impromptu drum solo using the desktop, a pen, and a pencil. She was just settling into her beat when someone answered the other line.

"Animal Control Services. Please state the nature of your emergency."

"Yeah, uh, I know this is going to sound kind of weird, but we've got, uh, like a yeti or something, I guess, in our store." She winced. She should've just said they had a big rabid dog. They might've believed her then. "I know how that sounds, but this is not a prank, I swear."

"Please hold."

Judy waited for the click and dial tone to replace the steady buzz in the earpiece. It didn't come. The clock on the wall ticked off the seconds. Maybe they were tracing the call right now and dispatching a squad car to arrest her. Or at the very least, give her a stern talking-to. Well, let them. When the cops got here, she'd just show them the yeti and it would become their problem.

"Cryptobiological Containment and Rescue Services. Can I have your name, please?" The woman sounded supremely disinterested.

Judy hesitated, but she figured it didn't make much difference at this point. "Judy Hines."

"And you believe you have a yeti in your freezer — is that correct?"

The words were beginning to lose their absurdity.

"Yes, I think so," she said, though she wasn't as certain as she had been five minutes before.

"Can you describe it?"

"It's big and white and eating all the ice cream," she said.

"What flavor?"

"What?"

"What flavor does it seem to prefer? Yetis generally go for rocky road. Now wendigos, on the other hand, prefer strawberry in my experience."

"What's a wendigo?" Judy asked.

"Like a yeti, except meaner."

Judy considered that this woman might be screwing with her. If Judy were working a lonely job in the middle of the night and got a crank caller, she'd probably do the same.

"It didn't seem to like vanilla." There was an awkward pause. "I am not making this up."

"Just stay out of its way. We've dispatched an agent. He should be there in fifteen minutes."

"I didn't tell you the address."

"We trace the emergency calls." The operator hung up.

Satisfied she'd done her job, she went to the front of the store. She shouted, "They're sending a guy, so I'll go wait for him and take a smoke break while I'm at it, Dave!" There was no indication he'd heard her, but he'd figure it out.

The night was cool, and she wished she'd thought to grab her sweater. It wasn't cold enough to bother going back. She sat on the coin-operated rocket, lit a cig, and waited.

She wondered about the yeti. It didn't make much sense for a mythical monster from the Himalayas to be in the Food Plus Mart freezer. She hoped the guy the city sent would know how to handle this. She doubted that pole with the loop of rope would be up to the task.

A white van pulled into the parking lot. The plain black stenciled letters on its side read MONSTER'S CRYPTOBIOLOGICAL RESCUE. The vehicle rolled lazily into a parking spot in the middle of the lot, though there were plenty of closer spaces available. A man in cargo pants and a T-shirt stepped out of it. The dim lot lighting kept him an indistinct blur as, whistling the theme to *Star Trek*, he went to the back of his van and retrieved something. He didn't look like much, and as he walked closer, he looked like even less. He was tall and lanky, with a narrow face. His hair and skin were blue. The hair was a tangled mess and could've passed reasonably for seaweed. He carried a baseball bat over his shoulder.

She didn't comment on his blueness. Like the inexplicable appearance of the yeti, it didn't seem odd. Like encountering an elephant at the beach or meeting an Aborigine at the mall.

She wouldn't expect it, but she wouldn't classify it as bizarre as much as unexpected. Her lack of a strong reaction struck her as stranger than anything else. But Judy made an art out of indifference, so she just chalked it up to not caring.

"Are you the guy?" she asked. "The guy the city sent?"

"I'm the guy. Are you the one who called?"

She nodded.

"Let's have a look, then."

Judy stabbed out her cigarette. "I don't think that baseball bat is going to do much against this thing."

"Lady, I don't recall asking you what you thought. How about I leave the delicate art of stacking canned goods in decorative pyramids to you, and you leave the yeti wrangling to me?" He snorted. "That is, if it even is a yeti."

He gestured toward the door and smiled thinly. "After you."

Judy flicked her cig into the ash can and led him to the freezer.

The yeti was still there. It'd done away with most of the inventory and was content to just sit on its big hairy ass and digest its meal.

"Yup. Yeti," said the guy.

"Told you."

"Good for you."

"How the hell did a yeti get in our freezer?" she asked.

"Tibetans make a pretty penny selling the young ones as pets. Then they grow up, and the next thing you know, some asshole drives them to a strange part of town and unloads them."

Judy frowned. "That stinks."

"What are you going to do? People are shit."

This was a philosophy that Judy shared, so she didn't argue. It did stimulate some empathy for the yeti, though, looking very much like a big fluffy teddy bear except for the claws and teeth.

"You aren't going to hurt it, are you?"

"I'm paid to bring them in alive." He pinned the bat under his arm and pulled out a small book from his back pocket. He flipped through the pages, nodded to himself, and with a marker drew a few strange marks along the bat.

"What are you doing?" she asked.

He glanced up with annoyance but didn't explain. The blue-skinned guy went into the freezer. He wasn't being sneaky. Just walked up to the yeti and smacked it on the back of its head with the bat. It wasn't a hard blow, but it seemed to do the job. The yeti's eyes fluttered and it fell over, unconscious.

The guy kissed his bat, took out his marker, and started drawing on the freezer floor. He drew a circle around the unconscious creature, and, after consulting with his pocket guidebook again, began drawing strange letters around its edges.

"What are you doing now?" she asked.

"You wouldn't understand it."

"Try me."

"Unless you've got a certified degree in runic studies with a minor in cryptobiology from the Greater New Jersey Community Collegius Arcanus, just leave me alone and let me take care of this."

He moved around the circle, drawing strange symbols. It took three minutes, and when he finished, he stepped back as the yeti disappeared in a flash. When the spots cleared from Judy's eyes, the yeti was gone. There was a small, fluffy rock in its place. The weird writing drifted off the floor and faded like smoke.

"What did you do to it?" she asked.

"Don't worry your pretty little head." He scooped the stone up and stuck it in his pocket. "Just transmogrified it for easy transport."

"So that's it?"

"That's it. Now if you could just accompany me to my van and sign some paperwork, I'll be on my way."

They started back.

"That was easy," she said. "I thought it'd be a lot harder than that."

"That's why they pay me the big bucks."

They were halfway down the stationery aisle when a tremendous clatter and crash echoed through the store.

"Is there anyone else in the store?" he asked.

"Just Dave."

Something roared.

"Another one?" she asked.

He pulled a small square of paper from his pocket. It had a lot of those weird not-quite-letters written on it. The paper folded itself into an origami hummingbird.

"Chester, recon," commanded the blue guy.

"I'm on it," said the bird, and it soared over the aisles on paper wings before quickly returning. "We've got a yeti in the canned goods aisle."

The bang of a shelf of Chef Boyardee brand beef ravioli being tossed to the floor made Judy wince. It depressed her to realize that she'd been working at the Food Plus Mart long enough to identify the brand and product solely by the sound. Spaghetti-Os had a tinnier echo, and green beans were more muffled.

"Shit—I just stocked that aisle."

The blue guy and Judy investigated canned goods. The yeti's cheeks bulged as it stuffed pasta, cans and all, into its maw. It was a hell of a mess. This creature was bigger than the last.

"This shouldn't be a problem," said the guy. "I can handle this."

Something growled behind them. Judy whirled and came

face-to-face with yet another yeti. This one bared its teeth at her and snarled. Its bloodshot eyes bore into her, freezing her in place. It knocked her aside with a glancing blow and seized the blue guy. He struggled, but the yeti lifted him to its jaws and swallowed his head. The guy flailed and twitched as the creature ambled away, sucking on him like a lollipop.

She didn't hear the man scream. Either he was dead already or his shrieks of pain were being muffled by a throat full of his own blood. The yeti stopped at the far end of the aisle and spit the man out. It hunched over him, growling and clawing. Scraps of cloth flew in the air, but the creature's body blocked Judy's view of the carnage.

"Oh, shit. Oh, shit." Judy froze, repeating the chant over and over.

A curious grunt came from the canned goods aisle. The second yeti's claws clicked on the tile as it drew closer. It snorted and sniffed.

She bolted for the front doors. They were only a dozen or so steps away, and the lumbering yetis didn't seem very fast. A can of peas rolled underfoot, causing her to fall. She struck her head on the discarded baseball bat and it rolled noisily across the floor.

The second yeti roared as it advanced on her. "Oh, shit, oh, shit!"

She'd always known Food Plus Mart was a dead-end job. She just hadn't expected to reach the end so soon.

The paper bird, now folded into a large vulture shape, fluttered in the creature's face. "Run, miss! I can't distract it for—"

The yeti grabbed the bird and threw it to the floor. The beast stomped on the paper several times.

Judy snatched up the baseball bat and clutched it in two

tight fists. The Animal Control guy had used it to knock out the other yeti. She figured she'd only get one shot so she had to make it count.

The yeti pounced.

She brought the bat up hard and smashed it across the jaw. There was an explosion of force. The yeti was blown back down the aisle. It flew fifty feet, landing with a thud beside the third yeti, the one mauling the Animal Control agent. The struck yeti stayed down, but the last one turned away from its victim and howled.

The strange writing on the bat glowed brighter. The weapon quivered in her grip. It was only a bat and the yeti was a hulking brute, but she felt invincible with it.

"Come on," she whispered through clenched teeth. "Nobody messes with my canned goods aisle, you son of a—"

The abominable snowman charged forward. Its feral roar dissolved her sense of power. Yelping, she pitched the bat at it. The weapon sailed through the air and struck the yeti right between the eyes.

The bat exploded in a crack of thunder. Splinters of wood flew like shrapnel, slicing her face and arms. A sizable chunk collided above her right eye, knocking her to the floor. Everything went hazy as she struggled to stay conscious for a few seconds.

"Miss? Miss?" Her vision cleared enough to make out the four-foot paper man standing over her. "Are you okay, miss?"

She sat up, and the sudden rush almost made her throw up.

"Don't try to stand. That's a nasty bruise on your head."

The yeti was dead. Its head was gone, blown to oblivion. There wasn't even any blood or brains left. Just a smoking crater. She glanced down at the chunk of scorched wood that had dented her skull.

The blue guy was beside her. "Are you okay, lady?"

"She might need medical treatment," said Chester.

She struggled to speak.

"She'll be okay," the guy said. "Chester, get the healing elixir from the van. The one in the yellow bottle. That'll fix her up."

"Sure thing, boss." The paper man folded himself into his hummingbird shape and flew away.

"But...but..." Judy covered her eyes as she assembled the thought piece by piece. "But that yeti mauled you."

He helped her up, keeping her steady. Her vision cleared. The guy's clothes were ripped, but there wasn't a mark on him. Not so much as a scratch.

"Why aren't you dead?"

"I'm blue."

Judy leaned on the guy to keep from falling over. "Huh?"

"I'm invulnerable to violent harm when I'm blue."

Maybe it was her spinning head or the way that he said it so matter-of-factly, but it made sense to her.

A vaguely Dave-ish blur appeared at the end of the aisle. "What the hell happened?"

"It's okay, Dave," she said. "We took care of it. Me and this guy the city sent. Uh, what's your name?"

"Monster," said the blue guy.

"Of course it is. Well, Monster, I really have to sit down before I puke, which I really don't think you want to happen. Unless you're also immune to dry-cleaning bills while you're blue."

They went over to checkout and found a stool for her. She leaned against the counter and closed her eyes.

"Shit," said Monster. "You killed one."

She opened one eye. "It was going to eat me."

"A dead yeti is hardly worth hauling in for alchemical harvesting," he said. "Thanks a lot."

"Sorry," said Judy, but she really didn't mean it.

The paper man returned and handed Judy a plastic bottle. "Drink this, miss. It'll help you feel better."

She took the squeeze bottle and squirted some in her mouth. "Ugh. This tastes like crap."

"That's the manticore bladder," said Monster. "But without it, a healing elixir isn't much more effective than a sports drink. So deal with it."

Judy grumbled, but her head did feel better. She slurped another mouthful.

Dave's exhaustion dulled him, and so when he shook his head and muttered to himself, Judy knew he was pissed. His store was a mess, and there was no way they'd get everything fixed before the next shift.

Monster said, "Soooo, what do we got here? Two healthy yetis..." He glared pointedly at Judy. "And one dead one."

She half scowled, half smiled. "It was going to eat me."

"Mmm-hmm."

"Screw the overtime," she said. "Dave, I'm going home."

He mumbled his approval. Or disapproval. Or indifference. Regardless of the exact sentiment, she was out of there.

Chester said, "Miss, we'll need you to sign some forms."

"Whatever. Just make it quick."

"I left the forms in the van, Chester," said Monster.

Rather than wait for Chester to go retrieve the paperwork, Judy followed him into the parking lot. While he rummaged around in the back of the van, she lit a cigarette.

"So how did that guy do that?" she asked. "Make that yeti into a stone and have the baseball bat explode?"

"I'd like to explain it to you, but I really don't understand the magic of this lower universe myself. Even if I could, you'd just forget it."

"I nearly got killed tonight. That kind of makes an impression on a girl."

"Oh, you'll sort of remember it, but you'll soon find the details a bit…fuzzy."

"Wait a minute. You're calling me a muggle, aren't you?"

Chester jumped out of the van with a clipboard. "That's not an officially recognized term."

She snatched the papers.

"I'm not a dumbass muggle."

"Whatever you say, miss. Though only muggles use the word *muggle*." His paper head had no mouth to smile with, but she sensed his condescending grin. She was tempted to flick her cigarette at him.

"There. All signed. Can I go now?"

"Certainly, miss. Have a pleasant night."

She tossed him the clipboard and headed toward her car. "And tell your boss he's lucky I don't sue his ass for giving me an exploding baseball bat."

Judy didn't see how she could ever forget this, and her contrary nature made her even more determined not to.

By the time she'd gotten home, she'd forgotten that vow.

Since dead things couldn't be transmogrified, Monster had to lug the yeti corpse back to his van. He slapped a few gravity-defying Post-it note runes onto the carcass to make it easier. Still, he found it annoying, especially since there wasn't quite enough room for a full-grown yeti in his van. He'd known that but decided to give it a try. Now the carcass's wide shoulders were caught on the shelves and cabinets that filled the interior, and its lower half hung out.

"Come on, Chester," he grunted. "Are you pulling?"

Chester spoke from somewhere on the other side of the corpse. "I'm not exactly the strongest paper gnome in the business. Maybe we should just call Hardy. He's got a pickup."

"Screw that. I'm not giving him a cut of my commission." Monster planted his hands on the yeti's ass cheeks and pushed. It slid in a little farther. A shelf tipped. Its contents spilled. Most of the forms fell in the interior, and a few plastic bottles with elixirs and potions bounced around.

"Stupid girl."

"Perhaps it's not my place to say," called Chester, "but she is a civilian. Under the circumstances, she behaved admirably."

"Shut up, Chester."

"Yes, boss."

Monster took a minute to catch his breath. It was too bad he wasn't superstrong green today. Would've made things a lot easier.

"So should I radio for Hardy yet?" asked Chester. "Or should I wait until the specimen is good and wedged?"

"Sarcasm doesn't become you."

"To be technical, I was being facetious, not sarcastic."

Monster wasn't really sure what *facetious* meant. The gnome had a bigger vocabulary than he did, and it bugged him. Not enough for Monster to actually try to improve his word power, but just enough to irritate. Kind of like a pebble in his shoe that moved around so that he felt it only once every dozen steps or so. Annoying, but not quite enough to induce him to unlace his sneakers and fish it out.

"Call Hardy," he said.

"You got it."

Monster sat on the wedge of fender not blocked by yeti hips. He reached into his pocket for a cigarette. Then he remembered he didn't smoke anymore, and even if he did, his shirt pocket had been ripped to shreds by his earlier mauling.

Chester appeared. The paper gnome held up a one-inch doll that chimed steadily. "You missed a call."

Monster took the doll, set it on the fender, and searched his pocket again for cigarettes that he knew weren't there. "Got any smokes?"

"Sorry. Fire and paper gnomes don't mix." Chester folded himself into a parrot and settled on Monster's shoulder. "Dispatch says Hardy is on the way."

Monster made a neutral gruntish kind of noise.

The doll continued to chime.

"If you're not going to check your messages, you could at least turn that thing off," said Chester.

"Can't turn it off," said Monster. "Only way to get it to shut up is to listen to the message."

The doll grew more insistent in its chiming.

"I don't know why you don't just get a cell phone," said Chester. "At least those can be set on Silent."

"Don't want a cell phone."

He didn't want a nagging doll either, but Liz had insisted. She'd said the doll was more reliable, and it didn't have to be recharged. The truth was that it was a lot harder to ignore the doll than a cell. The chiming would just get louder and louder and louder. Now that the doll knew he knew about the message, it would be even worse. It would also report his slow response time back to Liz.

The doll's chime changed to a shrill hiss. It was getting impatient.

"All right, already. Give me the damn message."

Liz's voice issued from the doll. "Hey, this is Liz. Call me."

"Thanks," said Monster. "Glad I didn't miss that one."

The doll hummed. "Hey, this is Liz. Call me."

"I got it."

"Call me."

"I heard you the first time."

"Call me."

Monster snatched up the doll. "Listen, you stupid little bastard, I got the message already! Shut the hell up!" He hurled it across the parking lot. The doll jumped to its feet and jogged back over.

"Wouldn't it just be easier to call her back?" asked Chester.

"Maybe."

Monster raised his foot and prepared to stomp the stuffing out of the doll, but he came to his senses at the last moment. Destroying the doll would release the minor devil contained within. Although it couldn't do more than one small malicious act before returning to the underworld, it could still be a pain in the ass. Last time he'd lost control and destroyed one of Liz's dolls, he'd gotten a boil on his nose. And the one before that had taken all the fizz out of his sodas for a solid month.

Of course, minor devils lived for stuff like that. It was the whole reason they allowed themselves to be bound. Inevitably, they'd be released to pull one of their malevolent pranks. For a devil, spending a thousand years in mortal servitude was always worth it if it got to eventually inflict someone with a case of sonic flatulence for a day. Nasty little bastards, and Liz loved them.

That should've been his first clue.

No, he corrected. Summoning a girlfriend from the Pits, that should've been his first clue.

The doll chimed in hopes of irritating Monster to destroy it, but he set aside his foot. "Nice try. Just connect me with Liz."

The doll rang three times. "Hi, this is Liz. I'm not here right now, but please leave a message after the beep."

Monster declined to leave a message. He snarled at the doll. "You knew she wasn't going to answer, didn't you?"

The doll shrugged. He picked it up and stuffed it deep into his pocket.

Twenty minutes later, a lime green pickup pulled into the lot and came to a screeching halt beside Monster's van. A large man, not exactly fat but tall, wide-framed, and doughy, got out. He wore a jumpsuit the same shade of green as his pickup. Other than his largeness there wasn't much about Hardy to notice except the full set of ram horns curling around his skull. Hardy claimed to be part demon, but it seemed unlikely. A lot of folks claimed to be part demon, but a lot of people claimed to have known Merlin too.

Monster nodded at Hardy. Hardy nodded back. They said nothing else as they worked together to extract the yeti from the van and load it onto the pickup.

"I want forty percent," said Hardy.

"Forty? Shit, I captured the damn thing. All you have to do is deliver it."

"Forty percent. And I'm doing you a favor. Alchemical harvest for a dead yeti won't even pay for my gas. The most valuable parts are the tongue, eyes, and fangs, and those are missing. You aren't holding out on me, are you?"

"Come on, Hardy. Look at it. The head got blown to bits."

"So no teeth?"

"I checked. They must've been disintegrated in the blast."

"What the hell happened, anyway?"

"A civilian got in the middle of things and misused a pacification rune." Monster patted the yeti. "The pelt is used in some cryo preservation enchantments. That's worth something, isn't it?"

"Maybe ten years ago. Forty. Take it or leave it."

"Fine."

"Great. Let me just go get the paperwork." Hardy fumbled around in the cab of his pickup. Monster thought he saw a bulge just above Hardy's ass, the telltale sign of a goat tail. It was far likelier Hardy was half satyr than part demon.

Monster pulled the doll from his pocket and tossed it under the pickup's rear tire.

Hardy lumbered over. He wasn't that fat and so there really was no reason for him to lumber that Monster could see. Unless

Hardy was trying to squeeze some hooves into size-ten sneakers. With a smug grin, he handed over the forms, and Monster signed them.

"You drive a hard bargain, Hardy."

"Just trying to make a living. You understand."

Monster climbed into his van and drove a safe distance from the doll while Hardy started his pickup. The vehicle pulled forward, squishing the doll. The devil's revenge was swift as all four tires blew out at once and steam exploded from under the pickup's hood. The engine sputtered to a halt.

Monster waved to Hardy and pulled into the street.

"Little much, wasn't that?" asked Chester.

"Hey, I owed him one. Last week he sprayed my underwear with chupacabra pheromones, remember?"

"And two weeks before that you replaced all his grimoires with Dr. Seuss books, if I recall correctly."

"Only because he phoned in that false gryphon call to keep me from scoring that cockatrice bag."

"And, if I remember correctly, a month before that, you—"

"Hey, I owed him one for the pheromones, and that's that."

"I suppose it would be a waste to remind you of the dangerously cyclical nature of these kinds of feuds."

Monster pulled the three yeti fangs he'd managed to scavenge from the Food Plus Mart and stuck them in the ashtray, smiling. "You suppose right. Not least because I don't know what the hell *cyclical* means."

Three scores in one call was an unexpected windfall. He wondered if the Food Plus Mart might be a hot spot. A change in architecture or street names could create an imbalance in the flow of magic, but usually the Bureau of Geomancy was on top of that sort of thing. He decided it must've been a fluke. Even in the world of magic, shit just happened sometimes.

Half past six in the morning, he decided to call it a night. One of the advantages of being his own boss. He had enough cash in his pocket and figured he'd wait to drop his bags in the afternoon. For now, he was just tired and ready to get some sleep.

It wouldn't be as simple as that. Liz would be waiting. She was always waiting. But it was either go home, sleep in his van, or get a motel room. His back was achy, and even fleabag motels cost money that he'd rather not spend.

He parked the van outside the house and sat there for a while, just looking at it. The lights were on. Liz didn't sleep. Demons didn't need to, and Liz was all demon, dragged up from the Pits. He'd dragged her up himself.

Demons were like people. They came in a lot of varieties. Though they were always evil or self-serving or, at the very least, obnoxious, they weren't all the same. On the surface Liz was warm, intelligent, and charismatic. She was also part succubus and had the perfect body to show for it. There were a lot of good things about having a succubus for a girlfriend. She cooked. She cleaned. She had a job at Sin Central Incorporated that brought in more money than he made, and she never bugged him about playing too many video games. And there was all the sex too.

But there was a real downside to having a succubus for a girlfriend. Little things such as spitting fire, superhuman strength, that slight brimstone scent that no amount of air freshener could ever quite mask no matter how many gallons of aerosol artificial pine stench she sprayed over everything. And there was all the sex too.

"If you hate coming home so much," said Chester, "why don't you just break up with her?"

He'd tried once. There were still scorch marks on the ceiling, and he'd had to buy a new television after she'd melted the old one. She hadn't hurt him. She never would, though she could've killed him easily enough. In her own way, she loved him, and he cared for her too. They just weren't a good couple.

But they were stuck with each other. He kept her out of the Pits, and she kept from tearing him to pieces as per the scorned woman clause of their contract. He reminded himself that should he ever find a way to escape this relationship, he would never again answer a personal ad in the *Weekly Underworlder*.

"See you tomorrow, boss."

Chester folded himself into a palm-size square. Monster stuck the paper in his pocket and went inside.

Liz was sitting on the couch. She didn't look up as he entered, just kept reading her *Cosmo*.

"Hey," he said.

"Hey," she replied. "How was work?"

He grunted.

"I made some spaghetti, if you're hungry."

He grabbed a plate and sat beside her. Liz didn't have horns, bat wings, or a tail, but her skin had a deep red tint, and her lips, eyelids, and hair were jet black. She looked like a sunburned Native American goth woman. Her tendency to wear clothing and accessories with flowers and butterflies usually added a touch of hippie to the mix, but today she was wearing one of his old T-shirts and nothing else. Fifteen months ago, he would've found the sharp hint of her nipples against the cotton and her naked perfect legs to be enticing. Now all he could think was that she was getting the scent of brimstone all over another one of his shirts.

She did it on purpose. She was slowly odorizing his wardrobe, marking her territory.

23

"What happened to you?" she asked.

"Yeti," he replied through a mouthful of spaghetti.

She nodded to herself, thumbing through the magazine.

He finished his dinner in silence. Then he tried to slip off to bed unmolested, but when he came out of the bathroom in his pajamas, she was waiting for him. There was a time when the promise of her carnal pleasures would've filled him with glee. Back then she would've been naked and oiled up and ready for action. Now she was still wearing his T-shirt and reading her magazine.

Liz's succubus nature meant that regular sex was necessary to keep her from getting cranky, but that didn't mean she necessarily enjoyed it. There were plenty of times when she wasn't interested in it except as a bit of exercise. And those times were more and more common lately. Maybe he wasn't a great lover, but she could've had the decency to fake some passion. Hell, she was a succubus. Wasn't that her job?

He went to the bed and lay down beside her.

"I don't really feel like it tonight, baby," he said.

She arched an eyebrow. "Oh, come on. It never takes long."

He was too tired to be insulted.

"Our contract specifically says intimate relations are to be supplied on a daily basis."

Monster didn't need to be reminded. When he'd signed the contract, he'd found special promise in that particular clause. He'd assumed it was meant to bind *her*. Now he knew better.

"I don't know if I can even —"

It was a weak attempt. Among Liz's supernatural talents was the ability to give a man an erection by her willpower alone. He could've been strapped to a bed of nails while mongooses chewed on his face. It wouldn't have made a difference. All she had to do was wave her index finger in a small circle and upward motion toward his groin and he would snap to attention.

Liz pulled his pajama bottoms down to his ankles without ceremony and climbed atop him. He made a halfhearted attempt to fondle her breasts but didn't even have the motivation to reach under the T-shirt. She kept reading her magazine the whole time. Monster occupied himself by scanning the articles titles on the cover. He was guessing she hadn't gotten to "Old Flames: Keeping the Spark" yet.

When she was finished, she got up and left the bedroom without so much as a "Thanks." Monster pulled his pajamas up and covered his head as the dawn light filtered through the curtains.

3

The red cat was at their door again.

Rob didn't like cats. He didn't hate them. He just didn't see why people kept them around. He also had the same puzzlement over dogs, snakes, hamsters, fish, and children. Spouses occupied a sort of subcategorization in his universe. Sometimes useful, but mostly a bother.

Over thirty years, Rob and Evelyn had developed an encyclopedia of unspoken communication. It was through this vast network of signals that their marriage endured — thrived — in a comforting familiarity and reassuring silences. The system had worked because they'd both come to conclusion that they really didn't like each other. The truth was that neither of them was very likable. They could be pleasant, polite, helpful. But they weren't charismatic or endearing, and a divorce and new marriage would only lead to the same place they were already at.

Everything had been going swimmingly these last twenty-seven years. Then the old lady had moved in next door, and now Evelyn spent three or four hours a day staring at cats, yammering about cats.

"It's out there again," she whispered. "It's sitting on the porch."

Rob sighed. "It's just a cat." While he had no use for cats, these particular felines, while numerous, weren't generally much of a nuisance. Once in a while, one of the little beasts might start howling in the middle of the night, but it was far less frequent and disturbing than the parties thrown by the swingers across the street.

"Have you ever taken a look at them?" asked Evelyn. "I mean *really* taken a look at them."

"They're cats. What's to see?"

"Their eyes. There's something wrong with their eyes." She peeked out the front-door window at the cat sitting on the porch. "And their shadows aren't right either."

"Jeezus, Evelyn. How much time do you spend watching those things?"

"And don't you ever notice that, except for this one, they always stay in her yard?" she said. "There's always ten or twenty out there, but they never get outside the fence."

"Who's complaining?" he replied. "She's got them trained."

"You can't train a cat to stay in a yard. It can't be done."

"Obviously, it can."

"Something destroyed my rosebushes. Explain that."

"I don't know," he said. "Raccoon, maybe?"

"Raccoons don't burn down rosebushes," she said.

"Burned? You think cats set fire to your rosebushes?"

"Not cats. Cat. *That* cat! Just look at it. It knows I know, and it's rubbing my nose in it."

Rob was beginning to doubt that spouses belonged in that subcategory after all. But at least her inexplicable paranoia gave him a reason to look forward to work. Eight blissful hours of middle management drudgery seemed almost like paradise compared to listening to Evelyn ramble on about her furry arch-nemesis.

He started to open the front door, but she slapped away his hand. "For God's sake, Rob, use the back door. It's out there."

"Oh, for cryin' out loud." He pushed her aside and opened the door.

The cat stood and stretched. It glanced at Rob and Evelyn but didn't seem very interested in either of them.

Evelyn hid halfway behind the door and a few steps away from the threshold. "If you were any kind of man, you'd confront her. Tell her that we know what she's up to."

"You aren't serious. You want me to go and yell at an old lady who has never done anything to us except have a cat that likes to sit on our porch?"

"And burns down rosebushes," she added. "And I think the beast ate the Newtons' dog. The one that disappeared a week ago."

"The Saint Bernard?"

She nodded.

The cat raised its head and licked its lips in a manner that even Rob had to admit looked very satisfied.

Evelyn moved a few steps back.

"Oh, for the love of Pete," said Rob. "Look, if I take the cat back where it belongs and tell them that we'd prefer they keep it inside, would that make you happy?"

He really didn't care if it made her happy, but he was hoping it might make her shut up. All he'd ever asked of her was a certain degree of bland agreeableness. It seemed ridiculous that one cat should destroy that. If it meant yelling at an old lady to restore her sanity and his peace, then he was perfectly willing to do so.

She smiled. Her smile always struck him as forced and counterproductive, more disturbing than reassuring. His smile was even worse, but at least he had the good sense to use it only on special occasions. He never inflicted it on his wife.

"Won't you?" she asked. "I can't stand the dreadful thing. If she could just keep it inside…"

Rob picked up the cat. It didn't try to run away. He didn't grab it by the back of the neck, but gently cradled it in his arms. This wasn't motivated by care or concern but by an awkwardness with touching living things. Whenever someone offered to let him hold their baby, which was thankfully a rare occurrence, he always excused himself to use the bathroom.

He strolled over to the neighbor's house, passing through the white picket fence around the neatly trimmed yard and colorful flower beds planted along the cobblestone path from the sidewalk to the door. The many cats on her lawn, at least a dozen, all raised their heads as he undid the latch and opened the gate.

The cat in his arms didn't squirm at all until he reached the quaint front door and knocked. Then it twisted loose and hit the porch. The cat waited patiently with Rob for the door to open.

He checked the time. He had another five minutes before rush hour really set in.

The door swung open and a tall young woman appeared. Her face was thin, and she didn't have much of a chest either. She made up for this with a nice figure and a pair of slender, athletic legs with just a hint of muscular power. Rob had always been a leg man, and he had a preference for brunettes. This woman's hair was long and shimmering, just the way he preferred.

"Oh, my — Pendragon," she said. "There you are! And who is this you've brought with you?"

The cat meowed once, then went inside without saying anything else.

"Wherever did you find him?" She smiled widely, displaying long white teeth that were just short of an overbite. They were not her best feature, but he was willing to overlook it.

"Your cat keeps —" he started.

"Pendragon," she corrected. "His name's Pendragon."

"Uh, yeah. Your cat, Pendragon, he keeps coming over to my house and bothering my wife."

"He has?" She gasped theatrically. "That's most distressing. Mrs. Lotus will be most upset with him. Come in, come in."

"I have to get to work."

"Oh, nonsense." The woman took his hand. "We must tell Mrs. Lotus. I'm sure she'll want to hear your story."

He started to protest, but he was at that point in his life at which two hours of traffic jam seemed a fair trade for five minutes of miniskirted legs. It wasn't as if anyone at the office would notice. The guy in the cubicle next to him still called him Ron. Rob might've been insulted except he'd never even bothered to learn the guy's name.

The young lady drew him inside and shut the door. There were a lot of cats. So many that they were perched on every piece of furniture and every other step of the staircase, under every table and in every corner. They were all quiet and none seemed very interested in him after an initial glance. Despite their overwhelming numbers, the house smelled of gingerbread and coffee.

"I don't believe we've been introduced," said the woman. "I'm Ed."

"Ed?" said Rob. "Is that short for something?"

30

"No, it's just Ed. Just a little joke, or so Mrs. Lotus told me. I don't get it myself, but I'm sure it's very funny." Ed laughed. It was rough and unladylike, and it ended with a snort.

"Rob," he said. "I'm Rob."

"What a pleasure to finally meet you."

"Do you live here?" he asked.

"Oh, yes. We all do. Mrs. Lotus has a weakness for strays."

She led him deeper into the house, past more cats and down a hallway.

"I've never seen you outside," he said.

"We're not usually allowed outside," she said. "Mrs. Lotus says that will change soon, but for now we're supposed to stay inside. That's why I'm sure she'll be ever so mad at Pendragon. He really should know better."

He wasn't sure what he'd stumbled into, but there was definitely something unwholesome going on in here. He didn't have the imagination to think of anything specific.

Ed led him into a cozy den decorated in shades of blue and suspiciously absent of cats. She guided him into a comfortable chair. "We were just about to have some tea. You must join us."

"I don't like tea," he said.

"Oh, but you'll love this. It's Mrs. Lotus's own special blend." She took the pot from the small table, poured a small cup, and handed it to him. "Just a sip."

She frowned. There was an ugly expression on her long face. Rob was more fixated on her legs as she uncrossed and crossed them. She poured herself a cup and offered a toast.

"To good neighbors."

He clinked his cup against hers and watched her slurp down her drink. Rob did the same. If he'd had just a bit more imagination he might've thought it was poisoned or laced with a

31

narcotic, but he wasn't really thinking about it. He tried not to think about most things, as the answers he reached were rarely comforting.

The tea tasted good. Very good. Like strawberries. He had another cup. Then another. Then two more. It filled his stomach with soft, comforting warmth.

Ed filled the room with small talk. He was only vaguely aware of it, but he nodded as if he were paying attention.

Pendragon walked into the room. The cat sat at Rob's feet. He meowed, and a small tongue of flame erupted from his throat.

Rob was taken aback, though he was feeling too good to make a big deal about it. "Did you see that?" he asked Ed.

"He has to do that sometimes. Set Mrs. Lotus's favorite tablecloth aflame the other day. Pendragon, you must be more careful."

"I guess Evelyn was right. The little bastard did burn down her rosebushes." Rob giggled. He felt better than he had in years. Better than he ever had in his entire life, which admittedly wasn't saying much.

Mrs. Lotus appeared in the doorway. He'd seen her a few times, even waved to her once or twice, but Rob had never seen her up close before. She was perhaps eighty, he guessed, and had long gray hair and wrinkles to show for it. Yet she was a striking woman, tall, lean, slight in frame yet powerful in presence. She wore a skirt that ended midthigh, and Rob noticed that her legs were impossibly long and well formed. They were the legs of a ballet dancer in her prime and didn't really fit on her.

"Hello," he said.

She didn't reply right away. Just nodded slightly to herself. And she didn't blink. Not once.

"Hello, Rob. So nice of you to join us."

"I know you'll be very happy here," said Ed. "Won't he, Mrs. Lotus?"

"Yes," said Mrs. Lotus. "Very happy."

"Happy," agreed Rob as he drifted off to sleep.

Lotus asked, "Now, Ed, what did I tell you about serving my special tea to uninvited guests?"

"Oh, I know, but he seemed so nice. And also, Pendragon invited him."

Lotus eyed the cat, who merely turned and sauntered out of the room without apology.

"I suppose there's no harm in it. I'll be back shortly, Ed. In the meantime, put our guest someplace more comfortable."

Ed eagerly picked up the cat snoozing comfortably in Rob's chair. "Where are you going?"

Lotus took the teapot in hand. "I'll be getting to know Rob's lovely wife over a cup of tea."

4

Monster's alarm went off, and the bright light filtering through the windows told him it was earlier than expected.

Without opening his eyes, he reached for it. His hand wrapped around the squealing doll. Another of Liz's damn devil dolls. He struggled to remember how to hit Snooze. He tugged on its arms and legs, but that didn't have any effect.

"You're supposed to be set for three," he grumbled. "It's not three, is it?"

The doll cut short its squeal. "At the sound of the beep, the time will be one minute after twelve in the afternoon." Its voice was loud and congenial with a hint of contempt, just like your average television announcer's.

The doll resumed squealing.

Monster tugged on all the limbs again and tried shaking it, but the doll continued. Fortunately, he was prepared. He rolled over and reached under the bed. He felt around in the junk under there and found a lockbox. He dropped the alarm doll

into the box and shut it. The squealing was not entirely damp-
ened, but it was muted. Monster had perfected this procedure
to the point that he could do it without ever opening his eyes or
having to wake fully. He rolled over and went back to sleep.

Or tried.

If the alarm was ringing at noon, then Liz must've reset it.
She must've had some errand she needed him to run.

"Screw that," he mumbled.

The doll continued its squeal of urgency. Despite his best
efforts, Monster couldn't overlook it.

"Goddamn."

Monster opened his eyes to discover he was purple today.
He couldn't remember the effect purple had on him, but he
did know he hated the color. He stretched out the kinks and
opened the lockbox. The squealing alarm doll sprang up.

Monster rubbed his heavy eyes and yawned. "What the hell
is it?"

The doll announced in Liz's damningly sweet voice, "Hey,
honey. Can you do me a favor and pick up the dry cleaning
today? Oh, and maybe get a few groceries before you have to
head off to work? There's a list on the fridge."

"Why can't she pick up her own stupid dry cleaning?"

The alarm doll only offered a sympathetic shrug.

Monster rose, took his shower, and ate some cold spaghetti
for breakfast. He found his color code book and looked up purple. There wasn't an entry. He'd never been purple. He hated
new colors. At least with the old ones, he knew what to expect.

Since he was up already, Monster decided to drop off his
scores. In addition to the yetis, he had eight other transmogrified cryptos that he hadn't cashed in yet. He stopped by the
Animal Control offices, gathered the stones in a sack, and
carried them inside.

He didn't use the front door. That only led to the cats and dogs section. He went around the side and down the alley into a small back door bearing the Cryptobiological Containment and Rescue Services logo, a muzzled dragon skull. The CCRS lobby was a drab gray room without furniture or decoration. The only door in or out was the one he'd used. There was a small plastic window where the payout clerk sat.

She wasn't sitting there now.

Monster pressed the buzzer beside the window, then paced the empty room a few times. The cameras mounted in the four corners of the ceiling followed him.

Monster pressed the buzzer again. He held the button down until the grinding hum of the device exhausted itself and sputtered to a halt.

The payout clerk appeared in a flash. It wasn't much of a flash. More of a pop, like a lightbulb burning out, accompanied by the smell of ozone, cigarette smoke, and too much cheap perfume.

"All right already," she said. "Jeezus—what do you want?"

Charlene was a fallen goddess, and the only remnants of her divine nature were her omnipresence and her third eye, accentuated by too much bright blue mascara and adorned with the cheapest false eyelashes available to woman or goddess.

"What took you so long?" he asked.

"Coffee break," she said. "Union rules."

Charlene's union was only her, but there was a lot of her to go around. She was the sole employee of the Department of Motor Vehicles, half the city's health inspectors, and had positions in several other departments. Monster was also pretty sure he'd heard her voice on the other end of a phone sex line one time, but he preferred not to dwell on that.

"What do you have?" she asked.

He emptied the sack and laid his collection in a row on the desk. She appraised the specimens, checked her computer, and prepared an offer. In the background, he heard the distant, ever-present sound of barking dogs and the screech of a green cockatrice. Something howled as if in terrible agony.

"Wraith," said Charlene. "Damn thing hasn't shut up since it was brought in."

"Isn't that a Spirit Supervision job?" asked Monster.

"Yeah, well, they're full up so they had to transfer it over here. Like we have the room for it."

She cut a check and handed it to him through the slot. "What about that dead yeti I turned in for alchemical processing last night?" he asked.

"It's in there," she said. "By the way, you're also getting three demerits on your license for that."

"What? But it wasn't my fault."

She fixed him with a vague stare that clearly indicated she couldn't care less.

"Yeah, yeah, whatever," he grumbled as he pocketed the check.

The loudspeaker in the corner near the ceiling blared with shrill static.

"Monster, we've got a call for you. If you want it."

It was Charlene's voice. One of her other selves was probably sitting in some office right now, staring at him on a grainy monitor. He glanced at the Charlene sitting at the payout window. She sucked on a cigarette, running a file across her nails and looking supremely bored.

"I don't work days," he said.

He glanced at Charlene to see if her lips moved as the loudspeaker voice replied, "One of my best day guys had a run-in with a gorgon. Until they de-petrify him, I'm shorthanded."

Monster hesitated. He still felt half-asleep, but he was here already. He might as well take the call, grab a few extra bucks.

"Sure."

"Great. We'll have Dispatch send you the details."

In his van, Monster woke Chester. The paper gnome didn't unfold all the way, only allowing his head to poke out of the square. "What time is it, boss?"

"Early. We've got a call."

Chester said, "I believe the terms of service were eight p.m. to six a.m. Three personal days a year, Hanukkah and Arbor Day off, and one floating holiday." He stretched. His body crinkled as the wrinkles smoothed out.

"Quit bitchin' and get the paperwork ready. If I've got to work, so do you."

Charlene came over the radio. She sounded a little more bored than usual, if that was possible, as she gave the details. Something small and hairy had popped up in a closet.

It took longer than it should've to reach the call. Monster wasn't accustomed to daytime traffic. He got stuck in a freeway jam, and it didn't improve his mood.

The Oak Pines apartment complex was a blankness that defied description. Four blocks of brick with eight apartments each. He parked his van and rummaged through the supplies in the back.

"That's odd," said Chester.

"Yeah." Monster found a five-by-five piece of cardboard. "What's that?"

"Trees can be either oaks or pines. I don't think they can be both."

"Fascinating." Monster gathered half a dozen markers of

assorted colors and stuck them in his pocket. "I'll be sure to notify the management."

Someone pounded on the van's back door. Monster threw it open and stepped out to confront an angry apartment manager. He leveled a finger at Monster and snarled.

"You can't park here. Residents only."

Monster glanced around. There were plenty of spaces available.

"The city sent me," he said.

The manager glowered suspiciously. "I didn't call the city."

Chester said, "Excuse me, sir, but we've been called about a possible closet infestation in apartment twelve. Possibly a troll or a wodwose."

Like any incognizant, the manager refused to acknowledge that he was talking to a paper man. Monster sometimes wondered how that worked, how the incogs perceived the universe. Did the manager substitute an easier image, like making Chester into a really short, very thin guy? Or did he just glance over the details and not even bother subconsciously making excuses? Even the cognizant weren't sure how it worked—not exactly. It was like trying to imagine how a bat used sonar to see the world. The result was easy to observe. The wiring wasn't. It wasn't really important to know, but Monster couldn't help but be curious sometimes.

However the manager justified or ignored it, he snatched the paperwork from Chester and spent a minute fuming over it. It satisfied him without lessening his unpleasantness.

He showed them to an apartment. He grew grumpier with every step, which was saying a lot. By the time he knocked on the door, he was a tense knot of awkward rage.

"I knew she had a pet in there," he said to Monster.

A young woman opened the door. The same young woman

from the Food Plus Mart. Her gaze lingered on Monster with vague recollection.

"These people are from the city." The manager jerked his thumb at Monster. "And they say you have some kind of illegal pet in there."

"Actually, sir, we believe it's more of an unwelcome pest," Chester tried correcting. "Miss Hines did call us, after all."

The man either didn't hear or ignored it. "You're not allowed pets."

Monster and Chester slipped into the apartment, but Judy blocked the doorway to prevent the manager from entering. They started arguing, though Monster deliberately avoided listening. He went to the kitchenette and helped himself to a glass of water, waiting for the discussion to end. The finish came when Judy abruptly slammed the door in the guy's face.

She fixed Monster with a curious look. "Don't I know you?"

"Last night," he replied. "You killed my yeti."

Slowly, realization dawned in her face. "Yeah, the abominable snowman. That's right." She frowned. "You're the guy with the paper man."

"Paper gnome," corrected Chester. "The guy with the paper gnome."

Judy squinted up at the ceiling. "I'd forgotten all about that. How could that happen?"

"It's the haze," said Chester. "Most human minds cannot process magic into their conscious long-term memory. It has to do with a nerve cluster at the base of the—"

"It doesn't really matter," interrupted Monster. "There's no point in explaining it because you'll just forget it all once we're gone. Where's the bogey?"

She led him to her bedroom and pointed to her closet. She'd jammed a chair under the knob to keep the thing contained.

"It's in there. I woke up this afternoon, and there it was. In my closet. Thought something had died in there at first. Because of that odor."

The moist odor of fresh crap and decaying flesh hung in the bedroom air. She pinched her nose. "Is it supposed to smell like that?"

Monster sniffed. "I don't smell anything."

"How can you not smell that?" She suppressed a gag. "Like wet burning dog hair covered in Tabasco sauce."

Nodding, Monster removed his color code book from his pocket and scrawled *Purple: Can't smell*. It would explain why Liz's leftover spaghetti had tasted so bland this morning.

"Can you describe it, miss?" asked Chester.

"I really didn't see it very well. Kind of looked like a monkey, but with a big head and covered in green hair."

"Troll," said Monster. "No big deal. We'll grab some stuff out of the van and —"

The closet crypto pounded against the door. Stubby, clawed fingertips felt along under the doorjamb.

"It's not going to get out, is it?" Judy asked.

"Trolls prefer the dark. I'll just get some bait and take care of this."

Chester went to fetch the bait while Monster laid down the piece of cardboard and began drawing his magic circle on it, checking his rune dictionary occasionally.

"You're purple," she said.

"I am?" He made a show of looking at his hand. "Wow, thanks for letting me know."

"Weren't you blue yesterday?" She dragged the reluctant memory to the surface. "Yeah, you were blue. So why are you purple today?"

"It changes whenever I wake up."

41

If there was any further explanation, he didn't offer it to her, and she was less concerned with the colors than the creature in her closet.

"Is this normal?" she asked. "I mean, this kind of thing with the sasquatches—"

"Yetis."

"Yeah, that. And now this thing in my closet. Is that normal?"

"Nothing's normal," said Monster. "*Normalcy* is just a word people made up."

"Says the purple guy," replied Judy.

Chester reappeared with a bag of jelly beans. Monster laid his magic circle next to the closet, poured a few jelly beans on the cardboard, and removed the chair from the door.

"Give it a minute," said Monster.

The closet door opened and a long crooked nose protruded from it. The large, dripping nostrils flared as the nose sniffed curiously.

Monster tossed a jelly bean beside the closet. It landed far enough away that the troll had to stretch out its arm to reach for it. The limb was even more crooked than the nose, and the fingers were thick and wart-covered. The troll snatched up the candy, shut the closet, and slurped it down noisily.

The door opened again and the troll's arm protruded farther, probing for more candy.

"Come on, you little bastard," said Monster. "I don't have all day."

The troll stumbled into the light.

Judy grimaced. "God, it's ugly."

The beast looked like a chimpanzee with a rat's face. Its entire body was bent and strangely shaped. Its torso appeared about three inches misaligned with its pelvis. Both its arms were twisted, but the right arm was significantly longer than the left. And its mouth was wide enough to nearly split its head open.

The troll pounced on the jelly beans, shoving them down its mouth. The magic circle beneath it flashed, and the crypto was transmogrified into a small green lump.

"Works like a charm."

"Uh, boss," said Chester. "Looks like we've got another one."

A new troll loped forward from the back of the closet. It was a little bigger than the last one. Its nose twitched, and its beady eyes darted around the room. This one didn't smell any better either.

"I got it." Chester poured some more jelly beans on the circle. The troll quickly gobbled these down and was transmogrified in the process.

Monster said, "So I'll just take these off your hands and—"

Two more trolls ventured into the bedroom. One was hairless with a bulbous blue ass, and the other was lumpy and piglike. The trolls rushed Chester, who threw the candy at them and folded himself into a spider and started climbing up the wall. The trolls snarled and fought over the bag.

Growls and an overpowering stench came from the darkened closet.

Trolls of various shapes, sizes, and colors began to fill the bedroom. A few wandered over Monster's magic circle and were transformed into harmless stones. But the circle's power faded and at last was consumed, leaving a few dozen wandering around the room.

Something big and red struggled to stick its egg-shaped head out of the closet, but its ears were too large. Its massive fingers wrapped around the doorjamb as it struggled to push its way through.

"What the hell is that?" asked Monster.

"You mean you don't know?" said Judy.

"I believe it's a kojin," remarked Chester. "Although I've never heard of one outside of Asia."

The snarling kojin pushed against the frame. Meanwhile, trolls trickled between its ankles. They were groggy in the light of day and confused by the odd surroundings. Trolls ate anything. Or rather, trolls would try to eat anything. They chewed pillows, strewn clothes, the end table, and carpeting.

"Hey! Give me that!" Judy snatched a lamp from a troll's jaws. "That was my grandma's."

The troll snapped up the end of the power cord and slurped it down.

"Damn it."

The closet frame cracked as the kojin thrust several of its arms into the room. It looked to have at least twelve. It made a clumsy grab at Monster but couldn't quite reach.

"Time for Plan B, Chester," said Monster. "We're going to have to seal them in."

They exited the apartment. Monster fished around in his pocket and grabbed a red marker. He scrawled a quick containment rune on the door.

"But you can't just leave these things in there," said Judy. "What about my stuff?"

"Sorry, miss," said Chester. "But we're required to in the interest of public safety—"

"Get me another black marker from the van," said Monster. "Left the one I had on me in the apartment. Not sure how long a red seal will hold trolls in."

Chester folded into a falcon and soared off toward the van.

"These doors are made of particleboard," said Judy. "It won't hold anyway."

Something, many things, crashed inside the apartment. The moist troll scent filtered under the doorjamb.

Monster scrawled the last squiggle of the rune just in time as something heavy, probably the kojin, thudded against the door. Several cracks appeared, and the hinges broke off. The magic, and only the magic, kept the door in place.

"How does that work?" asked Judy.

"It just works."

The cryptos on the other side continued their thrashing against the door, inflicting a steady increase in cracks and dents.

"Shit. It's not going to hold," said Monster.

"What's going on here?" The manager stormed toward them. "What are you doing to my apartment?"

Judy grumbled. "Look, asshole. All my stuff is getting eaten by trolls. I don't really need to hear any crap from you."

"Situation's under control," said Monster. "I'm afraid we'll have to call in a cleanup team. It'll be inconvenient, but better than having to deal with a horde of skin-eating trolls."

"They eat skin?" asked Judy.

"Among other things."

"Oh, no," said the bald man. "No, no, no! You can't do this! Who do you think you are? You can't deface private property like this!"

"Relax," said Monster. "It's non-permanent."

Chester appeared with a handful of markers.

Monster grabbed a black one. "Took you long enough."

The manager grabbed Monster's wrist. "Nobody marks on my doors without explaining just what's going on —"

The door crumbled into pieces. Only a residual magic kept the trolls from stepping over the threshold. However, it didn't stop the kojin from reaching out and seizing the manager by the head. His muffled scream was mercifully ended by a crushing squeeze. His body went limp and he was yanked inside to be devoured.

"Crap." Monster thought of the demerits he'd get for that.

The trolls were too distracted by their meal to notice that the seal had faded. Monster retreated to his van. Judy and Chester followed.

"Oh my God," said Judy. "They're going to eat everybody."

"It's not as bad as all that, miss," said Chester. "Even trolls don't enjoy the company of other trolls. They'll disperse instinctively and go into hiding from the daylight."

While Monster radioed in a report to Dispatch, trolls filtered from Judy's apartment into the parking lot. They were a rainbow of colors, and all different shapes. The stench was overwhelming. Judy pinched her nose. It didn't help. The odor burned her eyes, and she could taste it.

Out in the open, the creatures became less aggressive. They scampered in all directions, confused and blinded by daylight. They seemed lost now. Hideous as they were, Judy felt sorry for them as they ran about erratically. They darted into the streets, hid in darkened corners, or sought shelter under parked cars.

"Poor things," she said. "They must be terrified."

Her apartment burst open as the kojin managed to break free. There didn't seem enough room on its shoulders for its multitude of arms. The kojin had a tremendous belly and pendulous breasts. It looked as if the beast, with its staggering weight, had to struggle not to fall flat on its face with each step.

It paused to rub its eyes, but the sunlight didn't bother it like it did the trolls. It scanned the parking lot with a horrible, hungry sneer. Then its gaze fell on Judy and Monster. It wiped the drool from its lips with the back of one giant hand and lurched toward them.

"Oh, crap," said Monster.

Monster, Chester, and Judy jumped into the van.

"If you sit in the back, Miss Hines, you should be safe while we deal with this. No need to worry. We are professionals." Chester retrieved the thick crypto reference guide from below the passenger seat and started flipping through it. "Kobold, koerakoonlased, koguhpuk...kojin—here it is."

The creature was beside the vehicle. It clutched the van in its many arms. The squeak of a hundred powerful fingertips crushing the chassis followed.

Monster started the van and pushed the accelerator, but the vehicle didn't move. Its tires spun against the pavement. Thick clouds of smoke filled the air. The kojin sneezed, and the tremors of its great belly rocked the van to one side. It hung there, balanced on its two passenger-side wheels, for a moment before tipping over. The windshield shattered. Judy bounced around in the back. She was buried under a few pounds of paperwork. Plastic elixir bottles buffeted her, and a metal case smacked her just above the eye.

The hacking kojin fanned the air with its many arms.

"Chester, where the hell are you?" asked Monster.

The flattened paper gnome's voice came out in a muffle from beneath Monster.

The giant sniffed around the edges of the van. It bit into a tire and the rubber blew up in its face. In retribution, it tore off the rear bumper, then flipped the van again, this time putting it on its roof. The same metal case struck Judy in the hip.

Monster, having fallen on his head, struggled to right himself. "Chester, I could use a little help here."

Chester managed to squirm out from underneath Monster. "We need the baby."

Monster crawled into the back, but the van's inventory was in disarray. Judy struggled to work free of the chaotic jumble. A small gash on her forehead was oozing blood into her eyes.

Monster dug through the clutter. He found the doll just as the kojin reached through the shattered windshield and seized him by the leg. He didn't even have time to yelp before being dragged from the van. The kojin held him aloft. Rivers of drool dripped from its wide jaws as it prepared to bite off Monster's face.

Monster held up the doll.

The kojin stopped. Its small black eyes narrowed as it grunted curiously.

Monster pulled the ring on the back, and the doll squeaked. "Ma-Ma."

The creature's eyes went wide with delight, and it cooed. Its coo was more of a rough snort, but there was no mistaking the joyous expression on its hideous face.

Monster threw the doll as far as he could. The kojin dropped him and stomped its way over to the baby. Blissfully it scooped up the doll in one of its dozen immense hands. It drew the baby close to its chest and sat down on a sports car, crushing it beneath its colossal butt cheeks.

"Damn." Monster surveyed his ruined van. "I just had twelve more payments to go."

Chester tiptoed his way through the safety glass sprinkled on the asphalt. "You okay, boss?"

"I'll live." He nodded to the kojin. "How long will that doll keep her distracted?"

"Hours. Maybe days."

Judy shouted from inside the van. "Could someone help me out here? I think I smell gasoline."

It took Monster and Chester a few minutes to wrench open the van's back door because the frame had been bent. After that, it was another minute to dig Judy out.

Meanwhile, the giant grunted a heartfelt rendition of "Rock-A-Bye, Baby."

5

Monster helped Judy to find a seat on a car hood a good distance from the van. He didn't see any leaking fluids, but with no sense of smell, he figured it was better to be cautious.

"I put a call in to the Arcane Commission," said Chester. "They're sending a team over."

With a piece of chalk in hand, Monster went over to the kojin. He had to transmogrify it now before the Reds arrived and sealed off the site, robbing him of his score. He drew a wide circle around the creature. The kojin was too busy rocking the toy baby in its arms to care.

Judy twisted her head to one side and pressed the short sleeve of her T-shirt against the cut on her forehead. It'd nearly stopped bleeding, but she applied pressure to stop the red trickle dripping into her eye. She asked Chester, "Why is it that whenever you guys show up I end up with a severe head injury?"

"Our sincerest apologies, Miss Hines. Cryptobiological handling is an inexact science." He held up a clipboard. "We'll need you to sign some paperwork. Strictly standard procedure—"

"No way. I'm not signing anything. Not until I see a lawyer." She glanced over at Monster, still working on his magic circle. "How does that work? Magic."

"It just works," said Chester. "There's really no secret to it. Anyone can do it with the proper training. Of course, doing it well is another matter."

Monster paused to check his pocket dictionary.

"Could I do it?" asked Judy.

Chester hopped up beside her on the hood. "You could learn, but you couldn't remember for long. There's a nerve cluster in the human brain called Merlin's lobe. It has to do with magic perception. In most humans, the lobe is underdeveloped, almost nonexistent. Those types, called incognizants, can't even acknowledge magic, even when it's right in front of them. They just don't recognize it.

"The second-largest group, say about twenty percent, have it developed enough that they can recognize magic when they see it but they can't really remember it very well once it's gone. They're light cognizants. Depending on how light, they might recall small details or none at all. Some light cogs have managed to learn some basic magic, but nothing spectacular or reliable."

Judy pulled her sleeve from her sticky, clotted wound. "Well, can't I learn to be more aware?"

"Perceiving magic isn't a skill. It's a physiological condition," said Chester. "Can a monkey learn to drive?"

She didn't like the comparison, but she got the idea.

Monster completed the necessary runes on the circle and stepped back. In a soft flash, the kojin was transmogrified from a ten-ton ogre to a twenty-pound stone.

"I could do that," said Judy. "How hard is it to draw a circle on the pavement?"

"It's harder than it looks," said Chester.

Most everyone in the apartments worked days, and while the cars in the nearby streets slowed down to gawk at the overturned van, they didn't seem interested in stopping. She wondered if it was because they didn't want anything to do with magic or if they just didn't want to get involved. She heard sirens, so someone must've called the cops.

She slid off the car hood.

"Maybe you should stay off your feet, Miss Hines. That's a nasty bump on the head."

Her legs were a little shaky, but she needed a smoke. She paused before the missing wall that served as the entrance to her ruined apartment. The troll odor wafted over her, but nicotine called.

Paulie appeared. She didn't know most of her neighbors, but Paulie was a fellow night-shifter, so they'd run into each other a few times. They'd slept together a half dozen times, when they'd both been in the right mood at the right time. He was a tall, blond Nordic god from the waist up with cartoonishly thin legs. He had a habit of walking around shirtless. It wasn't to show off his perfect chest, powerful shoulders, and chiseled abs. It was just because he didn't have any shirts. She'd checked his closet the last time she'd spent the day at his place.

"Hey, Jude."

He always greeted her the same way. She'd assumed it was a joke, but she'd tested him and was pretty sure he didn't know one damn thing about the Beatles.

"Whoa." Paulie pushed his long hair out of his eyes and sniffed. "Smells like trolls. Hey, was that a kojin?"

She nodded.

"Cool. You don't usually see them outside of Asia, y'know."

"Yeah. Cool. Got any smokes?"

"You mean, like, regular cigarettes, right?"

When Judy wasn't horny, there wasn't much to appreciate about Paulie. Realizing he was magically cognizant annoyed her too. Although it did explain the strange herbs, those odd books on his shelves, and his collection of faerie skulls. Damn it. Why hadn't she noticed that before?

She had. Many times, she realized. But always forgetting afterward. Even now, the observations were slippery, trying to get away from her. She knew that she would forget again as soon as she wasn't consciously thinking about them.

It sucked.

She held her breath and ventured into her apartment. It was in shambles. In the three minutes or so that the trolls had been trapped behind that door, they had gnawed and broken every stick of furniture. The carpet was torn to shreds, and chunks of drywall were missing. Translucent, slimy troll droppings covered the floors, walls, and ceilings. Judy stepped in something wet and sticky.

It was the remains of the apartment manager. There wasn't much left. Just a few bones, a red stain, and some pieces of meat that had gone uneaten. She very deliberately forced herself to not take pleasure in that. It wasn't easy. Even though he'd made her life hell for months, her moral side knew he didn't deserve to die, but her emotional core wasn't willing to cooperate. She compromised by feeling just a little good about it, then feeling guilty about feeling good.

She picked her way through the apartment to her bedroom. Along the way she had to take in a breath, and the stench nearly caused her to black out. She considered turning back, but she'd gone this far.

Her nightstand had been devoured, but by some gracious nicotine miracle, a pack of cigarettes had survived. They had some slime on them, but not enough to deter her. She exited the apartment and gasped for air.

"Hey, Jude," said Paulie. "Since you're up, maybe you wanna come over to my place and watch a movie?"

"No, thanks. I'm not really in the mood."

"Cool." He stuck his hands in his pockets and nodded. He stood there with a blank look on his face. He could stand like that for up to fifteen minutes at a time. She'd clocked him once.

The cops had arrived, but they weren't regular cops. Their cars and uniforms were red. There were two squad cars and four officers. Two were questioning Monster. A third was surveying the parking lot. The fourth approached Judy.

"The Reds. Damn." Paulie turned his back to the cop and whispered to Judy. "If they ask, you don't know nothing about that mandrake root I got in my closet. And I was holding it for a friend anyway."

"Yeah. Sure." She shook the slime off a cigarette (arbitrarily and very consciously deciding it was merely drool and not one of the many other possible bodily fluids a troll might excrete), stuck it in her mouth, and fished around for a match.

The cop in red did some quick gestures with her hand, and a tongue of fire danced on her fingertip. Judy used it to light her cig.

"Thanks."

"Those things will kill you, ma'am," said the cop.

"Thanks for the tip," Judy replied absently.

If the cop recognized the sarcasm, she failed to acknowledge it. She was a dark-haired giant with a muscular swagger and a scar on her lip. She reminded Judy of a less pretty, more realistic version of Wonder Woman. Judy studied the badge, a seven-pointed star wrapped in a hexagon, on the Amazon's chest. Her name tag read M. GOODDAY. The cop put her hands on her hips and pulled her wraparound sunglasses down to the end of her nose. One of her eyes was ice blue. The other was a solid scarlet orb.

"Are you Miss Judy Hines?" Her voice was smooth and delicate.

Judy nodded.

Goodday flipped a notebook open. She wrote something down and wasn't looking at Paulie as she asked, "And you are, sir?"

He held up his hands. "I'm nobody. I didn't see nothing. I was in my apartment the whole time." He jammed his hands deep into the pockets. "I think I left some rice on the stove. I gotta go check it. See you, Jude." He skipped away. Goodday lowered her head and watched him go from under her hat brim.

"Would you please relate to me your recollection of the events, Miss Hines?" said Goodday.

Judy puffed on her cigarette. "Sure. There were these trolls and this...uh...big red thing. I think they called it a codger."

"Kojin," corrected Goodday.

"So there were these things," said Judy, "and they came out of my closet and ate the apartment manager. Guy was a dick, but that doesn't really make it right."

It was slipping away. She struggled to find her focus. "Shit, I can't remember the rest."

Goodday waved the fingers of her right hand in a small circle and poked Judy in the forehead. "Is that better, ma'am?"

The memories snapped back into sharp and perfect clarity. The details spilled from her lips in a steady stream, almost against her will. It was like recapping a movie she'd just seen that she wasn't particularly interested in. It took a few minutes. Goodday wrote it down without a single note of personal interjection.

"In your opinion, ma'am," asked the officer, "did Mr. Dionysus behave in a responsible manner?"

"Who?"

Goodday gestured over her shoulder at Monster. "Mr. Dionysus, the freelance cryptobiological rescue agent. Did he perform in a negligent manner?"

"You mean because of that guy getting eaten? I guess he's not responsible for that. If the moron had listened, he'd probably be alive still." Judy mulled it over. "No, it wasn't Mr. Dionysus's fault. Not really."

Goodday snapped her notebook shut and marched away. Judy wasn't sure if the interview was over, so she stuck around and smoked three more cigarettes while watching the Reds do their job. They talked to Monster for half an hour, then waved wands around the overturned van and parking lot.

Monster walked over and sat on the car beside her.

"Thanks," he said. "For telling them it wasn't my fault. Can't really afford more demerits on my license."

"No problem." She caught him staring at the pack of cigarettes on the car. "I'd offer you one, but I've only got eight left."

"It's all right. I quit." He glanced at the ruins of her apartment. The Reds were inside, using a staff dangling with charms to do some forensic work. "Sorry about your place."

She shrugged. "Sorry about your van."

She rubbed her temples.

"It's the memory enhancement," said Monster. "It'll give you a helluva headache in another twenty minutes."

Judy slouched and grumbled.

The Reds continued doing all that weird stuff that Judy didn't understand. They walked around the parking lot swinging pendulums, drew more runes, and took reports. It took two hours for them to finish, and in the meantime, Judy and Monster had to wait.

They didn't talk.

The Reds had Monster and Judy sign some papers and told them they could go.

"Is there somewhere we can reach you, ma'am?" asked Officer Goodday. "In case it's decided this incident needs further investigation."

Judy cast a look at her ruined apartment. Everything she owned in the world (admittedly, not much) was gone. Except for her car. She gave them her sister's phone number, not because she would be staying there. It was just easier.

Since his van was ruined, Monster was going to call a cab. But Judy offered him a ride. She knew that as soon as this night was over, she'd forget it. She wanted to hold on to it as long as possible. And having a purple guy in her passenger seat and a talking piece of paper in the back helped to keep her focused.

"How long have you been doing this?" she asked.

"Four years."

"Do you like it?"

"I don't know. Maybe. Sometimes. It's okay."

"How'd you get into it?" she asked.

Monster was beginning to regret not calling that cab.

"A girl," he said. "When I was getting my rune degree there was this chick in my Basics of Alchemy class. She was so fucking hot. I mean..."

His voice trailed off wistfully as he closed his eyes and chuckled to himself. After a minute, Judy forced a cough to bring him back.

"Sorry." He grinned. "I mean, she had the sweetest tits you've ever seen. And talk about an ass. Oh, man. And she could do this thing with her hand that—"

"Yeah," interrupted Judy. "That's great, but I really don't need to hear about it."

"But it was this trick, see? She'd curl her fingers like this and—"

She threw a disinterested glance his way, and Monster got the hint.

"So she was hot," he continued. "I mean, this girl was way out of my league. But she had this thing for cryptos. Wanted to become a vet. So I enrolled in some cryptobiology classes, trying to impress her."

"Did it work?"

"We dated for about a year. Then she decided she wanted to be a corporate enchantress. Said I didn't have any ambition other than to watch TV and drink beer. We broke up. I didn't feel like starting a new major, so I stuck with it. And here I am."

"Do you like it?"

"Pays for my beer and cable. Usually."

His attitude annoyed her. She was stuck in a world of drudgery and more drudgery with a little slogging and grinding thrown in on occasion. Maybe the world he lived in was much the same, but at least it had dragons in it.

"Can anyone do it?" she asked. "Catch monsters?"

"Okay, first of all," he said, "I am not a monster catcher. I'm a freelance cryptobiological rescue agent. And no, not everyone can do it. You have to have a license."

"How does someone get one of those?"

"There's a test. You'd never pass it."

Judy frowned. "I'm pretty smart. How hard could it be?"

Monster tapped his temple. "In twenty minutes, you won't even remember how to capture a kojin."

"Sure I will."

"Okay. How?"

Judy hadn't the faintest idea. She wasn't even sure what a kojin was. Something big, she thought. Red, maybe. Or black.

"It's not your fault, Miss Hines," said Chester from the backseat.

"What I want to know," she said, "is how all those trolls got into my closet in the first place."

"That's for the commission to determine exactly," said Chester. "But in cases such as this, it's usually just a spatial fold."

"Like a wormhole?" she asked.

Monster and Chester chuckled.

"What's so funny?" she asked.

"Nothing," replied Monster.

"No, really. What's so damn funny?"

"Nothing. Just, there's no such thing as wormholes. Science-fiction bullshit." Monster laughed. "Wormholes."

They passed the rest of the ride in silence. She turned up the radio and took account of her life. Nearly everything she owned had been eaten and excreted by trolls. Tonight she'd be working at a job she didn't care about with people she didn't like doing things that really didn't matter for barely enough money to pay her rent. Except now she didn't have rent. Upside in everything.

She pulled the car in front of Monster's house.

"Thanks for the ride." Monster, lugging the kojin stone, and Chester got out of the car and waited for her to pull away.

She started the car but sat there for a moment, still thinking.

Monster leaned in to the window. "Sorry about your apartment and your clothes and your furniture and . . . everything."

Judy, lost in thought, stared absently out the windshield. Monster fumbled for some other polite phrase, finally settled on a halfhearted "Take care now," and turned toward his house.

"Are you going monster hunting tonight?" she asked. "I mean, cryptobiological rescuing?"

He answered without turning back. "Not tonight."

He took a step away from the car.

"Why not?" she asked.

"Because I've had a hell of a day, and I just want to go home, watch TV, drink some beer, have sex with my girlfriend, and call it a night."

"Uh-huh. I was thinking maybe it was because you didn't have a van anymore because the koja ate it."

"Kojin," he corrected.

"Whatever. So do you have a car?"

There was always Liz's car. He could borrow that if he had to. If he got so much as a ding in the fender, she'd probably rip out his soul and eat it. He'd seen her do that once to some guy who cut her off on the freeway, though really she didn't eat the whole thing. Soul went straight to her hips, so she'd just taken a small bite out of it before giving it back. But Monster figured it would be better not to risk it.

"Because if you don't have a car," said Judy, "you can borrow mine. If you wanted to."

Monster handed off the kojin stone to Chester. The paper gnome wrinkled under the weight.

"What's the catch?" asked Monster.

"No catch. You just have to take me along while you work. That's all."

"I can't drag you around while I'm on the job. This is dangerous business. Every night I go out there, I'm taking my life into my hands. It'd be irresponsible. You wouldn't last the night. You'd get eaten or petrified or dissolved, and I'd lose my license." He shook his head and waved his arms to emphasize the point. "Thanks but no thanks."

Judy jumped out of her car. "You owe me."

"I owe you?" He barked a single, harsh laugh. "Lady, because of you my van was trashed, I nearly got devoured by trolls, and I almost lost my license."

"Almost," said Judy. "You *almost* lost your license, but you didn't. And you didn't because I told the Rubes—"

"Reds," corrected Chester.

"Yeah, those guys," said Judy. "The guys who would've already taken away your license if I hadn't lied and said you weren't responsible for what happened."

"She did kind of get you out of a jam," said Chester.

"Okay, forget it," she said. "Sorry I asked."

She climbed into the car and restarted it. She feigned searching for her last cigarette, fumbled around in her pockets for a while.

Monster slouched. He wasn't responsible for what happened at the apartment, and though it had been a bit dicey, he'd managed to keep things from getting worse than they could have been. The kojin could've done some real damage, eaten a few people, destroyed a lot more property. Monster had kept that from happening. But the Reds wouldn't have cared. If Judy hadn't vouched for him, they would've been more than happy to put the blame on him. It made their paperwork easier. She'd saved his license, some hefty fines, and maybe even some jail time.

He owed her. And maybe if he'd handled things better, she wouldn't have lost her apartment. Even if it wasn't his fault, she'd still had a lousy day, and he could relate to that. If she wanted a night of crypto hunting, it didn't seem too much to ask.

Monster threw open the passenger door. "Okay. You can come along. But let's get this straight. I'm not responsible for you, and nobody knows about it. Tomorrow night, if anything happens to you, I'm just walking away. No report. I didn't see nothing, and I don't know anything about it."

"Sure, sounds like a deal."

She offered her hand, and they shook on it.

"Tomorrow night, ten o'clock," said Monster. "Don't be late."

"Oh, I'll be here." She gunned the engine and sped away.

Monster took the kojin from Chester. The paper gnome had no eyes, but Monster had worked with Chester long enough to recognize his disapproval by the way he folded his hands on his hips.

"What? What is it?"

"Every night you go out there, you take your life into your hands?" repeated Chester.

"Well, don't I?"

"Whatever you say. Although I don't know if it's a wise idea to bring a light cog along in any case."

"What are you talking about?" Monster did a whiny imitation of Chester. " 'She did kind of get you out of a jam.' Isn't that what you said?"

"Yes, but that didn't mean I thought you should give in to her."

"Then why didn't you just keep your trap shut?"

"I don't know. I like her, I guess."

"You like her? What's to like about her? She's grouchy, bitchy, and hard to get along with. I can't stand people like that."

"No surprise there," Chester mumbled, but it was a stage mumble. The kind that could be heard across the street.

"What's that supposed to mean?" asked Monster.

"Oh, nothing."

Monster glowered at Chester.

"It's just, people don't generally like people who remind them of themselves. Or so I've read."

"Are you calling me bitchy?"

"I'm just remarking on something I've read. That's all."

Monster stood there and scowled unilaterally.

"None of it matters anyway," he said. "She'll forget all about it by tomorrow. Probably sooner. But at least for a few minutes she'll have something to look forward to."

"Wow. That's almost decent of you," said Chester. "In a minimalistic, barely-do-anything kind of way."

"What else could I do? Buy her a new wardrobe?"

"I wasn't criticizing. I was paying you a compliment. Usually you're too busy feeling sorry for yourself to notice other people's problems. Nice to see some empathy now and then. Maybe this Judy brings out something good in you."

"Her life stinks. My life stinks. I can relate. But that doesn't really matter." Monster shrugged. "She won't be back."

"I don't know. She seemed kind of determined."

"Hell, if you like her so much, why don't you go work for her?"

Monster tossed the kojin stone at Chester, who was caught off-guard, tipped over, and had his head flattened beneath it. Since he was flat to begin with, there was no noticeable effect.

"Put that someplace safe," said Monster. "And for the record, I am not bitchy. Guys can't be bitchy. It's a genetic impossibility." He walked away as Chester wiggled out from under the stone.

"Saved by a Y chromosome," mumbled Chester, this time to himself.

Liz sat on the sofa, stitching together another one of her devil dolls.

"Hey," she said. "Do you need some help with the groceries?"

Monster paused at the threshold. "Oh, crap. Sorry, I forgot."

"Oh, that's okay." She nipped off the end of a thread with her sharp teeth. "Did you at least remember the dry cleaning?"

He cringed. He had remembered, all right, but the clothes had been in the back of his van. It was possible they'd survived the crushing, but he'd left them there.

"Don't tell me you forgot." There was a little fire in her eyes.

"No, I didn't," he replied defiantly. "But there was this kojin, and..."

She scowled, and her fangs showed whenever she did. "Bless it, Monster—can't I rely on you to do anything?"

"There was this kojin, this huge Japanese ogre with a hundred arms—"

"I know what a kojin is. What I want to know is why it kept you from getting my dry cleaning."

"It wasn't my fault."

"It's never your sacred fault. You blessed mortals always blame everyone but yourselves for your screwups."

He adopted his soothing voice. "Take it easy, baby. There's no need for that kind of language."

"To Elysian, there isn't! I have a big meeting tomorrow. I was going to wear my blood red suit. Mr. Moloch himself said I should wear it to make a good impression. Said it brought out the flames in my eyes."

"Just start yelling," he mumbled. "Nothing brings out the flames better than that."

She was too busy seething to notice. Liz rarely lost control of her temper, but when she did, there was nothing to do but weather the storm.

"Do you know how long I've been waiting for this blessed promotion? Finally there's an opening in Marketing, and I'm not going to get the sacrosanct thing because you"—she glared, and the carpet under her feet began to smolder—"can't even blessing remember to pick up my blessed blood red suit."

Chester poked his flat head under the front door. "What do you want me to do with this kojin?"

"It was his fault." Monster pointed to the paper gnome. "Not mine."

Chester uttered a stifled peep and retreated. He knew better than to be nearby when Liz was mad. Paper and enraged demons did not mix.

She stalked forward and raised a finger to poke Monster in the chest, but changed her mind. "You know what? Forget it. Why do I even bother? I should know better than to count on you." She glanced down at the six footprints burned into the carpet. "That's just great. Look what you made me do."

The heat faded. She went to the sofa and started back on her doll.

Monster debated on whether to make up or not. Sometimes it was better to leave things alone, give Liz time to boil. When she burned hot, it was usually over quickly. Other times, she simmered with a low, steady heat that could build to an explosion, usually figurative, sometimes literal.

She didn't like to talk about it, but sin was a high-pressure job. It wasn't hard to get people to do bad things, but competition was stiff in her demon-eat-demon world. A demon was only as good as her last inspired atrocity, and even that didn't count for much.

She wasn't mad at him. He wouldn't give a damn about that. She was sad. That always bothered him. He didn't know why, considering his misery didn't usually register with her. But that was what she was, and regardless of the logic behind it, he was mildly fond of her.

"I'm sorry, baby. Really, I am, but there was this kojin and—"

"There's always something," she said.

"Don't get mad at me just because you're unhappy with your job," he said. "Maybe if you'd listened to me you wouldn't be in this mess. I told you that the temptation and corruption racket were pretty full up here. What'd you expect?"

It'd just slipped out, and he bit his lip.

"You never believed in me," she said softly.

He slid closer. "You said it yourself. It's an old devils' club. All the good jobs were taken centuries ago. You've only been upside for a few years now. You can't expect to make assistant to head of gluttony overnight."

She didn't look at him as she tossed the doll onto the coffee table. She folded her arms and frowned at her feet. "It's just frustrating. I know I'm qualified for that job."

"I know you are, too." He put his hand under her chin and raised her head toward his. "Remember that time we went to the pizza buffet and you hexed that guy to eat until they had to call the paramedics because they thought his stomach had split open?"

She smiled at him. "That was fun."

"And what about when you slipped those addictive ingredients into those bake sale cookies?"

"Oh, yeah." Liz slapped him playfully on the shoulder. "Those kids were tearing each other apart for that last one!"

"I'll never forget when that little girl broke that chunky kid's arm. What was it she screamed?"

Monster and Liz remembered in unison. "That's mine, fat-ass!"

They laughed, and Monster remembered how beautiful Liz could be when she laughed. Shame it always had to be at other people's expense, but nobody was perfect.

Liz was suddenly kissing him as she started to pull off his T-shirt.

"I want you," she whispered in his ear, and for the first time in a long while, he wanted her too.

They had sex on the sofa, and it was good. It'd been a long time since he'd seen any passion in her eyes. True, the passion didn't originate from him but from her fond delight of her own cruel accomplishments. But Monster wasn't picky.

Afterward, they lay sprawled on the sofa. It wasn't a comfortable fit, but they made do.

She almost immediately slipped back into a sullen mood. "I just know they'll give that promotion to that suck-up incubus in the mailroom. Blessed brownnoser."

Monster said, "Work sucks."

"Yes, work sucks."

She slid away from him. Liz wasn't much for cuddling in the afterglow.

"How are you going to work now?"

"I've got a ride," he said. "At least, for tomorrow."

"Who with?"

"Just some woman who wants to go on a ride-along."

"Really."

Liz's tone was flat. Not surprising. She wasn't the jealous type. She didn't need to be. Not when she could glimpse every lustful thought running through Monster's mind. And there was no way to actually have sex with another woman without Liz instantly knowing at a glance. One of the disadvantages of having a succubus girlfriend.

Not that it was an issue. Monster wasn't interested in Judy. Sure, he'd noticed she had a nice ass, and maybe she had a bigger chest than her loose T-shirt let on, though he couldn't be sure.

Liz fixed him with a knowing stare.

Monster quickly redirected his mind. "So what's on TV?"

"I stopped by the video store and rented a movie on my way home. We can watch it together."

He plastered on a forced smile.

"It's called *Red Fury*."

And for a moment he had hope of something involving commandos and machine guns.

"It's about this young boy and this wild horse who struggle against racism and..."

He zoned out after that.

*   *   *

68

Judy spotted a convenience store just a few blocks from Monster's house. It was her only hope.

She could feel the memories seeping to the bottom of her brain, becoming buried beneath more ordinary recollections. In a few minutes, perhaps less, she'd forget. Or at least stop thinking about it until something reminded her of it in a way she couldn't casually dismiss. She couldn't let that happen.

Judy ran a yellow light and bounced over a curb as she recklessly screeched to a halt in two parking places. A car that had been going for one of the spaces honked, but she ignored that. She had no time.

She ran inside the store and dashed to the short aisle of writing supplies. Quickly, she tore open a black marker and scrawled on her forearm in thick letters.

MAGIC IS REAL.

She grabbed a notebook and quickly started writing everything she could remember.

TROLLS ATE YOUR APARTMENT. PICK UP MONSTER TOMORROW AT 10. DON'T BE LATE. PAULIE KNOWS ABOUT MAGIC. CHESTER IS A PAPER MAN.

She filled a half page with these notes before she was interrupted.

"Miss, are you going to pay for those?" asked a kid in a blue and red shirt with a name tag labeling him a "sales assistant."

"Relax, junior. I'm not stealing them."

The kid didn't look entirely convinced, but he retreated to the safety behind his counter.

Judy grabbed a beef jerky, some orange juice, and a few other items that caught her eye. She went to the register and bought a carton of cigarettes too.

"Why'd you write on your arm like that?" asked the sales assistant while Judy pulled some cash from her wallet.

"Huh?" she said.

"Your arm. Why'd you write on it?"

"What are you—"

Judy read the words on her forearm. And she remembered.

She flipped open the notebook and scanned the contents and smiled. The details were fuzzy, but they were there. The trolls, the big thing with all the arms (red or black, she wasn't quite sure which), Paulie and his faerie skulls. It wasn't perfect, kind of like remembering something somebody had told her instead of something she'd experienced herself, but it worked.

It wasn't a permanent solution. Something better would have to be worked out in the long run. But for now, the act of writing the memories down and reading them allowed her to recall, at least to some degree. Why hadn't she thought of this before?

Maybe she had. Maybe there were notebooks full of reminders back at her apartment before the place was trashed by . . .

By something.

She glanced at her notebook and read her notes.

"Trolls," she said to herself, though she was looking at the sales assistant. "Trolls ate my apartment."

The look in his eyes and the way he backed away from the counter told her he probably thought she was crazy.

Chuckling, she paid for her items. He stuffed them into a plastic sack and pushed them across the counter toward her. When she reached for them, he jumped back.

"You don't know," she said, "because you can't see or remember. But I can." She held up the notebook and laughed. She turned toward the door and realized everyone in the store was staring at her like she was a madwoman. But she liked being left alone anyway, so it seemed like a perk.

She opened a pack of cigarettes, took one out, and lit it in the middle of the store. No one complained. Probably thinking she'd sink her teeth into their throats if they did. Judy held up her arm for everyone to see. She pointed at each word, reading it aloud in a calm, even voice.

"Magic. Is. Real." She tapped her temple. "And I don't care if there is something wrong with my brain—this time, I'm going to remember."

A mother pulled her children closer as Judy left the store. Everybody might think she was crazy, but they were the crazy ones. They were the ones without a clue.

She drove back to her apartment. When she got there, she was surprised to see it was in ruins, a big hole in her wall marked off with police tape, and a horrible odor coming from it. *MAGIC IS REAL,* the writing on her arm reminded her, and now she recalled that something supernatural had eaten her apartment.

She went to Paulie's apartment and knocked on his door. Loud music played, so she knew he was home. She pounded her fist as hard as she could. It took a couple of minutes for him to finally answer. He was naked. No surprise there. He was naked a lot. Thick smoke wafted out of the doorway. It smelled of pot and incense.

"Hi," she said.

He offered her a nod before turning and walking inside, leaving the door wide open. His narrow butt, flat and pale, didn't match his wide, tanned shoulders. She stepped inside the apartment and closed the door.

"Paulie, is it all right if I stay here tonight?"

"Mi casa es su casa," he said. "But you'll have to sleep on the couch. I already got two ladies here, and I ain't a machine. Want a beer?"

It was a rhetorical question. He brought her one.

"So, like, bummer about your apartment, y'know," he said as he twisted the cap off the bottle and handed it to her.

"Yeah, I know."

She took a drink, and he just kept nodding to himself.

A naked woman stepped out of the bedroom, and Judy was beginning to feel overdressed. The woman was tall and lean, a little on the bony side. She had wings sprouting from her back.

"This is Judy," said Paulie. "She's going to stay the night."

The angel nodded to Judy, who nodded back.

"Okay, so I'll be in the bedroom if you need anything, Jude," he said as the angel took his hand and pulled him toward the bedroom.

Judy sat down, and the couch cushions expelled a cloud of trapped, sweet-smelling smoke around her. She opened her notebook.

ANGELS ARE REAL, she wrote.

She heard a faint giggle and a moan beneath the loud music.

AND THEY'RE EASY.

Lotus was old. Older than the universe. And older than the universe that had come before that. And the one before that. She'd lost count of how many universes she'd seen come and go. They all tended to bleed together, follow the same basic trajectory from birth to collapse. The details might differ, but the end result was always the same. Chaos, then order, then chaos again. The chaos parts were safe and quiet, something she always looked forward to. It was those stretches of order that could sometimes make her endless life difficult. But even those instances were brief. She usually ignored them, finding ways to kill the time.

Since the dawn of this universe, she'd seen everything there was to see and been nearly everything there was to be. She'd swum the ocean depths as a plesiosaurus and spent several hundred years as cave moss. She'd been there to see the invention of the wheel, the first flint ax, several hundred ice ages repeated over and over again on planets now dead and long forgotten. On this planet, she'd been there for the rise of the Roman Empire, the fall of Camelot, every Chinese dynasty, the Dark Ages, the Enlightenment, the Industrial Revolution. She'd marveled at the wonders of the written alphabet, the discovery of fire, and Velcro. And she'd witnessed the horrors of Genghis Khan's conquering hordes, the Spanish Inquisition, and the Pet Rock craze.

She'd seen every wonderful advance and every boneheaded mistake of humanity and nature repeated ad infinitum to the point that the whole world felt like a script she'd read a thousand times before. And it was. Yet inevitably, despite these mistakes, the universe would continue to advance its own misguided agenda. Humanity was only the latest tool toward that goal.

She could not allow that. There was a balance to the universe, a way things were supposed to be. And every so often she had to remind the universe of that natural order. And if she had to remove humanity from the equation...well, it wouldn't be the first time a species had to be removed.

On the positive side, she didn't feel nearly as bad about this as when she'd had to undo the dinosaurs.

Lotus sat in her kitchen, drinking tea, communing with the stone. Everything was recorded within it because everything sprang from it. Without its vital energies feeding the existence of the cosmos, there would be no cosmos. If one bothered to look deep enough into the stone's depths, one could read the history of the atoms themselves, and of the tinier parts that made those atoms, and so on and so on. Vast and incomprehensible histories that were beyond imagining.

She wasn't interested in any of that. She already knew most of it.

The stone told her what she wanted to know, albeit reluctantly. It had grown resistant lately, even a bit tricky. It couldn't hide from her the information that the time was near for the next ascendency. Very near. Even without the stone, Lotus could feel it. She'd seen the pattern often enough to recognize it.

The ascendency was close. She was in the right place; the usurper lived somewhere in this city. And she knew the usurper's first name, but it wasn't quite enough to go on.

Judy was a very common name, after all.

8

Judy awoke clutching a notebook. At first she wasn't sure where she was, but the strange odors, and the soft melodies of Barry Manilow coming from the stereo helped to remind her. If those weren't enough of a hint, Paulie was sitting in the chair across from the sofa. He was staring at her with half-closed eyes. At first she thought he was naked, but he was wearing underwear. It looked a little too tight, and the spandex around his thighs and waist appeared to be cutting off his circulation. It didn't conceal much. Better than nothing, though, she decided.

She stirred. Her back was a little stiff after a night on his sofa. She couldn't remember why she'd spent the night here. Something had happened to her apartment, but the details were fuzzy.

Paulie had yet to react to her awakening. He just kept staring. She didn't know if he was really staring or if he'd just fallen asleep with his eyes not quite closed. She almost tested him but figured she didn't care.

The bathroom was occupied. She waited a minute, but had to get up and knock at the insistence of her bladder.

"Just a minute," a woman said on the door's other side.

Grumbling, Judy slid down the wall and sat on the floor to wait. She noticed a few white feathers scattered on the carpet. Maybe Paulie had gotten a bird. A big bird.

A woman stepped out of the bathroom. Her robe sat high on her shoulders, like she had a hunchback. The woman noticed a feather held in Judy's hand.

"Sorry, I'm molting."

Only half listening, Judy nodded before ducking into the bathroom. She emerged feeling refreshed and hungry. On her way to the kitchenette, she noticed Paulie was still sitting in his chair. He hadn't moved an inch.

His fridge was a wasteland of moldy leftovers. She found some milk, and after some scavenging, turned up some cereal, a bowl, and a wooden mixing spoon. She plopped down on the sofa while munching.

She picked up the notebook beside her with mild curiosity. The words *DON'T FORGET* written in bold marker. She flipped it open and scanned its contents. At first she thought it was a joke. But it was a damn elaborate one, considering the way the handwriting matched hers. Somebody must've gone to a lot of trouble.

The skinny woman emerged from the bedroom. She had jeans on but was topless. Probably because she couldn't get a shirt on over her wings.

Judy set aside her bowl and read through the notebook.

"Son of a bitch."

"Forgot again, huh?" The angel took a seat on the sofa and picked up Judy's cereal. "Sucks, I know. Gotta be annoying to keep forgetting."

"Yeah." Judy moved to the edge of the sofa because the angel's wings were taking up a lot of space.

"I'm Gracie," said the angel.

"Judy."

"So, I could show you a trick to help you with that. If you wanted."

"What kind of trick?"

"Just a magic thing."

"I can't use magic," Judy said. "Damn, I can't even remember it."

"Anybody can use magic," said Gracie. "It's not like it's rocket science or anything. What you need is a memory charm. Something simple, easy enough for even you to remember." She went to the shelf and found a book. "There should be something in here to handle it."

Gracie handed off the bowl to Judy. The angel flipped through the pages before arriving at her destination. "Here we are. Memory enhancement glyph should do the trick."

She found a marker on the coffee table and plopped down on the sofa. She leaned close to Judy and moved the marker to her forehead.

Judy blocked the tip with her palm. "What are you doing?"

"I'm helping. It's what I do." Gracie's golden eyes sparkled, and she smiled. She had a crooked tooth. "It's ... like ... kind of my job."

"I don't want to look like an idiot."

"What are you worried about? Most humans won't even notice it. Believe me—they miss a lot." She spread her wings and flapped.

"No, thanks."

Gracie capped the marker. "Suit yourself. No pinfeather off my wings. I don't usually help people like you anyway."

"Like me?" asked Judy.

"Not-nice people."

"I'm nice."

"Well, you're nice-ish." An embarrassed look crossed Gracie's face. "Let's just drop it."

"Let's do that," agreed Judy.

She finished off the rest of her cereal in angry gulps, stomped into the kitchen, and carefully balanced the bowl atop the pile of dirty dishes. She found a beer in Paulie's fridge but decided it was too early for that. Afternoon was morning for a late-shifter. So she went for a soda instead.

She walked back into the living room. Gracie was gone. Paulie was still sitting immobile in his chair.

Judy drank her soda and fumed. Nobody was really nice anyway. The word didn't mean anything.

Gracie returned wearing a backless shirt to accommodate her wings. "I'm sorry if I offended you. It's not like you're evil or anything." She disappeared into the kitchen. There was the unmistakable clatter of foraging in Paulie's fridge. "Are there any more sodas left?"

"Maybe. I don't know." Judy chugged the last half of her soda and crushed the can. She threw it behind the sofa just as Gracie returned.

"Now I feel bad. Let me make it up to you." Gracie's eyes went wide and soulful. "Pretty please."

"Nobody is going to notice?" asked Judy.

"Some people will notice. But most won't."

Judy considered the offer, but she didn't see any other choice. She would forget otherwise. Even the notebook by itself could only slow the process. It couldn't stop it. If she wanted to remember, she'd have to take radical steps. She consented.

Gracie drew the memory glyph on Judy's forehead. After it

79

was finished, Judy remembered again. It was a weird sort of memory, distant and without details.

"That's all you have to do?" asked Judy.

"Yep. Should work fine, although there are side effects you should—" Gracie checked her watch. "Oh, darn. I've got a transubstantiation in twenty minutes." She prodded Paulie in the shoulder and his eyes snapped open. "You've got to give me a ride."

"Can't you just fly, babe?" he asked.

"In this smog? Forget it." While Paulie went to find some pants, Gracie pounced on Judy, seizing her in a powerful hug. "Good luck with your memory stuff."

"Thanks."

Paulie and Gracie left. Judy was relieved that he didn't comment on the markings on her face. Maybe they weren't as bad as she imagined. She checked herself in the bathroom mirror. The glyph occupied all of her forehead. It was hard to miss. She reminded herself that most people weren't even as magically aware as she was, so it didn't matter how much of her face was covered in special enchanted doodles. Heck, maybe even people who could recognize magic might not notice it. Maybe it was invisible.

"Are you using the bathroom?" asked somebody behind her. " 'Cuz I really need to go."

It was Paulie's second lady friend from the night before. She was short, a little chubby, and appeared to be human. Though Judy wasn't willing to take these things for granted anymore.

Judy stood in the doorway, scrutinizing the woman's every reaction, trying to decide if the mark was visible to her. But she seemed more interested in getting past Judy than in looking at her face.

"I really need to go." She pushed Judy aside.

"Nice glyph," the woman remarked before shoving Judy out and slamming the bathroom door.

Judy bought a baseball cap an hour later.

She wasted the rest of the day watching television in Paulie's place. She called in to work to tell them she wasn't coming. She didn't even bother faking sick. Nobody cared.

The memory glyph worked. She didn't forget about magic, about the trolls and the existence of angels. And she didn't forget to pick up Monster at ten.

He wasn't ready.

Judy sat on the porch and smoked a cigarette while waiting. Monster appeared fifteen minutes later. His skin was gray tonight, and his hair was stark white. He hadn't shaved. Short white fuzz formed an inverse shadow on his chin.

"Are you ready?" she asked.

"Sorry, I just assumed you'd forget. How did you remember?"

"Somebody showed me a trick."

"Memory glyph?" said Monster.

"Whatever works." She adjusted her cap, pulling it lower. "Where's the paper man?"

Monster patted his shirt pocket. "Are you sure you want to do this?" he asked.

"I'm sure."

They got into her car, and he pulled a devil doll from a pocket and propped it on the dashboard. He yanked on its left arm and twirled its feet until he tuned in to the right frequency.

She started the engine. "Where to?"

He told her to head toward the center of the city. That way the odds of being nearby to any call were increased.

"So what happens when you're gray?" she asked.

"I can shoot lightning bolts from my fingertips," he said. "Stings like hell, though."

"Why do you change colors anyway?" she asked.

"About three years ago, I was bitten by a basilisk. That usually kills you. But if you're very, very lucky, and the anti-venom treatment doesn't make you into a puddle, then it leaves you with an unstable enchantment. So now I change color whenever I go to sleep and wake up and have different enchantments depending on what color I am. Also, I'm immune to all poisons and toxic substances."

"Must come in handy in your line of work."

"Yeah, almost makes the two months of daily, cripplingly painful alchemical injections worth it."

"And your girlfriend is red too."

"Yes, she is."

"Why is that?"

"Because she's a demon," he said. "I agreed to let you drive me around for one night, but I didn't say anything about answering a lot of questions. So who showed you the glyph?" he asked.

"An angel."

"Let me guess. Her name was Charity. Or Chastity. Or Modesty. Still can't figure out why angels all have stripper names." Monster paused to listen to some of the noise filtering through the doll. A chimera was reported downtown, but they were too far away to have a shot at that. "Did she tell you about the side effects?"

"Of course she did," Judy lied.

"And you're okay with that?"

"Nothing's perfect," she said.

"I guess you're pretty serious about this then. Most people freak out when you mention aneurisms and premature memory loss."

Judy took some time to process the information, being very sure to keep a neutral expression.

"It works for now. I'll figure something else out when I have to. Is this all you do all night? Drive around?"

"What'd you expect?"

"I don't know. Just something more than this."

"Nope. This is it," he said. "It's a lot like war. Long stretches of boredom interrupted by brief moments of terror."

Half an hour later, the radio doll announced a bag only ten minutes away, but Monster didn't call in for it. "If I had my van, it'd be no big deal. But I don't have the supplies to bag a gwyllgi."

"Here's what I don't understand," she said. "I can get the concept of magic. I mean, it's not like I hadn't heard of the idea before. And trolls and yetis and stuff like that. But why can't I remember when I run into it?"

"Before adolescence, all children are light cognizants," said Monster. "That lets you pick up the basic concepts. Later, when Merlin's lobe is reabsorbed, it's in there." He tapped his temple. "Even if you think it's only make-believe."

"Then how do I know what's real and what's not?" she said. "When I was a kid, I had an imaginary friend named Sharon. She was a stegosaurus. Was she real?"

"I doubt it."

"Why? Aren't dinosaurs real?"

"They were. At least, I think they were. But then again, unicorns were never real, so who knows?"

"How can I trust anything?" Judy asked. "If my memory is so unreliable, how can I even be sure this conversation is taking place?"

"You can't."

"I should just stop trying?"

"I don't know what to tell you," he said. "You're in the worst place to be. Being a light cog sucks. I'd tell you to stop, but it wouldn't make much difference. You'd still keep running across magic, remembering and forgetting over and over again. That's just the way it is. Sorry to be the one to break the news to you. Although I'm probably not the first one. Probably won't be the last either."

She snarled.

He considered telling her the truth. It would get better. Her lobe would continue to decay over time until she became a full incog no longer having to deal with light cog confusion. The downside was that light cogs had a much higher likelihood of crippling senility and/or mental illness in their golden years. He elected not to mention any of it out of vague sympathy.

Judy pulled in to a convenience store. She announced she was getting a candy bar and jumped out of the car before Monster could say anything else that might annoy her. She was beginning to think he was right. Just forget the whole thing and get on with her life. Occasionally she might run into something strange, get a glimpse of this other world. She must've done it all the time, if these last few days were any indication. It hadn't hurt her so far to just let it go.

Even if she did find a way to remember, she couldn't do this job, and she wasn't sure she wanted to. She didn't know why she was bothering. It was more frustrating than anything else.

She wasn't in the mood for a candy bar, but she'd said she was going to buy one, so she just grabbed something randomly from a shelf. There was a short line at the checkout. Three people were ahead of her, and the lady at the counter was buying lottery tickets with all the care and eye for detail one usually saves for bomb disposal.

"How many Lucky Duck Bucks do you have left?" she asked the clerk.

"Ten."

"Oh, that's good. The last ten are usually the lucky ones." She turned and repeated it to the customers behind her.

Judy tensed, squeezing her candy bar into a misshapen lump within its wrapper. The petite woman in front of her sighed with annoyance. The lottery lady was unaware of these signs and continued her methodical task.

Judy tore open the wrapper and took a bite. It didn't have nuts. She hated chocolate without nuts. Grimacing, she forced herself to swallow and realized now that she'd opened it, she was going to have to pay for the damn thing.

Judy grabbed a magazine off a rack and flipped through it without reading it. The line still hadn't moved an inch when something weird got in line behind her.

The creature was short, with pale, scaly skin and pointed ears. It had a tail too. It was wearing slacks, a nice jacket, and a tie. And it was buying a six-pack of beer, a bottled water, and a hot rod magazine.

It caught her looking at it and nodded. "Hello."

"Hi." She buried her nose in her magazine. Now was not the time to panic. She'd been waiting for a chance to see if she could make it as a cryptobiological handler, and now the opportunity was right in her lap. Whatever this thing was, it wasn't human.

She stole a glance over her shoulder. The creature smiled and nodded again. Judy, nodding back again, appraised it. It wasn't very big. Only about five feet, and couldn't have weighed more than a hundred pounds. It didn't have claws, and its teeth didn't appear sharp enough to be dangerous. The tail might be a problem, but she was pretty sure she could take it. She'd taken some judo at the Y and knew a few pins that should be easy to execute on this runt.

She thought about getting Monster, but then he'd just push

her aside and take care of it himself. She had to prove to him that she could do this. And she had to prove it to herself. If she captured one damn supernatural creature, she could claim that this night wasn't a total waste. If nothing else, she could scrawl a memory glyph on her forehead occasionally and remember the night she captured a sea elf. Or whatever the hell this was.

By the time Judy got to the front of the line, she had a plan. She couldn't know for sure if this creature had any special powers. Maybe he could breathe fire or turn things into gold. Maybe if she captured him he'd grant her three wishes. Whatever he might be capable of, her best bet was to take him off-guard. She paid for her candy bar, stuffed it into her pocket, and walked out the door. The store had a glass front, so she sauntered casually around the corner, where she waited.

Monster was fiddling with the radio doll and hadn't noticed her exit. So much the better, she thought. Now he'd feel like an idiot for missing the creature right in front of his nose.

The sea elf exited the store and by a stroke of luck turned her way. She pulled back into the darkened corner, listening to his approaching footsteps. Just as he came into sight, she threw herself into him. There wasn't much of a struggle, and soon she had him down on the pavement. There was some squirming and swearing from both of them. His flailing fist smacked her in the throat. She gagged but managed to force him onto his stomach and twist his arm behind him.

"Ow!" he screamed. "What's wrong with you, you crazy bitch?"

"I caught you, you little…whatever the hell you are! I caught you!"

While the creature unsuccessfully struggled to free itself, Monster got out of the car and stood before Judy.

"What are you doing?"

"I caught something." She pressed the weight of her knee into the creature's back. "See? It's not human!"

"I knew it!" said the creature. "I knew it wasn't any different here. Land of the free, my ass. I've got a green card!"

The possibility that she'd made a horrible mistake came to Judy slowly. She was still working it out when Monster suggested she should release her capture. She did so with reluctance, and the sea elf stood, glaring.

"I'm sorry, sir," said Monster. "This has all been a misunderstanding."

The sea elf scooped up his magazine. Several pages had been torn out in the scuffle.

Monster took Chester out of his pocket and instructed him to deal with the elf while Monster took Judy aside.

"Why did you do that?"

"He's a creature," she said. "I mean, look at him."

"I knew this was a bad idea. Just because he's not human doesn't mean he's a cryptobiological."

"It doesn't?"

"There are four general classifications: human, animal, cryptobiological, and parahuman. Guess what he is?"

The sea elf ranted at Chester, who continued to try to calm him down.

"My job is to capture cryptos. Nothing else."

"Why didn't you tell me this before?"

"I didn't think you'd be going nuts and tackling anything with pointed ears."

"How can I tell the difference?" she asked. "Those trolls looked kind of like people, didn't they?"

"A good rule of thumb is, if it's standing in line to buy beer, it's probably not a threat to public safety. You'd better hope Chester can smooth things over. Otherwise, you're probably going to jail."

After a few minutes, Chester's efforts seemed to have an effect. Chester came over to Monster and Judy. "He's willing to forget the whole thing on a few conditions. He wants fifty dollars and a new magazine."

"I just spent my last buck on a candy bar." Judy turned out her pockets and discovered a chocolaty mess. "Crap, I just bought these jeans."

Monster paid off the sea elf. "No hard feelings, pal."

"I'm really sorry," said Judy.

"It's all right," said the elf. "These things happen."

He held out his left hand to her. She was a little thrown by that, but rather than risk offending him, she offered her left, and they shook. Grinning sinisterly, he squeezed, and a sharp point of heat pricked her palm. The sea elf released her and ran off.

"Let's get out of here before you do anything else stupid," said Monster. "By the way, you owe me fifty bucks."

The radio doll reported a gargoyle in an attic that was nearby. Monster called in for the bag and gave Judy directions.

By the time they got to the house, the heat in her palm had become a bothersome itch. She scratched it and noticed an odd-shaped spot on her left hand. "What the hell?"

"Oh, that's just the mark." Monster grabbed his bag and got out. "Stay here. This shouldn't take long. Keep an eye on her, Chester."

"Mark? What mark?" asked Judy, but Monster was already on the front porch, so she turned to Chester.

"What mark?"

"The mark of the curse," said Chester. "The curse that the

parahuman put on you. You shouldn't ever shake with the left hand."

"You couldn't have warned me earlier?" she asked.

"Sorry. Didn't want to make a fuss." He checked her hand. "Doesn't look too bad, a minor misfortune hex. Doubt it can do much except inconvenience you for a few minutes once it activates. But it might be smarter to look both ways before crossing the street in the meantime."

The door to the house opened and Monster stepped inside. Judy stared at the house while drumming her fingers on the steering wheel.

"Screw this."

She got out of the car. Chester folded himself into a parrot and landed on her shoulder. "I wouldn't recommend that, Miss Hines. Probably smarter to stay in the car while the curse is still in effect."

"You said it was no big deal."

"It's not. Unless you put yourself in a bad spot."

"I came to see stuff, not sit in the car."

"I didn't really want to say anything, but you've made several dumb decisions tonight. Maybe you should take a moment to consider if this might be another one."

He had a point. The only reason she had this bad luck curse was because she'd done something stupid.

"But if it's a misfortune curse, how do I know if I go back to the car that it won't blow up or something?" she asked.

"That's far too improbable," said Chester. "The curse doesn't have the strength to circumvent plausibility. It just pushes small events in certain disadvantageous directions. The odds that the car should explode are remote. The odds that you'll pick up rabies from a gargoyle bite are significantly higher."

Judy went back to the car, lit a cigarette, leaned against the hood, and waited for Monster.

"Why did I do this?" she asked herself aloud. "What was the point?"

"You were curious, Miss Hines. Like a monkey obsessed with opening a puzzle box."

"I'd really appreciate it if you'd stop using monkey analogies."

"Sorry."

"So what do you get out of this?" asked Judy.

Chester said, "This body is not my true form. I'm actually a sixth-dimensional entity using this paper construct to interact and interface with this plane. In the process, certain energies, for lack of a better word, are transferred back to my home dimension. These energies, though abundant on this plane, are dwindling in my own, making them a valued commodity."

"Just another working stiff," she said.

"Aren't we all? But it's not a bad gig. I just bought a house and am sending one of my progeny to the Translucent Spheres of Supremacy. She's majoring in quantum duality mechanics with a minor in accounting."

"So you're married, then?"

"In a manner. My true nature is hard to explain in terms you could understand."

"Because I'm a monkey," said Judy.

"I never said that."

"But you were thinking it."

"I don't judge," said Chester. "I rather like you lower entities. You've done quite well for transient globs of possibly sentient protoplasm."

"Possibly sentient?"

"The jury is still out."

Monster exited the house.

"Did you get it?" asked Judy.

"Got them. There were two." He held up two gray rocks in his palm. "Surprised you stayed in the car."

"Didn't want to get rabies."

Monster chuckled. "Gargoyles don't carry rabies."

Judy brushed Chester off her shoulder. He folded himself into his gnomish shape and shrugged.

"Are you ready to go?" asked Monster.

"Yeah, I'm ready."

Judy took a long drag of her cigarette before flicking the stub at Chester. It bounced off his paper body, burning a small hole in it.

"What was that about?" said Monster.

"Nothing to worry about, boss," replied Chester. "You get used to it in this job. Protoplasm can be touchy."

Monster didn't answer a lot of calls, going after only a few. He offered excuses, saying he didn't have the right equipment, that it was too far, or the rescue fee wasn't worth the trouble. But Judy knew he was just taking the easy ones because he didn't want her getting in the way. The few calls he did answer were simple stuff: some gremlins (resembling scaly hamsters), an attercroppe (a snake with arms and legs), and a grylio. The grylio looked like a polka-dotted iguana, but Monster warned her that it was extremely venomous. He was immune, so it wasn't much trouble for him, even if it did sink its teeth into the tender flesh between his thumb and forefinger. But he was used to getting bitten and just slapped a Band-Aid on the wound.

"Guess we should call it a night," said Monster as the first hints of dawn lit the sky.

"Guess so," she agreed.

Monster studied her out of the corner of his eye. She was down, and he supposed she had the right. She'd had a bad run of luck lately, and it didn't look to be getting any better in the future. Incognizants ignored the magic around them with ease, but light cogs had a rough time in this world, always struggling to make sense of things they couldn't quite grasp but couldn't quite forget either.

Monster pulled in to a diner with a pasted-on 1950s sensibility.

"Want some breakfast?" asked Monster. "On me."

"Sure," said Judy, without enthusiasm. She wasn't hungry, but she wasn't in a rush to get back to Paulie's place.

The diner was all chrome and neon. The Big Bopper played on the jukebox. Maybe later in the day it might've been charming, but after a long night, it just seemed tiresome. Most of the other customers were starting their day while Monster and Judy were finishing theirs. Nobody seemed to really care about anything other than coffee and breakfast. Surprisingly, the drowsiness of the customers didn't seem to register with the waitstaff, all of whom appeared overjoyed to be working there.

A teenager, looking very much the part in poodle skirt and sneakers, flashed a gleaming smile. "Hi, I'm Chipper."

"I noticed," said Judy.

Chipper tittered, and it was probably the first time Judy had seen someone ever legitimately titter. "Right this way!"

She sat them at a booth, took their drink orders, and skipped away. She skipped back, and Judy was mildly impressed that someone could skip with two mugs of coffee without spilling a drop.

"I'm sorry, ma'am," she said. "This is a No Smoking building."

Judy tapped the cigarette on the table. "Have you ever watched any old movies?"

Chipper nodded. "Yes, ma'am. I love them."

"Then you'll notice that everyone in old movies smokes. All the time. Even when they're in church. Hell, even when they're in intensive care, they're lighting up. So if this is an actual *authentic* fifties dining experience, then I think it's reasonable to expect that I can smoke."

Chipper's smile never faded. "We aren't going for the total experience, ma'am. I mean, if we were going to be accurate, all the black customers would have to be seated in the back of the restaurant. And we wouldn't want that, now, would we, ma'am?"

"She's gotcha there," said Monster.

Chipper took their order, managing to squeeze in two more *ma'am*s in Judy's direction, before skipping off into the kitchen.

"Sorry it wasn't more exciting," said Monster finally, "but that's just not the way this works. Usually."

"I noticed."

Around three in the morning, Judy had decided that Monster's job was just as boring as her own. Dragons and sorcery didn't really change the nature of the world, and working stiffs were just the same whether grocery clerk or monster catcher.

"Even if you could get certified," he told her, "it wouldn't matter. There's not much call for the job anymore. Cryptos aren't common enough to make a living at this. I don't even earn enough to pay my rent most months. Not without a little extra help from my girlfriend. It's just the way the world is going. Cryptos are just like any other animal. Gotta have space to live. The more space we take up, the less for them. Some can adapt, but most are disappearing. Pretty soon, it'll be one bag a night.

"Not that that's a big deal either. The cognizant birthrate is falling too, and in two or three hundred years no human alive will be able to understand magic. It'll probably always be around in some form, but who's gonna notice? Probably be replaced by numerology, astrology, tarot cards, all those things humans like to think of as magical but really aren't."

Judy had gone through a phase as a teen, had had a shelf full of books about signs and planetary alignments and all that jazz. It would've been nice to think she could've been on to something.

"It seems like you've had plenty of business lately," said Judy.

"There's always surges. Usually two or three a year. This one's a little earlier than predicted, but that's not unusual."

"So what are you going to do?" she asked. "What are your plans when all the cryptos dry up?"

"I don't know. Haven't thought about it."

"Aren't you worried?" she asked.

"I don't know. Maybe." He stared into his coffee, gruffly feigning indifference. "Do you ever wake up and think, *What the hell happened? What am I doing?* And you realize that everything's all screwed up and it's probably your own damn fault but it's too late to fix it and you just have to learn to live with it because there's no way you're going back to school or dealing with the rat race or starting from the ground up. Because that sounds good, sounds like it should work, but if you weren't such a screwup in the first place you wouldn't be in the mess you are now. So why bother starting over? Because you're still a screwup and that's not going to change, no matter how you want it to."

She could relate, all right. It was all the stuff she tried not to think about in her own life. She glanced around the diner and noticed that same making-it-day-by-day posture in at least half the customers. We couldn't all be Chipper, so optimistic and bright, jaunty because tomorrow was certainly going to be a better day, and usually today wasn't all that bad. Judy's life wasn't even that bad. Just not very good, which in some ways was even worse. When you were at the bottom, you could work your way up. When you were at the top, you could gaze forward to the future with optimism. But the middle was tough. The middle was where it was too easy to be lazy and cynical at the same time.

Sometimes, she thought the starving people had it easy. Then she realized how idiotic that thought was and only felt worse about herself.

She stared into her own cup.

"Eh, I try not to think about it," said Monster with a forced smile. "I'm half hoping my demon girlfriend kills me before I have to."

"Sounds like a plan," agreed Judy.

"What can I say? I'm an optimist. So what about you? What are you going to do now?"

"I don't know."

She really didn't. Not a clue as to what her future might hold. She'd probably erase her memory rune, forget the past few days, and just go back to the Food Plus Mart and work there until she died. It wasn't the best plan, but at least it was simple.

Chipper brought forth their food. Judy was in a bad mood and would've preferred her breakfast swimming in grease, with ham like rubber and bacon like overdone toast. But everything was perfect. The eggs were fluffy. The bacon was crisp. The ham was succulent. It didn't lighten her mood—only made her more aware of her bad attitude.

"More coffee, ma'am?" asked Chipper, already pouring a fresh cup.

Judy forced a smile. "Thanks."

"No problem, ma'am." Chipper skipped away.

"I swear, if she calls me 'ma'am' one more time..."

Monster chuckled. "Ah, she's just a kid. Give her a break. She'll have plenty of time to get bitter and angry."

Judy found some consolation in that possibility. Not that she was optimistic about it. Some people went their whole lives without getting their hopes crushed.

She hated those people.

A terrible racket rose from the kitchen. It sounded as if the chef had dropped every pot and pan then smashed all the dishes. A busboy came running out of the swinging doors, leaped over the counter, and landed hard on his face. Wiping the blood from his nose, he continued to flee.

"There's a giant dog in the kitchen!" he screamed.

Something howled. It didn't sound like a dog.

"This sausage is really good," said Monster.

Half the customers had risen from their seats and were moving toward the exit. The other half were uncertain, waiting to see what would happen.

"This place is really great," said Monster. "Don't know why I haven't tried it before."

More kitchen staff fled in a mad rush, and by now most of the other customers had gotten the idea.

Judy fixed him with a stare.

"What?" he replied. "I'm off duty. Let somebody else handle it."

Someone in the kitchen screamed.

"At least let me finish my eggs," he said. "They got the yolks just right. I mean, look at these yolks. Do you know how hard it is to find a place that makes yolks like I like them?"

The unidentified creature thumped the wall and roared. Almost like a lion's roar but with a strange warble at the end.

Monster pushed his plate away. "Okay, okay. I'll take a look."

Another person filtered out of the kitchen. "Oh my God! It's going to eat Chipper!"

"There's no rush," said Judy.

Monster was already up and heading toward the door. Judy decided to follow.

The kitchen was in a shambles. Pots, pans, and broken dishes were strewn everywhere. The sink had been crushed and was gushing water. There wasn't much room, and the giant beast took up most of the space.

Though it had a dog's head, it wasn't a dog. It was huge and black, with scaly skin. Its body was that of a walrus, complete with the thick tail, but it had legs, four of them. Each foot ended in a wide paw.

It had Chipper cornered, but its bulky body was wedged between the fryer and the grill. The waitress had climbed atop a refrigerator and was safe for the moment. The beast's tremendous size kept it from reaching her.

"You should do something about it," said Judy. "Use one of your magic letters or something."

"Until I know what it is, anything I try will probably make it worse," he said. "Do me a favor and get my reference guide from the car."

While Judy retrieved his guide, Monster watched the creature menace Chipper, edging closer and closer. It lashed out with a large paw, nearly knocking over the refrigerator and sending Chipper toppling into its jaws.

"Hey!" he said. "Hey, you dumb thing!"

The creature turned its head, eyed him, then returned its attention to Chipper.

Against his better judgment, Monster grabbed a nearby fork

and flicked it at the beast. The creature failed to notice, and the refrigerator teetered after another swipe. Chipper screamed.

Monster pointed one finger at the creature's tail end. He narrowed his eyes and forced out a lightning bolt. Just a little one.

"Ouch." He sucked his finger. "Son of a bitch, I hate that."

The beast turned from Chipper and threw another annoyed glare at Monster. It bared its teeth and uttered a growl.

The beast paused, unsure whom it wanted to eat more. Trapped by its cramped quarters, it went back to Chipper, the easier snack. It managed to tip the refrigerator. The results didn't please anyone, the beast included. The refrigerator crashed onto its head. Chipper tumbled onto its back.

The first thing in the manual was to remove any civilians from the area of risk. Monster didn't usually follow the manual, but he didn't need another casualty on his record. One was just bad luck, but two in two days usually meant a board inquiry.

"Miss, come this way," he said soothingly.

Chipper, eyes wide with terror, kept her death grip on the creature. Monster swallowed his annoyance. He took a step forward, closer to the creature's giant fish tail. It twitched limply now, but it could start swinging with crushing force at any moment.

He held out his hand to her. "Come on," he said. "Come on."

Trembling, she reached toward him.

The beast sprang to life. Chipper was thrown off, striking Monster with enough force to knock him to the floor, which was fortunate, as the creature's tail would've crushed him where he stood otherwise.

Chipper scrambled roughly over him. Her knee mashed his sternum, and she stepped on his arm. He swore as she dashed out of the kitchen.

"You're welcome," he groaned.

The creature snapped and growled at Monster as it struggled to turn around. He backed out of the kitchen. Judy was in the empty diner with his crypto guide.

"Took your sweet time." He ignored the thrashing and roars as he took a seat and flipped through the book.

"Should we maybe get out of here?" asked Judy.

"Oh, it's fine. The thing is so stuck in there that it'll never get out."

"And the trolls in my closet weren't anything to be frightened of either," she said.

"You wanted me to handle this, so I'm handling it. Anyway, I'm betting this thing is pretty rare, and I'm not willing to pass up the score. You can go if you want. It'd probably be better if you did."

"I'm staying."

"Suit yourself." He skimmed the identification indexes. Since he didn't know what this thing was, he had to work his way backwards, using distinctive features. It wasn't hard to identify. Even in the world of cryptobiology, there just weren't that many dog-headed seal beasts.

"Az-i-wu-gum-ki-mukh-ti."

"What kind of name is that?" asked Judy.

"Inuit. It isn't usually seen outside of Greenland. In English, it's often referred to as a walrus dog."

"That's original," said Judy.

The az-i-wu-gum-ki-mukh-ti howled.

"Walrus dog sounds almost cute," said Judy, "and that thing is not cute. So now that you know what it is, can you capture it?"

"No problem." Monster picked up a napkin holder, a cube of aluminum, and traced a rune on it. He consulted his pocket dictionary.

"You'd think you'd have memorized those by now," said Judy.

Monster ignored the comment. Rune magic was just writing, but with a thousand-letter alphabet and rules of grammar and punctuation that were nearly beyond human comprehension. It was the shorthand of the universe, and the universe wasn't particularly bright when it came to interpreting it. A rune spell that could humanely incapacitate one yeti could blow the head off another. And he didn't want to kill the walrus dog.

He completed the rune, satisfied it would do the trick.

"Now what?" she asked.

"Now I throw this at it, freeze it in a block of ice. I make the world safe for greasy-diner-goers everywhere, and get a few bucks for my trouble."

"You said it's from Greenland, right?"

"Yes."

"Well, isn't Greenland the one with all the ice? What if it doesn't freeze?"

"Actually, Iceland is the one with all the ice," he said.

"No, it isn't."

Monster spoke through a tightly clenched jaw. "It doesn't matter. Even if Greenland is the one with the ice—which it isn't, because that would make no goddamn sense—this isn't regular ice. This is magic ice."

"Are you sure about that?"

Muttering obscenities, Monster entered the kitchen. Judy didn't follow, and that was probably a good thing, since he was very tempted to push her into the walrus dog's maw before freezing it. The creature had managed to turn itself halfway around and had destroyed the kitchen in the process. The counters were uprooted; half the tile floor was knocked loose. Broken dishes littered the floor, and water was spurting from several broken pipes. The stove was knocked askew, but Monster didn't smell any leaking gas.

No lightning bolts, he reminded himself.

The walrus dog snapped at him, but it wasn't much of a threat. When it came to land mobility, the thing was definitely more walrus than dog. It lashed out with its paws but came up short.

Monster tossed the napkin dispenser at it. It bounced off the az-i-wu-gum-ki-mukh-ti's black scales without leaving a mark. A blue flash engulfed the creature, and by the time Monster's vision cleared, the walrus dog was encased in a block of ice.

Judy entered, and Monster smiled smugly at her. "See? Frozen. No problems."

"I take it, then, that it's supposed to be doing that?" asked Judy.

The walrus dog shimmered. Its scales lightened as it slowly absorbed the ice around it.

"It's nothing to worry about." Monster flipped through his dictionary. "I'm on top of it."

The glow increased as the ice thinned enough for the creature to twitch its tail.

"Yeah, I can see you've got it all under control. Good luck with that."

She went to the front door. The handle snapped off.

Her left palm itched. The misfortune hex had struck. She pushed on the door, but it was designed to open inward and didn't budge. She tried getting her fingers between the doorjamb, but the seal was too tight.

The light coming from the kitchen and the raspy breaths of the walrus dog did not inspire Judy with confidence. Monster appeared through the swinging doors.

"We should get out of here." He stopped at the front door.

Judy held up the handle.

Monster went to the door on the other side of the restaurant. That handle broke off too.

She scratched her palm. It was itching like mad. "Sorry."

He shoved his shoulder against the glass door.

"I already tried that," she said.

The walrus dog howled.

Monster picked up a napkin holder, cocked back his arm, and hurled it into the door. It bounced improbably off the glass and smacked Judy in the head, knocking off her hat. She stumbled back and fell over a chair.

"Son of a bitch!" she grumbled. Despite the sudden throb in her skull, she was painfully aware of the itch in her palm.

The walrus dog pushed its way through the swinging kitchen door. The rune spell had transformed it into a living ice sculpture. Little pieces of ice cracked off its body with its every movement, but the shards were replaced with a steady refreezing. The az-i-wu-gum-ki-mukh-ti got stuck halfway through the kitchen door. It dug its frozen claws into the tile and struggled to pull itself the rest of the way through.

"This isn't fair," said Monster. "It's your bad-luck hex. Not mine."

Judy righted a chair and sat. She was having trouble concentrating, and her knees were weak. But she was getting used to functioning with head wounds, so she was aware enough to keep her wits about her but dulled enough not to be frightened by the prospect of being eaten by an ice sculpture.

"What about a lightning bolt?" she asked.

"Does that do anything to ice?" said Monster.

"I don't know. But it's not normal ice, is it?"

Only the walrus dog's hind legs remained stuck, and it was wiggling those free. Judy wasn't that worried. The thing was too big and clumsy to be much of a threat, and the transformation to ice hadn't helped it any. They could probably outmaneuver it fairly easily, but her aching skull reminded her that nothing was easy right now.

Monster leveled his hands at the walrus dog, closed his eyes, and unleashed a blast from all ten fingers.

"Ow, ow, ow, ow, ow, ow, ow, ow."

The creature absorbed the lightning, drawing it into its body. The ball of electricity crackled in its heart. The beast bayed, and voltage leaped off it. The diner's lights exploded in a shower of sparks. Monster sought cover behind a booth, and Judy, having regained some semblance of balance, joined him.

"Great idea," said Monster.

"Don't get mad at me. This is your job, not mine. And if you'd listened to me in the first place and not tried freezing the thing, we wouldn't be in this mess."

"If I'd ignored you in the first place, I'd still be finishing my eggs."

They chanced a peek. The walrus dog had freed itself and was advancing in their direction. It was getting slower if not weaker. It batted aside the tables in its way.

"We could run around it," suggested Judy. "I bet there's an exit in the kitchen."

"If we get anywhere near it, we'll be fried," said Monster.

"We could bash it with a chair. Maybe stun it enough to get past."

"Everything in this place is metal. Not sure striking a living lightning generator with a metal rod is a smart thing to do."

A single paw trod into view. Monster and Judy jumped back against the wall as the crackling walrus dog raised its head, with a maw of jagged ice shards, and howled.

The howl ended in a whimper as its jaw fell off. Fissures

split the az-i-wu-gum-ki-mukh-ti's huge tail, and it shattered. The creature tried to raise a paw. The limb broke apart. The walrus dog attempted to keep its balance, but its frozen limbs weren't able to keep it from falling, so it rolled to one side. The electricity in its heart fizzled, and the az-i-wu-gum-ki-mukh-ti exploded in a glittering burst. Frost covered Monster, Judy, and the diner in a thin coat.

"Is it dead?" asked Judy.

"What do you mean, is it dead? Of course it's dead." Monster wiped the ice from his face. "Damn, I guess I lost the collection fee on it. Not even good for parts."

Monster and Judy found the back door out of the diner through the kitchen. They went around to the front, where most of the customers and employees were standing around in mild confusion. Chipper was still flushed and wide eyed, on the verge of madness, and Judy forced herself not to smile at the perk-deprived moppet.

Judy guessed the combination of danger, chaos, and magic caused the stupefying effect. Monster ignored the crowd and got into her car without saying a word. But Judy thought she should say something to ease the crowd's bewilderment. Without her magic rune, she'd have been just as confused.

She cupped her hands around her mouth and yelled to the crowd, though not too loudly. The bump on her head was still throbbing. "It's okay, folks. It's all taken care of. The, uh, the big dog is dead. It won't hurt you. You can all go in and finish your breakfast now."

Much to her surprise, they seemed soothed. Probably because the crowd was eager to pretend that the walrus dog attack had never happened and to get on with their otherwise dreary lives. A few of the braver or incognizant employees and customers headed toward the diner.

Judy started the car. "Should we maybe stick around? In case the cops have any questions?"

"Are you nuts? Let's just get out of here before we get into any more trouble."

She glanced at the diner's frosted windows. "Guess you're right."

"You're bad luck, you know that?" said Monster on the drive back.

"It wasn't my fault. It's that hex that elf put on me." She glanced at her hand, still slightly itchy, but at least the mark had vanished.

"It's not like you weren't a jinx before you got that. I've only known you two days, and I've been nearly eaten by a yeti, trolls, a Japanese ogre, and some Greenland walrus monster. Not to mention losing my van."

"It's not like it's been all rainbows and puppy kisses for me." She touched her bruised and cut forehead.

"If I were you, I'd wash that glyph off my face and move on. Before I ended up dead. Or worse."

One more head injury and she'd have to use her fingers and toes to count to twenty. Her life was hard enough without the possibility of brain damage. Monster was probably right. She resented him for the advice, but she couldn't argue.

She dropped him off at his house.

"Sorry things didn't work out like you hoped," he said.

"I don't even know what I expected," she replied, more to herself than him.

Monster sucked his teeth noisily to cover the awkward silence.

"Forget it. Not your fault. At least you let me come along. You didn't have to do that. I wouldn't have changed my statement, y'know. To the Reds. You aren't as bad at this job as you think."

"How would you know?"

She laughed. "I guess I wouldn't. Not really. But all I know is that every time I've been around you, I've been nearly killed. But I haven't actually been killed. And that's probably thanks to you. You might be a screwup, Monster, but considering what you do for a living, you can't be that big a screwup. Otherwise, you'd be dead by now."

"Thanks."

"Don't thank me for telling the truth," Judy said. "Guess I won't see you around, huh?"

"Guess not."

The conversation had ground to a halt. Monster muttered a quick "Take care," then grabbed his bag and headed up the sidewalk and waved at her without a backwards glance.

She muttered as she lit a cigarette.

She sat in the idling car and smoked two cigarettes.

"Fuck it."

She used her sweaty palm to wipe the glyph from her forehead. It didn't remove it, merely obscured it, but she felt the slight disorientation as the haze settled on her mind. Or maybe that was just the concussion.

Judy stopped by a convenience store to purchase some aspirin for her aching skull. The clerk behind the counter asked her about the purple swelling and smudge on her forehead. But by then she didn't remember much of it, and what little she did recall she didn't believe.

What Judy believed was irrelevant to the universe. It wasn't as if it were hiding things from her. It just didn't care to share certain information. Judy was a tool, a linchpin in a cosmic engine. And an engineer didn't usually bother explaining himself to the nuts and bolts. He just screwed them into place and let them do their job.

Judy was in communion with the most primal aspect of creation. She just didn't know it. Her thoughts and desires were broadcast to the heart of the universe. But the signal was lousy, and most of those thoughts never reached their destination. And the few that did were garbled and all but unrecognizable. Judy's will was a remote control with bad batteries trying to guide a massive universe more comfortable with pushing galaxies around than with the subtleties of daily human life.

The resulting chaos was understandable and only getting worse as the signal grew stronger every hour. Had Judy been aware of it, she might have taken more care in even her most casual thoughts. It wouldn't have made any difference, but at least she could've tried.

Lotus was perfectly aware of this, though. She sat in her cozy den, staring at the strange letters scrawling across the stone tablet's surface.

Ferdinand glanced up from her crossword puzzle. The muscle-bound woman paused in her steady, noiseless gum chewing. "I hate when she does that," she said.

"Does what?" asked Ed, sipping her tea.

Lotus could sit there for days sometimes, looking into the stone's depths, never moving. Both Ed and Ferdinand knew she was doing something, and they assumed it was terribly important. And that was all the thought they gave to it. It wasn't in their nature to wonder. They just followed orders. If they'd ever tried to gaze within the stone themselves, they would've seen nothing worth noticing.

But Lotus saw the patterns within the patterns, the way it all tied together and how it was designed to turn out.

She also saw something was missing, an anomaly she couldn't

account for. The stone was working against her, but it wouldn't make any difference. In only a few hours, less than an instant as Lotus measured time, she would know where to find Judy. And she would fix things, keeping everything on track despite the universe's attempts to screw it all up.

That was her job, and after several billion years, she was quite good at it.

10

As Monster was getting ready for bed, Liz was getting ready for work. She had on a new red suit. It wasn't as nice as her other one, he noted to himself, but he didn't admit that to her.

"How was your night?"

"Don't ask," he said.

"Poor baby." She gave him a quick hug and a peck on the cheek. "Don't wait up. I'm going for drinks after work."

"Have fun," he said, but she was already out the door.

Monster slipped into his pajamas. He didn't feel that tired and decided to recline on the couch, watching some TV until the urge to drift off to bed hit him. There was nothing on. Just morning news shows, which he watched with half interest.

"Twelve dead in a subway fire," said the stoic news reporter. "Back to you, Brad."

"Terrible when tragedies like this strike." Brad nodded sagely. The camera angle changed, and a goofy grin crossed his face. "Now to a story about a woman in Arizona who makes decorative art out of tinfoil!"

The morning-news segues kept everything in check. Twelve people dead, but that didn't stop seventy-seven-year-old Anne O'Grady from making her shiny masterpieces of crumpled foil. He fell asleep on the couch.

He awoke a few hours later as something rattled around in the other room.

Rubbing his sore neck, he noted his new color: golden. He didn't have to check in his book for that. When he was golden, he became invisible when his eyes were shut. There was no way to control it. Every time he blinked, he'd vanish for an instant.

There was a clatter, as if the medicine cabinet was being emptied onto the floor.

Still drowsy, Monster rose from the couch and checked the noise.

"Liz, is that you?"

A low growl issued from the bathroom. Monster stopped.

A goat stuck its head into the hallway. The crypto turned its eyes toward Monster and bleated, then stepped into view. It had a goat's head but a humanoid body, naked and hairless. It wasn't very big, only about four feet tall, but its squat frame was powerfully built.

Monster kept his cool. "Where did you come from, little fella?"

The goat monster launched itself forward, ramming its horns into Monster's gut and knocking the breath from him. He fell to the floor, gasping.

The goat grumbled as Monster vanished before its eyes.

"You little bastard."

Groaning, Monster stood. The goat creature charged forward.

Monster turned to one side and took a glancing blow to his ribs. The goat hopped onto the couch and bleated, baring its teeth.

Monster clutched his aching side. "Look, you little shit. Don't make me hurt you."

The goat shifted its weight back and forth in an unfriendly manner. Monster closed his eyes. The goat grumbled. He heard it sniffing for him.

He didn't know where this thing had come from, how it had gotten into his house. He wasn't sure what it was. He'd never seen one of these short, goat-headed beasts before. Monster had been handling cryptos for years now, and it was rare for him to run across unfamiliar specimens. But it seemed to be happening more and more lately.

This one didn't seem that dangerous, but his ribs were aching and he hadn't caught his breath yet. Having no familiarity, he couldn't be sure how to handle it. Some cryptos could be scared by a show of force. Others were provoked to attack. It was trying to sniff him out, but he didn't know if that was because it was aggressive or scared. Probably both. He tried to put himself in the goat's place, finding itself in a strange environment, confronted by a large, potentially hostile animal. It was probably just panicked.

He opened his eyes again. Just a little squint, which made him semi-visible. The goat was glaring at him. It clicked its long, pointed teeth together with a staccato clicking, but it didn't attack.

"I don't want to hurt you, little guy," said Monster, as softly as possible.

The goat bleated softly. It twisted its head to one side, nostrils flaring, teeth chattering.

"Can't we be friends?"

The creature's ears fell flat. It squared its shoulders. Its legs tightened to spring.

Monster shut his eyes, and the goat started sniffing.

He ran through his choices. There was an annoying creature in his house, and he was unprepared to deal with it. He could feel his way through the living room to the front door, then lock the thing inside. Then he could call for backup and have the city send someone to pick it up. It'd be the smartest thing to do.

He wasn't about to do that.

The goat thing was irritating but not tremendously danger-ous so far. As a professional, he should be able to handle this without any help. If he called the CCRS for assistance, he'd end up catching hell from the other freelancers for months. Worst of all, somebody else would get the collection fee, and if this thing was rare, it had to be worth something. He wasn't sure the world needed angry, naked goat-headed beasts, but if the Preservation Foundation was willing to protect the greater prickly sluggoth and the farting drake, then this goat thing was probably deemed worth saving.

The goat's suspicious snorts drew closer. It apparently didn't have a great sense of smell, but it knew he was still here. And it wasn't happy about it.

Monster decided locking it in the house wouldn't be such a bad idea after all. Then he could come up with a plan to catch it. He tried to remember where he'd thrown his work satchel with his identification guide, rune dictionary, and a few writ-ing tools. And Chester, his paper body folded into a neat, sleep-ing square.

Monster made his way by memory to the other side of the room, away from the goat. He moved slowly so as not to attract its attention. He banged his shins against a potted fern. He'd forgotten about the damn plant. Liz had just gotten it a week ago. She was obsessed with plants. Specifically, trying to keep them alive. Her demonic nature made them all wither beneath her touch. Even a cactus that a florist had branded unkillable had fallen to her care. But she hadn't given up yet.

The goat leaped across the room and attacked Liz's latest leafy victim. Bleating and clicking, the goat wrestled with the fern, throwing fronds in the air. The distraction allowed Monster to open his eyes and scan the room. His satchel was by the front door. The goat stood between him and his goal.

It perked up, chewing a mouthful of fern. Monster shut his eyes, but the goat had worked itself into a frenzy. It jumped and managed to grab him. It blindly butted and bit at its invisible opponent. Fangs sank into Monster's shoulder, and he screamed.

The goat was stronger than it looked, and now that it had him, it wasn't keen on letting go. Monster spun around the room, locked in combat. He grabbed the thing by one of its horns, keeping its snapping teeth at bay. The goat growled, spraying Monster's face with sticky saliva. Monster tripped over the couch, tumbled backwards across the cushions. He wrestled with the thing for a minute. He was stronger than it, but it had a hell of a grip.

Monster reached out with his free hand for something to use. His hand fell on a pillow, one of those useless down pillows Liz insisted on keeping on the couch. The kind that cost way too much and constantly had to be moved around when you sat because they just got in the way.

He shoved it in the goat's face. The creature ripped it to pieces in two bites. White down went everywhere, much of it in Monster's nose and mouth. The goat hacked and snorted. Its grip loosened and he pushed it away, rolled off the couch, and grabbed the first heavy thing he saw: the potted fern. Sneezing, he swung it down on the goat's head. The pot shattered. Soil and fluff went everywhere. The goat, protected by its horns and thick skull, barely noticed.

Both Monster and the goat spent another minute sneezing and coughing. Dirt, fronds, and fuzz hovered in the air like a chunky fog. Blinded by all the dust in his eyes, Monster attempted to navigate his way to the front door again. He tripped over the coffee table, which he was certain should've been a few more inches to the right.

Monster sat up and found himself face-to-face with his opponent. It sneezed one last time, and snot spattered his face. Monster doubted becoming invisible would work this time.

He spotted a devil doll sitting on the coffee table's edge. With one arm he fended off the snarling goat and seized the doll in the other. He pushed the doll into the goat's face, and, having not learned its lesson with the pillow, it snapped off the doll's head in one bite.

The devil doll's retribution was swift and effective. Every particle of down and dirt in the air wrapped itself around the goat in a thick coating, covering the creature from head to toe. It broke away from Monster and clawed at the layers. Every bit it tore away only bounced back to stick to it anew. Every furious snort and growl was an exhalation of feathers and dust, orbiting briefly before being drawn back into place by supernatural gravity.

Monster straightened. It was some small miracle that the devil doll hadn't included him in its curse. He'd been close enough and just as responsible for its destruction. But minor devils weren't picky, or especially bright. They didn't care who they hexed so long as they got to hex somebody.

The goat, looking very much like a stuffed animal wandering

drunkenly around the living room, stumbled back and forth, bumping into the walls, tripping on its slippery, feather-coated feet.

Monster checked his shoulder. The wound was shallow, but bloody. He hoped there wouldn't be any side effects coming his way. The bites were always the most dangerous. He'd known a crypto handler who'd been bitten by a sea serpent and now had to drink ten gallons of water a day. And another who could only speak in riddles after a nasty run-in with a sphinx. Monster's own condition wasn't so bad compared to that.

The goat was incapacitated for the moment, but Monster wasn't taking any chances. He grabbed his satchel, limped outside on his bruised shin, closed the front door, and sat on the porch. A quick glance through his guide identified the goat thing as a crypto rarely seen outside of Ireland. And not often there either.

Monster found Chester and woke the paper gnome.

"Damn it," said Chester. "It clearly states in my contract that I get—" He unfolded himself. "Wow, what happened to you?"

"Gaborchend," said Monster. "It's still in the house."

"This is your house, isn't it?"

"Yep."

"Isn't that a little…odd? A cryptobiological rescue agent being attacked by a crypto in his own home?"

Monster hadn't thought about it. He'd been too busy fending off the gaborchend at first and too tired afterward to care. "It's just a coincidence."

"Pretty odd coincidence, boss."

"All coincidences are odd. That's what makes them coincidences."

"Guess you've got a point there," said Chester. "We should get you patched up."

"What about your time off?"

"I've got a couple of minutes to spare."

"Uh-huh."

Chester folded his hands on his hips. "You're supposed to say thanks now."

"Thanks."

Monster found a healing elixir in the refrigerator. The best-used-by date had expired a little more than a month ago, but it was all he had. It tasted awful, and he didn't get the expected energy boost. But his wounds stopped bleeding and the rejuvenation magic tingled.

The stumbling gaborchend wasn't cooperative, but the curse of stickiness had grown to include a lamp, a throw rug, and several magazines. It was fairly simple to draw a transmogrification spell and slide it under the blind, stumbling creature. The curse didn't end with the transformation, though, and Chester attempted to pry the lamp from the transmogrified stone while Monster checked his wound in the bathroom.

The elixir was working, though it wasn't helping with the pain. The wounds hurt, but he could deal with it. He'd been bitten and scratched enough in this job to get used to it.

Monster returned to the living room just in time to see Chester yank the lamp off the gaborchend, only to have it fly across the room and shatter on the floor.

"Sorry."

Monster appraised the damage to the living room. It wasn't terrible. Might've looked worse, but nearly all the down and dirt was still stuck to the transmogrified crypto. There was some blood on the couch, though. Liz wouldn't be happy about that. Or her fern.

Chester struggled with the throw rug. "I'm telling you. Something's up."

"There are a dozen crypto incidents a day in this town," said Monster. "Just the law of averages that some would happen to an off-duty rescue agent."

"I'd buy that if this were an isolated incident," Chester said. "But after these last two days, I'm not so sure. First, there's that supermarket score. Three yetis in one spot. Then there were the trolls and kojin in Miss Hines's apartment. Now this. Anything else strange happened recently?"

"No, nothing. Except that walrus dog at the diner while you were asleep."

"I wasn't asleep," said Chester. "Technically, when I'm in this particular quantum state, I'm closer to sleep than anything else. Really, your world is more of a dream to me."

"So I'm your dream?"

"Could be." Chester grunted and wrestled with the rug, working it half free. "And I myself am very likely merely a dream of a much higher entity. And so on and so on and so on."

"Where's it end?"

"What?"

"The dreamers. Which dreamer is the last?"

"There isn't a final dreamer," said Chester. "It goes on forever."

Monster plopped down on the couch, right on top of the feathers and blood and gaborchend drool. He squirmed before reaching behind him and throwing aside another of Liz's damn extraneous pillows. "It can't go on forever."

"Why not?"

"Because nothing lasts forever."

"Who says? Your mistake, indeed the mistake of your inherently finite senses, is to view the universe as an extension of yourself. You expect that, like you, it should have a beginning, a middle, and an end. But what you fail to understand is that everything you consider to be you, except for that rather silly imaginary part you call consciousness, is merely bits and pieces borrowed from the universe, and to the universe it will all return. You had no beginning, and you will have no ending. Everything that is you has always been and will always be." Chester stopped philosophizing and thought for a moment. "Unless, of course, your entire universe is just a shared dream of my species' universal unconscious, in which case you'll probably cease to exist if we're all ever awake at the same time."

"And what if the dreamers of your universe ever wake up?" asked Monster.

"Then we're both screwed."

With a final determined grunt, Chester wrenched the carpet loose. It sailed free and smacked Monster in the face.

"Sorry."

"Do me a favor, Chester. Dream me a beer."

The paper gnome retrieved Monster's beer. "Maybe someone put a curse on you."

"I think I'd know if I'd been hexed," said Monster. "And there's no hex that can summon a bunch of cryptos. Not one that I've ever heard of anyway."

"Maybe it's a new development. We should check your body for any marks."

Monster didn't feel like getting off the couch, but he supposed Chester was right. If someone had hexed him with some kind of crypto attraction curse, it would be better to know. It wasn't the worst curse for a crypto handler to have, but if it kept interfering with his off-hours, then it'd have to go.

He went into the bathroom and took off his shirt. A glance in the mirror confirmed nothing on his chest, back, or arms. He took off his pants and checked his legs. Nothing out of the ordinary there either. If there was a curse, there should've been some kind of mark.

Monster pulled down his underwear and had Chester take a look at his ass. "See anything?"

"Nope. Wait. Nope. That's just a mole."

Monster pulled up his pants. "See? Told you. No curse."

"It was just a theory."

Something thumped in the bathtub, as if someone had thrown an anvil into it. Monster pulled back the shower curtain. A gaborchend was in the tub. It wasn't the same one. Its left horn was cracked and chipped, and it seemed as shocked to find itself there as Monster was to see it. It bared its teeth and growled.

"I suppose that's just a coincidence too."

Judy went back to Paulie's place, but either he wasn't home or he wasn't answering his door. After banging on the door for four minutes, then waiting another ten, she decided she'd probably have to find someplace else to crash today. She wished she'd taken the time to actually have a few friends.

She couldn't remember when she'd become so isolated from the rest of the world. It wasn't that long ago, during her first and only year of college, that she'd had plenty of friends. So many friends and parties and good times that her grades had gone to hell. She'd failed to meet her scholarship requirements, and her dad couldn't afford to help with both Judy's and her sister's tuition costs. There just wasn't enough money to go around, and Judy wound up the loser in that deal. Now here Judy was, nine years later, no education, a crappy job, no apartment, and no money. It'd all gone wrong somewhere. How could she have made so many stupid decisions? It couldn't all be her fault. Not all of it.

She waited another half hour for Paulie. He never showed.

*   *   *

Judy didn't call ahead. She knew everything Greta would say, and Judy knew that she would have to hear it all. No way around that. But if she had to hear the "talk" on the phone, odds were that Judy would just get disgusted, hang up, and end up in a cheap hotel for the day. If she was going to be annoyed, she might as well get something out of it.

Greta lived in a perfect house. It had a perfect yard, perfect flower beds. The driveway was perfect too. Not a single crack in the smooth, unstained concrete. There wasn't a fleck of falling paint on the perfect walls, and even the lawn gnomes were perfectly arranged in the four corners of the front yard. It was the house that Barbie dolls lived in. Judy had always been more into G.I. Joe. Her ideal house would look pretty much the same as Greta's, except there'd be a secret lever you could pull to reveal a command center, a helipad, and maybe an anti-aircraft gun or two. Greta probably had all that hidden in there somewhere. Greta had everything.

Judy rang the doorbell, which chimed a lilting tune. Something classical. Probably Beethoven. The door wasn't answered right away, and Judy wondered if Greta had already left for work. She found herself hoping Greta was still home as much as she hoped she was gone. All possible futures involving the answering or non-answering of the door before her seemed equally fraught with peril.

The door opened. Greta was in her power suit.

Judy forced a smile. "Hi."

"What's wrong?" It was more of an accusation than a question.

"Nice to see you too, sis." Judy wrestled with her grin, trying to keep it from transforming into a scowl. "I need a place to stay for a couple of days."

"Okay. Sure. Come on." Greta stepped aside and made a half-hearted welcoming gesture. "But you'll have to put that out first."

Judy took a final drag on her cigarette and stubbed it out in the potted plant on the front porch. She crossed the threshold with a shudder. Greta's house was more like a museum exhibit than a home. Weird art hung from the walls, and strange sculptures occupied the corners.

"You've redecorated," said Judy.

"Three years ago," said Greta, sounding again as if Judy had done something wrong.

Judy ignored it. She had enough experience. "I miss the masks. So where are Chuck and Nancy?"

"Nancy has already left for school, and Chuck is out of town on a business trip until Tuesday." Greta went into the kitchen and began going through papers, adding some to pockets in her briefcase, removing others.

Judy went to the refrigerator and picked through the inventory. There weren't any leftovers. The disposal of day-old foodstuffs was a religion for Greta. There was no place for them in her neat and tidy universe. There was nothing to eat or drink.

"Don't you have any soda or anything?"

"We don't drink processed sugar in this house. Chuck has an allergy, and it makes Nancy hyper."

Judy found a bottle of orange juice. She was tempted to drink directly out of the bottle, but the only reason to do that would've been to annoy her sister. And Greta was giving Judy a place to crash, so she could at least play by her rules.

"How's the kid?" asked Judy. "She's — what — ten now?"

"Nine."

"She can read, right?"

"At a tenth-grade level."

"Cool." Judy poured the juice into a tumbler and gulped it down in a long swig. "That's good, right?"

Greta sighed. "So what happened this time?"

"I lost my apartment."

"You could've asked me for help if you couldn't make your rent."

"No, I mean I *lost* it. As in, it was destroyed."

"What do you mean, destroyed?"

"I mean destroyed. Ravaged. Demolished. Obliterated. Annihilated. Gone. Along with pretty much everything I own. Except for my car and these clothes I'm wearing."

"What? How did that happen?" Greta finished sorting papers and closed up her briefcase. "Was there a gas explosion or something?"

"No. It wasn't anything like that."

"What was it?"

Judy tried to remember, but the memory was slippery. Thinking about it gave her a bit of a headache too.

"I don't know. I think it was a wild animal attack."

"Animals? Like dogs or something? How the hell did dogs get into your apartment?"

"It wasn't dogs."

"What was it?"

Judy shut her eyes and dredged her memory but came up with only the vaguest details. None of them made much sense. "I don't know. Maybe it was dogs."

Greta gave her that look. Judy was all too familiar with it. It was accusing, disappointed, and suspicious all at once.

"You're always doing this," said Greta. "You show up with

some ridiculous excuse that doesn't make a damn bit of sense and expect me or Dad to bail you out."

"I do not."

"Yes, you do. Remember that time you got in that car accident?"

"That wasn't my fault."

"And we're supposed to just believe you hit a cow in the middle of the city?"

"It wasn't a cow," said Judy. "It was . . . something else."

"And what about when you burned down that Burger King?"

"I didn't start that fire. I am not an arsonist. That therapist Dad sent me to said so, didn't she?"

"Someone started that fire."

"Wasn't me."

"What about that motel room you destroyed on your senior-year field trip?"

Judy only distantly remembered that, but she was fairly certain that hadn't been her fault either.

"It's just bad luck," said Judy.

"That's a lot of bad luck for one person."

"You don't think I know that? Just the other day at the grocery store I was nearly killed by wild animals."

"More wild animals?" Greta fixed her with that look again.

"Wolves or lions or apes or something. If you don't believe me, you can ask my boss. He was there."

Greta appeared unconvinced.

Judy grabbed the phone. "Here. The city even sent a guy. I bet if you call that'll show in their records."

Greta took the phone and hung it up. "Maybe later. One of us has a job to think about."

"I have a job."

"Yes, I'm sure that aisle stocking is a rich and rewarding career?"

Greta's attempts at sarcasm always sounded more like questions. Judy let it slide. The arguments were always the same. She wasn't interested in them anymore.

"Damn. I'm running late, and I'm driving the carpool today. Just stay as long as you need to get back on your feet," said Greta, sounding far more put upon than Judy deemed appropriate. "Nancy has a sleepover after school. Help yourself to whatever is in the refrigerator."

"Thanks," said Judy. "None of that stuff was my fault, you know."

There was no way for Greta to understand. She'd always had the charmed life, never had to deal with this...stuff. Judy struggled to come up with a better word for it, but that was all she had. It was just a bunch of stuff that didn't make much sense and that she couldn't remember clearly. If she ever got a job that gave her decent health insurance, she might look into getting her brain scanned. In the meantime, it'd be nice if once, just once, Greta had some of her own...stuff to deal with. Nothing terrible. Just a little misfortune to show how easily a perfect life could go off track.

Never happen, thought Judy.

Mary got into Greta's car. "You're late."

Greta shrugged. "Sorry. Family crisis."

Mary turned her head and stared out at the horizon to illustrate her complete lack of interest in Greta's personal life. Greta wasn't too keen on discussing it herself, so she was happy to let it drop.

"Don't mention it to Jeanine," she said, as if she had to. Mary wasn't much of a talker. They'd been carpooling for two years now, and Greta knew absolutely nothing about Mary except that she had a son (name: unknown), she didn't eat marshmallows, and she liked to read Danielle Steele novels.

Jeanine, on the other hand, loved to talk. It wasn't that she was self-centered. She just despised silence. If there was a quiet moment, she just had to fill it. She was already talking the moment Greta's pulled her car to the curb.

"Hey, ladies. You're tardy." Mary's remark on Greta's lateness had been an accusation, but Jeanine's was playful. She winked in the rearview mirror. "Maybe I should give you a detention slip."

Greta didn't find her comment particularly funny, but it was an honest effort, so she smiled back and nodded.

Jeanine greeted Mary cheerfully. Mary offered a terse reply, and they were off.

"Sorry. Didn't get out on time," said Greta.

"Don't worry about it," replied Jeanine. "These things happen. Not like it's the end of the world."

Mary grumbled. The end of the world was probably the only excuse she'd accept, and then only grudgingly.

Greta sped a little. There was a five-minute window to avoid the morning rush. If she could beat that, they could make up for lost time. It might even appease Mary.

They didn't make it. There was an accident that slowed traffic to a crawl. The cars crept along in the exhaust-choked morning air. Jeanine talked the whole while about everything and nothing in particular. Greta did her best to carry some of the weight of the conversation to keep things pleasant as Mary continued to stare, brows furrowed, out the windows.

Something bumped into Greta's car. She thought the driver behind her had carelessly smacked her bumper. But then the roof creaked.

"What the hell?" asked Jeanine. "Pigeons?"

If it were pigeons, it would have to have been a heck of a lot of them, judging by the bend in the roof.

"What's that?" said Jeanine, pointing to the back window. A lion's tail swished back and forth from above.

Greta was too focused on the possible jungle cat sitting atop her car to notice the traffic pull ahead. The driver behind her honked his horn to remind her. She eased forward slowly, nearly banging into the car ahead of her as the lion shifted its weight.

They drove for several more minutes. Everyone was quiet. Greta and Jeanine exchanged curious glances as the lion remained above them, while Mary appeared no less annoyed or concerned than before.

"We should do something," said Jeanine. "Shouldn't we?"

Greta agreed, but she wasn't sure what.

"I'm calling 911." Mary flipped open her cell phone. "Yes, I'd say this is an emergency. There's a lion on our car, and I've got a meeting in half an hour."

While Mary discussed the situation with the dispatcher, Greta decided it might be wise to pull off the freeway. The next exit was three miles away through sluggish traffic and two clogged lanes. No easy feat, even without a lion on one's car. But it turned out not to be so difficult. Greta discovered that a lion on the roof was as effective as a police siren.

Off the freeway, Greta tried speeding up to persuade the beast to jump off her car. It only secured its grip by digging its claws into the roof. They sliced into the interior. Rather than risk having her roof torn off, she slowed to a stop and pulled in to a convenient strip mall parking lot.

"We'll wait here," said Greta.

Mary gave the dispatcher their location and hung up. Impatiently and with great annoyance, she dialed to inform work she'd be even later than expected.

"Should we get out?" asked Jeanine. "Maybe we can make a run for it."

"It's a lion," said Greta. "We can't outrun a lion."

"Maybe it won't chase us."

Mary lowered her phone. "Do you mind? This is an important call."

Jeanine whispered, "I bet it won't chase us if it's not hungry."

"It's probably hungry," Greta said. "How many gazelles are there in the city for it to catch? Don't they always say you should stay in the car no matter what in those animal safari parks?"

"This isn't a park," said Jeanine.

"The logic still applies. Stay put. Sit still. Wait for help."

Greta didn't feel much safer in the car. The gashes in the ceiling proved just how thin a layer of protection the automobile provided. But she reasoned that if the lion was indeed hungry, it would probably go after one of the tasty morsels walking around in the open. She expected everyone to run and hide, but a surprising number of people seemed unimpressed by her situation. They gave the car a wide berth, but it was more of an uncomfortable avoidance that showed in their expressions than outright fear.

A pair of huge paws slapped on the windshield. Spider web cracks appeared in the safety glass.

Jeanine stifled a shriek. Greta kept her cool, and Mary glared at the rogue animal atop the roof while arranging for a cab ride.

Mary said, "That's right. Twelfth and Main. Twenty minutes? Make it ten and I'll throw in an extra twenty bucks."

The lion shifted its weight, causing the roof to buckle in the back. Jeanine grabbed at her door handle. She was in such a panic, she couldn't quite figure out how to open it.

"Don't go out there," said Greta.

Jeanine finally threw open her door. Greta grabbed at Jeanine but couldn't stop her from running. She dashed away without glancing back in her mad scrambling flight. Greta was certain the predator, by virtue of its instincts, would pounce on Jeanine and begin devouring her. At least it would give Greta a chance to get away. She felt a little bad for thinking that, but she was just being practical.

Jeanine did not get eaten alive. She never once looked back, just kept running as far and as fast as she could. The lion remained on the roof.

Greta was relieved and disappointed at the same time. Relieved that Jeanine had not been devoured. Frustrated that there was still a lion on her car and she wasn't sure what to do about it.

"Where the hell is Animal Control?" she said.

"Where the hell is my cab?" said Mary.

They sat quietly for a few minutes more before the lion finally made the decision for them.

Roaring, the beast raked its claws across the roof, shredding it even further. Half of a giant paw poked its way into the car. With another stomp, it shattered the windshield. That was enough to spur the passengers into exiting.

They each flung open their door and ran for it. Mary bolted in one direction, Greta another. She made it only a few steps before tripping and falling. The asphalt scraped the palms of her hands as she tried to catch herself. She barely felt the pain and was on her feet. Something slammed into her from behind and knocked her to the ground again. A shadow fell across her. Greta spun around, her arms flailing wildly.

"No!" she shouted defiantly, drawing on her basic self-defense lessons at the gym. Be strong, be intimidating. Hit the attacker in the vulnerable points. Run like hell. It was basic strategy but seemed as practical to use against a lion as a mugger.

But it wasn't a lion. It looked mostly like a lion, but it had a giant pair of feathery wings. Its face was that of a human woman, though about twice the size of Greta's. Her passing knowledge of mythology allowed her to recognize a sphinx when she saw one.

"No!" she shouted again, readying herself to jam her fingers into the sphinx's eyes as it ripped her apart. She might not accomplish much, but at least she'd go down fighting.

The sphinx sat. It smiled and licked its paw with a giant blue tongue.

Greta took a cautious step backwards.

The sphinx spread its wings and roared. It lowered its head and rose on its haunches as if to spring. The impulse to run hit Greta, but she'd never make it. Instead she stopped moving, and this seemed to satisfy the sphinx, who reclined and returned to licking its paw.

"Where does an eight-hundred-pound gorilla sit?" asked the creature.

"What?" replied Greta.

The sphinx glowered as a low rumble of disapproval rolled from the back of its throat. It flew like a shot to Greta's car and with a casual swipe of its paws smashed a headlight and gouged deep slashes in the driver-side door.

Greta made a break for it. She didn't get far. The sphinx was on her in a moment, knocking her to the ground again. The creature seized Greta's leg in its mouth and dragged her with relative delicacy back to the car.

"What is it that demands an answer but never asks a question?" asked the sphinx.

Greta bit her lip as the sphinx raised an eyebrow and tapped its claws patiently.

"What is it that demands an answer but never asks a question?" asked the sphinx again, this time sounding a touch impatient.

"Damn," said Greta. "I don't know."

She wasn't surprised to find the sphinx displeased with the answer. Neither was she terribly shocked when it proceeded to slash her car's tires and shatter its remaining windows. She didn't bother running. She was pretty sure the sphinx would just catch her and drag her back again.

Satisfied with its latest acts of vandalism, the sphinx sat before Greta and asked, "If Train A leaves New York traveling at two hundred miles per hour..."

"Oh, come on," said Greta. "That's not even a riddle. It's a math problem."

"...and Train B is leaving New York traveling at one hundred miles per hour..."

Greta found a pen and small notebook in her suit pocket and hurriedly scribbled down what she could remember.

"Could you repeat the question?" she asked the sphinx.

The creature frowned and turned its head at an angle, puzzled.

"I missed some of it," said Greta. "I know I can get the answer if you just repeat the question."

"Is that your final answer?" asked the sphinx.

"What answer? I didn't answer."

The sphinx wheeled and leaped on the car.

"I didn't answer!" said Greta.

The sphinx seemed not to care. It tore a bigger hole in the roof and reached inside to rake its claws across the front seat. Then it squatted and urinated on the upholstery. With a satis-

132

fied grin, it hopped before Greta, who was determined to get the next riddle right, even if it was too late to save her car. She could smell the sphinx urine from here, a heady mix of ammonia and tuna fish.

"What is the final digit of pi?" posed the sphinx.

"I don't know. Nobody knows," said Greta aloud without thinking about it.

The sphinx turned toward Greta's ruined automobile.

"Wait, wait."

The sphinx glanced over its shoulder and raised an eyebrow.

"Eight," answered Greta.

The sphinx sat down, folded its wings, and yawned. It didn't move toward Greta's car, and in fact, seemed to have lost interest in everything except its own grooming.

"Eight?" said Greta. "Was that right?"

The sphinx wrinkled its nose at her but didn't reply.

A van pulled up beside her. A man leaned out of the passenger-side window. "We have a call about a sphinx. Is this it?"

Greta nodded. She hadn't called, but the huge mythological creature sitting just a few feet away answered the question.

The man and his partner, a short, dark-haired woman, exited the van.

"Did you answer a riddle?" he asked.

"Yeah," said Greta. "Then it just sat down."

"Yup, they'll do that," said the woman.

The woman had Greta fill out some paperwork while the man mixed together a potion. He poured it into a squirt gun and doused the sphinx with the green concoction. The sphinx fell asleep and shrank to the size of a house cat. He stuck it in a cage. It all seemed to make some kind of sense to Greta, though exactly what kind, she couldn't say.

"What demands an answer but never asks a question?" said Greta.

"Telephone," replied the woman.

Greta completed the paperwork just as a cab appeared.

"Are you the lady who called for a cab?" asked the driver.

"Uh, sure. Yeah, that's me." She was just glad to get out of there, away from that weirdness. At work, some people asked what happened to Jeanine and Mary. She had no good answer, only a hazy memory that didn't really gel. She was ready to get to work and put it behind her.

She discovered her office was inhabited by a flock of miniature gargoyles. They'd opened her drawers and upended her furniture. They'd torn the carpeting to pieces, and two were busy gnawing on her computer.

Quietly, Greta closed the door and decided to take an early lunch.

Some experimentation showed that gaborchends had a particular weakness for Cheez Whiz, and it wasn't difficult to lure the second goat creature out of the bathroom and onto a transmogrification rune.

"I think this all has something to do with Miss Hines," said Chester.

"Why would you think that?" asked Monster.

"I don't know. No good reason. Just an intuition. This crypto surge seems out of place. And it started with the grocery store incident."

"That's arbitrary," said Monster. "I run into cryptos every day. It's my job. And activity rises and falls. It has to start somewhere. It's easy to notice a foreign element and jump to a wrong conclusion."

Chester folded himself a mouth and eyebrows so he could gape.

"What?" asked Monster.

"That was surprisingly cogent," said Chester.

Monster was half pleased, half annoyed by the compliment. "I'm not an idiot."

"I didn't say that. It's just strange for you to think things through like that."

"I have my moments. So I'm right?"

Chester replied, "Probably. Usually a coincidence is just a coincidence. But sometimes it's not. And maybe this time it isn't."

"And maybe it is. Your Judy theory falls apart if you really think about it."

"I don't see you coming up with anything better," remarked Chester.

Monster wanted to disagree but couldn't find a strong counterpoint. "I guess we should check it out. Just to rule it out." He put on his T-shirt and pulled a shoe box from under his bed. He rifled through the box's contents, pulling out a tin car about an inch long and a folded piece of paper.

"What's that for?" asked Chester.

"Transportation. We're not going to figure this thing out just sitting on our butts."

"A little small, isn't it?"

"Har har," said Monster blankly.

"They rent cars."

"That costs money."

They exited the house, and Monster laid the toy car in the street out front. He unfolded the directions and read the three-minute activation chant. In a flash, the tiny toy became a full-size automobile, depending on how lax your definition of *full-size* was. It was bigger, at least. Big enough to hold Monster and Chester and a passenger or two. The wheels were still made of tin, and it lacked windows.

"You can't be serious."

"What are you worried about?" said Monster. "It's not like you can actually die. The worst that happens is that I have to get you another paper body. Anyway, it's perfectly safe."

A goat-headed creature sprang through the windowless gap on the passenger's side of the car. The gaborchend pounced on Monster. He rolled across the lawn, fending off the creature's snapping jaws.

"Hang on, Monster!"

Chester folded himself into a miniature rhinocerous and charged forward, knocking the gaborchend with enough force to rattle its senses. The gaborchend stumbled around in a daze. Monster jumped on it and pinned it beneath him. The creature was strong, but he managed to keep it held to the ground.

"I'll get the Cheez Whiz," said Chester.

Monster pressed his forearm against the back of the gaborchend's neck as he held one flailing limb with one hand and the other crushed beneath his knee. "Take your time."

After they finally managed to transmogrify the gaborchend, Monster was more willing to consider Chester's not-a-coincidence theory.

"What's going on, Sherlock?" asked Monster.

"I'd say someone is trying to kill you."

"By sending goat beasts after me?" Monster tossed the transmogrified gaborchend back and forth between his hands. "They're not very dangerous, really. This is three so far, and I'm not dead."

"Maybe they're not trying that hard."

"That settles it then. It can't be Judy. She has no reason to want to kill me."

"She was just trying to deal with her situation and you kept telling her she was wasting her time."

"She was."

"Whatever you say."

"I was being honest."

"Uh-huh."

"What? I should've lied to her?"

"You could've been more...delicate. She was going through a rough patch."

"And I was helping her deal with it."

"By being honest," said Chester.

"Exactly. What's so wrong with that?"

"People don't always need honesty."

"Not my problem."

"Not to be disagreeable," said Chester, "but you've got a couple of transmogrified gaborchends and a chunk out of your shoulder that say otherwise."

"So she's summoning cryptos to kill me. I've never heard of anyone who could do that. Much less a light cog."

"There are more things in heaven and earth than are dreamt of in your philosophy."

"Huh?"

"It's Shakespeare."

Monster scowled. "I had to read *Julius Caesar* in high school. Had to memorize that stupid Mark Antony speech."

"Yes, I'm sure the trauma of premature exposure to high literature has left lasting psychological scars," said Chester. "Regardless, I'm thinking Miss Hines doesn't know she's doing this. Not consciously."

"How the hell did you come up with that?" asked Monster.

"It's a simple inductive process involving higher-function logic and hyper-observational talents. It's not something I could explain. Some humans have a lesser version of it. They mistakenly label it intuition."

"Yeah, I get it. You're a superbeing from the sixth dimension. Great for you until someone lights a match," Monster said. "You're suggesting this comes from her id?"

Chester folded himself a jaw to gape again.

"Hey, I'm not an idiot," said Monster. "I know some stuff. I've read a few books."

"Comic books?"

"No. I saw it in a movie, okay? *Forbidden Planet*. Great movie."

"It's based on a Shakespeare play, y'know," said Chester.

Monster shrugged. "Well, it's still a great movie. What do you think? If I find her and apologize, my gaborchend problems will end?"

"Couldn't hurt. Why don't you give her a call?"

"I never got her number. I don't suppose that superior not-exactly-intuition-but-close-enough of yours knows it."

"It's not a psychic phone book."

"And yet you expect me to keep believing you're a higher being."

They got into the car. Everything in the interior, including the seats, was made of tin.

"It doesn't have any floorboards," observed Chester, pointing to the unobstructed view of the street below.

"Stay in your seat then."

Monster started the car. Its engine roared as the tin chassis rattled. It was a rough ride, and the car wasn't even in motion yet. He lowered his goggles and wrapped a scarf around the lower half of his face to keep from swallowing any bugs along the way. The car lurched forward, immediately striking something.

They didn't have to get out to see what they'd hit. Monster rolled the car forward until a freshly stunned gaborchend passed into view.

Monster just kept going.

The ride was as smooth as could be expected from a car with tin wheels and no suspension. Chester flattened himself against the seat and held on to avoid being blown away by an unexpected breeze, which wasn't strictly necessary since he didn't blow away easily. But he wasn't taking any chances. By the time they reached Judy's apartment, Monster's butt had gone numb and his fingers were red from holding on to the thin ring of metal that served as a steering wheel. Next time he'd remember to grab a pillow and some gloves.

They stood before Judy's ruined apartment, marked off by police tape.

"Really should've gotten her number," said Chester. "Would've made things a lot easier."

The faded troll stench was still strong enough to make Monster wrap his face with his scarf as he ventured inside. He risked only as far as the living room, finding a scrap of sock that should've been enough to link a decent tracking spell before returning to the parking lot.

"You'd better be right about this, Chester," he said. "If Judy isn't connected to this, then I'll probably be dead pretty soon, buried under a pile of goat men."

"It's just a hunch."

"What happened to that legendary superbeing hypersensitivity?"

"The thing about that," admitted Chester, "it works better on my home plane."

Monster glared. "Stop covering your paper ass and keep an eye out while I write the tracking runes."

Paulie's apartment door opened. Shirtless, he emerged with Gracie on his arm.

"Hey, aren't you that guy?" asked Paulie. "That guy who, y'know, was here when that thing happened?" He stared off blankly for a moment. "Y'know, that thing with the things."

"That's me," said Monster as he drew a circle on the pavement with some chalk and dropped the sock into it.

"You weren't very nice to Judy," said Gracie.

"He's not very nice to anyone, miss," said Chester.

Monster stopped flipping through his rune dictionary. "Do you know her?"

"Sure," said Paulie. "Judy's cool."

"Do you know where she is?"

"Sorry, dude."

"I know where she is," said Gracie. "She left a note."

"She did?" asked Paulie.

"I meant to give it to you but forgot."

"Great," said Monster, abandoning his tracking spell. "Where is she?"

Gracie frowned. "I'm not telling you. You're a collaborator. Don't try to deny it. You stink of demons."

"I don't stink." Monster pulled his T-shirt collar under his nose and sniffed. "So maybe I do stink a little."

She stepped forward and cupped his chin. "Your aura is totally, like, saturated with orange and teal. You could clear that up with some volunteer work. A little less dairy would help your karmic resonance too."

"My girlfriend is a demon," admitted Monster, "but I don't really like her."

Gracie scowled. "That's even worse."

Two gaborchends emerged from Judy's apartment. Grumbling, Monster ran to retrieve one of the many jars of Cheez Whiz he had stashed in the car.

"I realize Monster isn't exactly the most pleasant guy in the world, miss," said Chester, "but he does a lot of good, despite himself."

"Oh, really?" asked Gracie. "Like what?"

"He's rescued hundreds of endangered cryptos."

"I have," said Monster as he emptied two cans of Cheez Whiz onto the parking lot. The gaborchends momentarily forgot him as they lapped up the snack.

"That's his job," said Gracie. "That really doesn't count."

"Like hell it doesn't," said Monster, quickly beginning a transmogrification circle around the creatures. It wasn't easy to draw the chalk runes on the pavement while squirting processed cheese into the gaborchends' snapping jaws.

Gracie said, "Being a good person is more than just not being a bad person."

Chester shrugged. "I guess she's got you there then."

Monster completed the spell. The gaborchends transmogrified in a flash. He collected the stones and stuck them in a bag with the rest of his collection, then pulled out his wallet and counted a few bills.

"If you tell me where she is, I'll give you ten bucks."

Gracie snatched the money from Monster and handed him a slip of paper.

Went to my sister's, read the note. *Please, please, please, call me there.*

There was a phone number but no address.

Monster went to his car and found his phone doll. He tugged on the doll's arms to dial the number and waited for someone to pick up.

"Hello?"

He recognized Judy's voice.

"Judy, it's me. Look, we have to talk."

There was silence on the line.

"Are you still there?" he asked.

"Yeah, I'm here," said Judy. "Who is this?"

"It's Monster."

More silence.

"I don't know anyone named Monster."

Monster lowered the doll and covered it with his hand. "Shit. She's forgotten." He put the doll back to his ear. "Remember that incident at the supermarket and your apartment?"

"Uh...yeah?" But her tone meant she didn't remember much.

"I'm the guy you spent last night with." He sighed. "The Animal Control guy."

"Uh...yeah?"

"We have to meet."

"We do?"

"We have to talk."

"We are talking."

He lowered the doll and swore.

"Let me give it a try." Chester took the doll. "Hello, Judy. This is Chester. You probably don't remember me very well, but..." He nodded. "Yes, the assistant, that's me. I'm sorry, but there's been an oversight on our part. Frankly, we goofed. I've got some papers here that need to be signed. It's not essential, but it'd get us out of a bind. Shouldn't take more than five minutes, I promise."

"So?" asked Monster.

"She's thinking it over."

"What's to think over?"

"She doesn't remember much, but I'm betting she remembers that bad things tend to happen when you're around."

"Yeah, okay," said Judy.

"What would you do without me, boss?" Chester got the address and handed the doll to Monster. "I don't know how to hang this dumb thing up. You really should get a cell phone."

Monster twisted the doll's head and headed toward his car.

"Thanks for your help," said Chester to Paulie and Gracie. The gnome folded himself into a crane and flew after Monster. The tin car rattled its way out of the parking lot.

Gracie held up her newly acquired ten bucks. "C'mon, baby. Taco Bell is on me tonight."

Three gaborchends slinked out from behind Paulie's multi-colored van.

"Sorry, guys," she said. "You just missed them."

Judy's temporary residence was all the way across town. It was not a pleasant ride. Monster's teeth were chattering so hard that he wouldn't have been surprised to have chipped one or two, and he couldn't feel his ass anymore. But he was getting used to it.

"My legs have gone numb," said Chester. "I think that ride damaged my nerves."

"You don't have nerves," said Monster.

"Must be psychosomatic then," said Chester. "Still isn't a pleasant sensation."

Monster knocked on the door, noticing several unseen things rattling in the bushes on the front lawn. One unfortunate gaborchend clung clumsily to a high tree branch. Its disgruntled bleats showed it wasn't happy to be stuck up there.

Monster knocked harder.

Judy threw open the door. "Jeezus, all right already. Give me a . . . Hey, you're yellow."

He stepped inside and shut the door. Then locked it.

"I didn't invite you in," said Judy.

"Recon, Chester. There could be more in the house."

Chester folded himself into hummingbird shape and flitted away.

"Is that a paper man?" asked Judy.

Monster scanned the peephole. Five gaborchends were making their way across the lawn now. "Let's not get distracted. This would be a lot easier if you hadn't removed that memory glyph."

"What?"

Several goat creatures pounded against the front door. Déjà vu struck Judy then. Not quite strong enough to help her remember everything, but a few things fell into place.

"You're the guy who catches weird things!"

"Cryptobiologicals."

Chester flew back. "There was something in the closet. Didn't take a close look, but figured it would be safer to put a chair under the knob. Also, there's a couple more in the backyard, and I'm pretty sure there's something in the attic too."

A gaborchend slammed into one of the long windows on either side of the front door. Judy pulled back the curtain. The goat-headed creature ran its lips and tongue across the window, spreading drool.

Monster quickly scrawled out a memory rune on a sticky note and tried to place it on Judy's forehead. She blocked.

"What are you doing?"

Several things thumped around in the attic.

"We don't have time for this," said Monster. "Stick this on your head so you can remember."

"Remember what?"

A creature pounded from the inside of the oven while another bleated from beneath the living room couch.

"This could become a problem," said Chester.

Monster attempted to put the note on her face. Judy slapped his hand away.

"I didn't want to do this," said Monster, "but we just don't have time to screw around. Sorry if I accidentally hurt you."

He tried to pin her arms. Judy punched him in the breadbasket. In the middle of his painful exhale, she kneed him in the groin. Gasping, he collapsed.

"Take it easy on the poor lady," said Chester.

"Hey, where'd he go?" asked Judy.

Monster, eyes closed and invisible, managed to drag himself across the floor and behind Judy. He reached around and slapped the rune on her forehead.

"Ow, you poked my eye, you son of a..." She lashed out, catching him in the cheek with her elbow and knocking him to the floor again. "Hey, I remember! I remember everything!"

"Great." Monster thought he tasted blood, and he wasn't sure, but maybe a couple of teeth were loose. "You didn't have to do that."

Judy rubbed her closed eye. "You could've been more careful."

The gaborchend under the couch had managed to pull itself halfway out. It bleated and snapped at Monster.

"The master bedroom was all clear last time I checked," said Chester, leading the way.

They shut the door and listened to the increasing volume of the growls.

"What's going on?" asked Judy. "Where did all these things come from?"

"You did something," said Monster.

"Did what?"

146

"We don't know," said Chester, "but we think this is all related to you, so you might be the cause of it."

"Actually," said Monster, "I didn't think you had anything to do with it."

The growls of gaborchends increased in volume and ferocity.

"But I'm beginning to change my mind."

"Cause of what?" asked Judy.

"All these creatures," said Monster. "The trolls and the yetis, the walrus dog, the kojin. And now these gaborchends. You must have done something."

"Like what?"

"Like a spell. Have you done any spells recently?"

"No."

"Did you read any weird books? Drink any odd liquids? Maybe run over a gypsy or sign any contracts?"

"No."

"Don't just answer," said Monster. "Think about it."

"I'm telling you, no."

"Rub a lamp? Steal cursed Aztec gold? Behead an evil wizard? Anything at all?"

"No, I haven't done any of those things. I'd think I'd remember if I did."

"We have to check you for marks," said Monster. "If you're under a spell, odds are it'll leave some kind of mark on you."

"Where?"

"It could be anywhere," said Chester.

"Right," said Monster. "We'll need you to get undressed."

"Wait a minute," she said. "Is this some sort of magical come-on? Did you set all this up just so you could get in my pants? Because it ain't gonna happen, so you might as well call your goat beasts off."

"Don't flatter yourself, lady," said Monster. "I've already got a girlfriend, and she's a lot hotter than you. Now take off your shirt."

She glared, tightening her hands into fists. "Make me."

Monster lunged, and Judy punched him in the nose. She stomped on his foot. He hopped on one leg, which promptly fell out from under him when she kicked his knee.

"Son of a bitch." He wiped the blood from under his nose.

"Y'know, you're really not very good at this," said Judy. "You should take some self-defense classes."

A gaborchend crawled out from under the bed. Another stepped out of the closet. Monster and Judy retreated to the adjoining bathroom. It wasn't a full bath, just some minimum square footage with a mirror and a toilet. She sat while Monster stood pressed against the door.

Chester's flattened body squeezed under the doorjamb. "Thanks for waiting, guys."

The gaborchends thumped against the door.

"Not to be too obvious, but we're running out of places to hide," said Chester.

Judy massaged her temples. The memory glyph was already giving her the buzzing ache in her skull. The steady beating of the door and incessant bleating weren't helping either.

"Wait a minute. I just remembered." She pointed to the note on her forehead. "This thing will kill me eventually."

"Not right away," said Monster. "There's really not much risk at this stage."

She wondered if the buzz was the first sign of an aneurysm.

"I needed you to remember," said Monster. "I had to take the chance."

"That's easy for you to say when it's my life."

She stood and pushed him against the door. He knew she could take him. He had the bloody nose and sore jaw to prove it.

"Listen up, asshole. I don't know why you think any of this has anything to do with me. I'm not the monster hunter. I'm just some loser who works at a grocery store, doesn't have any friends, and may be about to have a stroke. I don't appreciate you coming here and accusing me of...whatever it is you're accusing me of. If this has anything to do with anyone, it's got to be about you. And I don't appreciate you endangering my life and bringing these hell-goats with you because of some dumbass theory you've got. The best decision I made in the last two days was forgetting all this crap and getting on with my life. So do me a favor and leave me the hell alone."

The racket of a dozen enraged gaborchends ceased instantly.

Tense with rage, she grabbed him by the collar with both hands. She spoke softly through clenched teeth.

"I never want to see you again. Is that understood?"

He nodded. Slowly. He was afraid that if he dared open his mouth, she'd bite off his tongue. He swallowed his fear and a little nervous vomit.

Chester slipped his head under the bathroom door. "They're gone."

A quick scouting of the house proved Chester correct. The musky, oily scent of the gaborchends clung to the air. The bedroom furniture was askew and there were track marks in the carpet. But there wasn't a single creature to be found.

"This doesn't make any sense," said Monster. "They couldn't have just vanished."

"Sure, they could've," said Judy. "It's magic. It does all kind of weird shit like that. Now get out of my sister's house. Or do I have to make you?" She cracked her knuckles.

"Okay, okay." Monster threw up his hands. "Hell, you just had to ask."

She flung open the front door, catching a tall, black-haired woman by surprise. The woman's hand was poised to knock. She lowered it.

A second, hulking woman thrust her way through the doorway. She had big ears, huge nostrils, and a long, thick face. Her swollen, muscular limbs and massive upper body would've put the most steroid-enhanced bodybuilder to shame. She moistly chewed on a wad of gum.

"Who the hell are you?" asked Judy with a sigh.

"I'm Ed," said the dark-haired woman. She gestured to her giant friend. "And this is Ferdinand."

"Ferdinand?" repeated Monster.

"It's a joke," said the giant, without a hint of humor. "You're Judy, right?" She glanced at the photo. "Yeah, you're her."

She moved toward Judy, who responded by socking Ferdinand in the face. Ferdinand didn't notice the blow, but Judy clutched her hand to her chest in pain. Ferdinand seized Judy in a headlock.

Monster stepped forward but stopped as Ferdinand fixed him with a glare.

"We ain't gonna have a problem, are we?" she asked with a snort.

"No, no problem." Monster stepped back.

"Good." Ferdinand blew a large bubble then swallowed it down. "I'll be waiting in the car, Ed."

The giant, dragging Judy helplessly along, trundled through the door and toward a waiting automobile parked in the street in front of the house.

"Hello, I'm Ed," Ed said with a grin. "And you are?"

"Monster. And this is Chester."

The paper gnome waved. "Hi."

"It's a pleasure to meet you," said Ed. "Really, it is."

"Where are you taking her?" said Monster.

"Oh, I'm afraid I can't tell you that. Mrs. Lotus gave very clear instructions." Ed winced. "Oops. I suppose I shouldn't have said that." She laughed, mouth wide, braying, before covering up her face sheepishly. "I guess it doesn't really matter. Mrs. Lotus said we were supposed to—how'd she put it?—sanitize the scene. I think that's the way she put it."

"Now wait a minute..." Monster moved toward Ed and received a foot to the gut as his reward. Her kick was so hard, he was sure he felt something delicate and necessary pop inside.

He closed his eyes tight, vanishing, as he struggled to catch his breath.

"Hey, that's a neat trick!" said Ed. "Too bad you won't get to show it to me, but Mrs. Lotus doesn't like me out of the house for too long, so I guess I better get going. Really, I'm so, so, so sorry about having to do this."

She pulled a small red serpent from her pocket. With a deft flick of her wrist, she twisted off its head and tossed the corpse onto the carpet.

"Have a great day." Ed left, shutting the door behind her.

"This could be a problem," said Chester.

"Is she gone?" Monster dared open one eye and spotted the serpent, twitching with fresh life. "Aw, shit. That's not a hydra, is it?"

"I'm afraid so."

The serpent twitched again and two heads sprang from its neck. It also swelled to double its original size.

"Aw, shit," said Monster again. It was a sentiment worth repeating.

The venomous, double-headed serpent slithered toward him.

13

The hydra launched itself through the air like it was spring-loaded. Monster raised his forearm. Instead of sinking its two sets of fangs into his throat, it bit his arm. He would've been dead right that moment except for his immunity to venom. He didn't even notice most poisons, but there was a slight burn in his veins from the hydra's potent one. The fangs hurt a hell of a lot more. Monster flailed his arm, trying to shake the creature.

"Careful," said Chester. "You don't want to—"

One of the hydra's heads lost its grip, and as Monster snapped his arm suddenly, the serpent's second head popped off. The creature struck the wall hard and fell onto the carpet. It twitched a bit as two more heads sprouted from its missing neck, bringing the total to three.

Monster pulled the clinging head from his arm. "Crap, that stings."

"You have to be careful with the heads," said Chester. "The heads come off really easily."

"Yeah, I know," said Monster.

"Kind of like anole tails."

"I know."

The hydra was nearly through with its latest growth spurt. Monster closed his eyes.

"That won't work," said Chester. "Hydras hunt by smell."

The hydra threw itself forward. Monster ducked aside, and it flew over his head and landed on the couch. He grabbed the first thing available, a hardbound coffee table book, and used it to smash the hydra. He struck it several times. The cushions put a bounce in each blow. The headless hydra lay across the couch.

It was only a temporary reprieve. The heads would grow back and the serpent would get bigger. The only thing that could be relied on to kill a hydra was fire. Monster ran into the kitchen.

The stove was electric. He didn't have time to wait for the burner to warm up. He threw open the only door he saw in the kitchen. It was a pantry. Dead end.

"Chester, see if you can find some matches."

Chester folded himself into a monkey and began opening drawers and cabinets with both hands and feet. The red serpent, now grown to the size of a Saint Bernard, slithered into view in the archway between the living room and kitchen. Venom dripped from their jaws, and for the first time Monster regretted his immunity to poison. Instead of receiving the mercifully quick death from the toxins, he was going to be torn apart.

The hydra's new heads didn't appear to be getting along very well for the moment. They snapped at their neighbors, keeping it distracted.

He could make a run for it, but the sudden obvious movement and noise would be sure to alert the creature. With six heads, the odds were that one would catch him. Or he could stand here, perfectly still, until it sniffed him out.

"How are those matches coming along?" he whispered.

"Not so good." Chester opened a drawer. The hydra squeaked slightly, and one head turned toward the kitchen. It narrowed its nearsighted yellow eyes and flicked its tongue, tasting the air.

Monster, moving very slowly, removed a notepad and pen from his pocket. He scribbled a sloppy rune. There was no time to double-check in his dictionary. He could only hope he remembered it correctly.

The alert head rasped a warning, and four of the remaining five turned their attention to the kitchen with an inquisitive hiss. The sixth head was too busy devouring a bowl of waxed fruit to join in.

Monster tore out the piece of paper. It grew warm in his hand.

The serpent slithered into the kitchen. The many heads searched the countertops and cabinets, sniffing in various directions. One drew close to Monster. It flicked its tongue once, twice. Then opened its mouth to alert the others that it'd found the prey.

Monster held out the paper. The hydra snapped it up and swallowed. The head went up in flame. It howled and writhed. The flailing, flaming head whipped wildly, setting the kitchen cabinets ablaze. It brushed Monster, searing his shoulder. Chester folded himself into a hummingbird shape and tried to get out of the way. One of his paper wings caught fire, and, cursing, he flew out of the kitchen, leaving a smoking trail.

The flaming head's neighbors were soon ablaze. Lashing about in a panic, the serpent backed up. Its red scales glowed bright scarlet as the heat radiating from its body and from the many fires it was spreading thickened the air. Having a demon for a girlfriend kept Monster from being overwhelmed by the atmosphere. Geysers of flame exploded from the hydra's skin. It was growing again, more rapidly than ever. In less than a minute, it'd probably be too big to fit in the house. If he didn't make a break for it now, he'd never get past the thing.

The hydra's huge body blocked the alcove out of the kitchen. The only alternative left was to climb over the counter between the kitchen and the living room. He flung himself through it, banging his hip and shoulder in the attempt and falling ungracefully on his face on the other side. There was no time to notice the pain. The hydra's long tail, now completely on fire, smashed the floor beside him. It raised up and looked as if it might crush him before swinging away, knocking the flaming sofa through a wall.

"Owowowowowowowowowowow," screamed Chester as he spun around in small circles on the floor, trying to beat out his wing before it consumed all of him.

Monster snatched up Chester and ran through the spreading flames, out the front door, and onto the lawn. He tossed Chester into the grass and stomped on him until the paper gnome was extinguished.

"Okay, okay!" shouted Chester. "I'm out already! You can stop!" He sat up. There was a hole in the left side of his body. He touched it gingerly and black flecks crumpled from the edges. "Ouch."

The hydra's whipping tail of flame smashed through the house's wall, causing one side of the blazing structure to collapse. The serpent's burning heads burst through the roof. A tower of fire shot three hundred feet in the air.

Monster and Chester put some distance between themselves and the conflagration. They ducked behind the tin car just as the hydra exploded. They crawled under the car to avoid all the flaming debris raining from the sky. It fell for a few minutes.

"What did you feed that thing?" asked Chester.

"Fire rune," said Monster. "But it shouldn't have had that reaction."

"Sometimes I wonder how you ever passed your rune certification."

"We're still alive, aren't we?" They crawled out from under the car and surveyed the hole where the house had stood.

"At least it's dead," said Chester.

"Yeah. Too bad, though. A hydra score is worth a lot of money."

"Should we call the fire department?"

"I'm sure someone already has." Monster checked his burnt shoulder. It wasn't too bad, though it stung painfully to the touch.

A cab pulled to the curb, and a woman stepped out. From the edge of the sidewalk, she surveyed a blackened kitchen sink sitting in the grass.

"What happened to my house?" she said quietly.

"You must be Judy's sister. I'm Monster, and this is Chester."

"Hi." Chester waved.

Greta said, "I came home early because I was having a really weird day. A lion destroyed my car." She tried to remember. "I think it was a lion. And then there was some other...stuff. I don't know. I just wanted to come home early, drink an espresso, maybe watch a movie. But now my house is gone."

"It was either us or the hydra," said Chester. "We're really sorry about this, miss."

"Thank you." She studied Chester for a long moment. "Are you a paper man?"

"Paper gnome."

"My mistake." She nodded to herself. "I think I'll go wait over there until the fire department arrives. If that's okay with you."

"Sure. No problem."

Greta walked away and didn't look back as the sounds of sirens drew closer.

14

Judy wouldn't have minded being kidnapped nearly as much if her abductors had had the decency to bring a properly sinister vehicle. There was something vaguely insulting about being thrown into a purple minivan against your will. They could've at least had the presence of mind to tint the windows.

Ferdinand sat in back with Judy. The giant woman kept her iron grip on her prisoner's neck.

"Ouch," said Judy. "You don't have to squeeze so tight."

Ferdinand snorted and looked out the window. For a few minutes, there was only the sound of her chewing gum.

"Mind if I turn on the radio?" asked Ed from the front.

"No easy listening," said Ferdinand.

Ed didn't turn it on.

"You don't mind, do you?" asked Ed of Judy.

"Whatever."

Ferdinand squeezed tighter. Judy could barely breathe.

"No reason to be rude," said Ferdinand.

"Sorry," croaked Judy. "Being kidnapped puts me in a pissy mood. I'm funny like that."

Ferdinand frowned. Her nostrils flared and her ears twitched.

"You're not human," squeaked Judy through her constricted windpipe.

"Eh, close enough." Ferdinand loosened her grip from suffocating to merely bone cracking.

Judy rolled her eyes. "Oh, hell, this is more of that stupid magic crap, isn't it?"

"I'm afraid so," said Ed.

"Now sit back and shut up," said Ferdinand.

"Please," added Ed.

Judy did as she was told. Once she knew this was all about magic, she decided she wouldn't even try to understand it. She'd just ride it out. It wasn't as if she had any choice. Ferdinand was too powerful to resist. She just hoped they weren't planning on sacrificing her to some forgotten god, making her a mummy's bride, or feeding her to a dragon. She wasn't too worried. They usually wanted virgins for that stuff.

Ed turned on the radio, tuning it to a classic rock station. It didn't seem right to hear someone whistle along with Led Zeppelin, but Ed managed to pull it off.

Judy kept her eyes forward. She kept her whole head forward. Trying to turn it only encouraged Ferdinand to tighten her grip. Judy watched the minutes tick by on the digital clock in the dash. Twenty-two minutes later, the minivan pulled into the driveway of an unassuming two-story house. It was well kept but unremarkable, with little to distinguish it from its neighbors, all of which were identical in nearly every way. Same fence, same yard, same arched roof and stone walkway to the front door. They were different colors at least, though obviously the list of approved colors was limited to shades of green and blue.

This house did have one noticeable difference. Cats. And lots of them. A dozen roamed the front lawn. They all perked up to watch the minivan enter the garage. There was something in their eyes, an eerie sense of expectation, that didn't register right with Judy.

Ed turned back and flashed a toothy grin at Judy. "Okay, we're here! Everybody out!"

They exited.

"This way, please," said Ed.

Ferdinand released Judy, who saw her chance. She dashed for the nearly closed garage door. With some luck, she could roll under it and run to one of the nearby houses. This was a suburb. She had a decent shot of finding some help out in the open.

A red cat slinked under the door, into Judy's path. It meowed, spitting a gout of flame. Judy jumped back to avoid being burned, and the door lowered shut with a metallic finality.

"Thanks, Pendragon." Ferdinand seized Judy roughly by the wrists and twisted her hands behind her back. Judy struggled, mostly for the sake of her pride.

"That wasn't very nice, now, was it?" asked Ed.

They followed Pendragon into the house. There were more cats inside. Lots of them. None breathed fire, though. She wondered if that was because they were normal cats or just well trained. Her captors hustled her through the house too quickly to see many of the details, but what little she did see reminded her of her grandmother's house. Except this place smelled like gingerbread, not cigar smoke. She didn't spot any velvet Elvis paintings either.

They shoved her into a room that was trying way too hard to

be charming. It was all blue and pink with shelves screwed into the walls. All too small to hold anything useful, just knick-knacks and commemorative plates. The entire history of the Napoleonic Wars and the Broadway musical career of Ethel Merman were on display. A thriving rubber plant sat in one corner.

"Stay here," said Ferdinand.

"I'm really sorry," said Ed, "but we'll have to lock you in. I don't really feel right about it, but, well, y'know...after what you just did, I'm afraid you've left us no choice."

They shut the door, leaving Judy in her cell. She flopped down in a padded armchair and propped her feet on an ottoman. She spotted a kettle of tea along with two cups on the table beside it.

The plant's leaves rustled. A pair of cats, one white, one gray, slinked out from behind the rubber tree and rubbed against Judy's ankles. The gray one jumped into her lap, and she scratched it between the ears.

"Hello," said Judy, half expecting the cats to say something back.

The door opened, and an elderly woman with long gray hair entered. She wore a casual flannel top and a pair of slacks. Nothing fancy. She looked eighty, but she glided across the room like a ballet dancer. Poised and graceful was the only way to really describe her. Despite her wrinkled skin, she brimmed with vitality. But she wasn't very big. Judy figured she could push the woman down and run past her without much problem. She tensed at the edge of her seat.

Pendragon trotted in after the woman. The red cat, licking his chops, gave Judy a look that dared her to make a run for it.

Judy decided she preferred staying to avoid having her eyebrows burned off.

The old woman smiled very slightly. She plucked the white cat off the floor, holding it in her arms. "I trust Rob and Evelyn have been pleasant company. They've adjusted quite well. Much faster than I expected, and now they're so much happier this way. Isn't that right, Evelyn?"

The white cat half meowed, half purred.

"Can we dispense with the nonsensical small talk and just get down to it?" asked Judy. "What am I doing here?"

"No reason to be hostile now, dear. I'm merely the guardian of the stone. What I have done is only in the name of preserving the rightful order."

Lotus removed the Post-it stuck to Judy's forehead.

"Will you look at this?" Lotus shook her head slowly. "Such sloppy work. Have the arts succumbed to such inferior magic? It's enough to bring a tear to this old woman's eye."

Pendragon turned his back on Judy for a second, and before she could talk herself out of it, she took advantage of the opportunity. She jumped out of her seat and kicked the fire-breathing cat across the room. He yelped, spitting a fireball that blackened the battle of Waterloo.

"How ridiculous," said Lotus. "Why do they so rarely cooperate?"

Judy punched the old lady right in the throat, who took the hit without flinching. A backlash knocked Judy into her chair and left her dizzy.

"I should have warned you that nothing can hurt me as long as I guard the stone," said Lotus.

Judy was still shaking off the weird magical repercussion of her poorly-thought-out escape attempt. The haze was coming back. It slammed down over her perceptions of the situation. It was just too much to absorb, too quickly.

Pendragon stalked forward and hissed.

"They always have to learn the hard way, don't they, Pendragon?" Lotus sat in the other chair beside the table and poured herself a cup of tea from the pot. "Care for some?"

"I hate tea."

"I think you'll like this. It's my own special blend. Specially brewed to help you with that memory problem of yours, dear. And, if I do say so myself, it is delicious."

Lotus poured Judy a cup and set it before her. The entire process was almost mechanical in its precision.

"Go on, drink it. You'll be glad you did. It will help you remember. For a few hours at least, and with far more vibrant clarity than any shoddy runesmanship can provide."

"And there are no side effects?"

Lotus said, "You won't be able to spell anything for a day or two, and you might have trouble riding a bicycle. But even the most perfect magic isn't a free lunch. As I see it, you have two choices. You can either drink the tea and begin to understand what is happening to you, or you can not drink it and stay as confused as you have been your entire life."

Judy contemplated the cup.

"It's your choice, really," said Lotus.

Judy, once again seizing a moment before she had time to think it through, drank down the tea. There was a twinge in her brain. She knew it was impossible for the brain to feel anything by itself, but that's how it seemed. Like a spark fired at the base of her skull, activating some unused portion of her mind, clearing out the fog and dust.

She asked for another cup, and Lotus was all too happy to comply.

"Tell me something, Judy: do you ever wonder where it all came from?"

"No, I can't say that I have," she admitted.

"The cosmos, I mean," said Lotus. "The totality of what you and I would label, for lack of a better word, the universe."

"No."

"Not at all?"

"Not really," said Judy. Everything seemed sharper now, more in focus. It was like she was seeing things for the first time. She noticed an odd shape to Pendragon's weak shadow. It was hard to identify, but it didn't match up. It was long and thin, and two triangles (*Wings?* she wondered) were attached to it.

Lotus picked up her cup, took another sip, and pondered her tea for a few moments.

"Would you like me to tell you?"

"You mean, the meaning of life?"

Lotus chuckled. "Oh, no. I never said that. I can't really tell you the meaning of life. As far as I can tell, it really doesn't have one. Not that I know this for certain. Just a feeling. No, what I'm talking about is the origin of the universe, how it came to be."

"You know that?" asked Judy skeptically. But not too skeptically. She'd seen enough in the past few days to believe nearly anything possible.

"Of course I do," said Lotus.

Lotus's kitchen was large and welcoming. It smelled of fresh-baked cookies, and every surface was pristine and sparkling. Roosters and hens decorated the wallpaper, and there were a few knickknack shelves screwed into the wall with ceramic kittens on display. A few cats slept in the corners, under the quaint kitchen table, and on the windowsills. A large, fat gray feline sat on the counter.

"Ernst, you know better than that," scolded Lotus. She lifted the rotund cat off the counter and set it down. He meowed in protest. Except it wasn't a meow but an elephant-like trumpet.

"Don't be like that. You know it's not feeding time yet. Go on, now. Scoot, scoot." She gently prodded the cat with her foot. All the other prime sleeping spaces were taken, so Ernst trundled his way out of the kitchen. There was no other word for it. He trundled. He swayed back and forth and his little gray tail swished lazily. It was hard to find a shadow, but Judy was certain the dim reflection in the shiny linoleum belonged to a miniature elephant.

"You must really like cats," said Judy.

"I think I prefer parrots, to be perfectly honest, but it's too late to start over at this stage. I'm sure I'll grow very fond of them in a few hundred thousand years. I didn't particularly care for primates at first, and that worked out all right. For a while, at least."

Lotus removed an apple from the refrigerator, set it on a cutting board, and with a few deft cuts sliced it into six pieces. She offered one to Judy.

"No. Thanks. I'll take a beer if you have one."

"Sorry, but I don't drink alcohol." Lotus frowned very slightly. "Rather nasty habit. I can offer you some juice."

"Pass," replied Judy. "So what's going on here? Where's this stone thing that everyone keeps talking about?"

"It's more than just a thing," said Lotus. "It is the life force of the very universe itself. The stone is responsible not only for the birth of everything you would call reality, but for the continued existence of that reality. It is the beginning and end of creation, the great wheel of life, the endless serpent eating its own tail."

"Sounds keen." Judy never had much tolerance for that New Age bullshit. The tea hadn't changed that.

"Yes," agreed Lotus. "Keen, indeed."

"So where is it?" asked Judy.

Lotus brushed aside the apples and held up the cutting board. She whispered a few words that Judy didn't understand. The wood darkened and became a shiny black slate with swirls of blue and red.

"That's it?" said Judy.

"You sound disappointed."

"I expected it to be, I don't know, bigger or something. So this is the most important thing in the universe?"

"Considering that there would be no universe without it," said Lotus, "I have to say that's correct."

"And you use it as a cutting board?"

"It's indestructible. My countertops aren't. It also makes an excellent nutcracker."

"A hundred and one uses, huh?" said Judy.

"No. Really only four." Lotus counted them off on her fingers. "Cutting board, nutcracker, universe creator, and paperweight."

"Probably could steady a wobbly table with it too," suggested Judy.

"Probably," agreed Lotus, "but that hasn't come up yet."

"Can I hold it?"

"Be my guest, dear."

Judy took the stone. It was a little warm, though not exceptionally so. It vibrated too, but not in a truly perceptible way. It was more a vague sense of vibrant energy. Strange shapes carved themselves into the slate. They reminded her of Monster's runes.

"What's that mean?" she asked.

"Oh, just the stone reacting to you. It not only sustains the universe but records what happens within it. You hold in your hands the source of all knowledge. Everything that has ever occurred is written somewhere within the stone."

"It knows the future?"

Lotus chuckled. "Nobody knows the future. It hasn't happened yet. But anything that has happened or is happening now is observed and recorded within the stone. Of course, for that very reason, it's also largely incomprehensible. Imagine everything within the universe placed within a single, disorganized volume."

Judy scanned the incomprehensible writing. It shifted and stirred, and the more she concentrated on it, the more it seemed to react. She thought she could almost read it. Almost...

"This is God?" asked Judy. "I thought He'd be taller."

Lotus offered an insincere smile. "Yes, very amusing. I've never cared for flippancy, you know."

"Sorry if I offended you," said Judy. "I'm usually more polite to my kidnappers, but so far my week's been really shitty."

"Oh, is that what you think? Kidnapped? Really, how absurd." Lotus laughed. "You aren't a prisoner. In fact, you're free to go whenever you please."

"Right. I'm supposed to believe that? After Muscles over there dragged me across town against my will and threw me in a locked room?"

"Ferdinand can be a bit heavy-handed, I agree," said Lotus, "but I assure you that this wasn't an abduction, merely an invitation. Perhaps more forceful than decorum permits, but that was only because it was so important for us to finally meet."

"You could've just sent a letter," said Judy.

"Far too impersonal. Plus, I needed to talk to you. But by no means are you forced to remain here against your wishes."

"So you're saying I can just leave? Walk out the door?"

"That's right."

"And you won't have Muscles or the fire-breathing cat get in my way?"

"Heavens, no. Although I do hope you'll stay just a little longer to hear the nature of my proposal."

"And what if I'm not interested?"

"That's a bit hasty considering you haven't even heard what I have to say. But what I plan to do can't be done without your cooperation, so it's entirely up to you."

She turned her back on Judy, and rinsed the stone in the sink.

Judy glanced over her shoulder. Ferdinand had stepped aside, and Pendragon was under the kitchen table, more interested in cleaning his paws than watching Judy.

"But ask yourself," said Lotus, "is there anything out there that you want to have? You can leave, go back to your life of confusion, frustration, and disappointment, never really understanding all the little things that will continue to happen to you. Ignorance is bliss, I suppose. But you won't be ignorant. You'll know. Somewhere, in the back of your mind, you'll know. And every day, you'll find yourself asking questions you can't answer. But if that's the life you wish, far be it from me to deprive you of it."

She dried the stone with a towel and put it back in its place. Judy could feel the stone from across the room. That subtle vibration remained in her palm as if she still held it.

She leaned against the counter. "Okay, let's say I'm interested. What exactly do you need my help for?"

"With your help, I'm going to fix a few things."

"What things?"

"Everything. We're going to correct the universe, ensure that everything remains as it should." Lotus smiled, this time quite sincerely and in a manner that Judy found a touch unsettling, though she couldn't say why. "Doesn't that sound wonderful?"

It was always hard dealing with the regular police and the Arcane Commission at the same time. Technically, the Reds were just a special division of the regular force, the way Crypto-biological Containment and Rescue Service was a subdivision of Animal Control. There were liaisons between the departments meant to keep things running smoothly between the cognizants and incogs. But it complicated things when both were involved. Reports had to be filed for both offices, doubling the paperwork. All the magical details only confused the Blues, who were eventually happy to pass Monster off to the Reds, where he gave his statement again to a commission detective.

Detective York had an angular body and a face that was mostly beard and eyebrows. He looked over Monster's statement from across a desk.

"And what's your relationship with Miss Hines, again?" asked the detective.

"Friends," said Monster.

"And why were you visiting at her sister's house?"

"Because of the gaborchends," said Monster.

"Yes, the gaborchends," said the cop. "The gaborchends Judy Hines was somehow responsible for."

"Somehow," agreed Monster. "I know that it doesn't make sense, but I've got a bag full of transmogrified goat cryptos to prove that I'm not making that up."

"Mmm-hmm," said York.

"I've got witnesses. Those two people at the Oak Pines apartments. One's an angel, so she should be trustworthy. And my assistant, Chester."

"Yes, we'll look into that," said the detective noncommittally. "By the way, the clerks in Otherworld Immigration tell me they're having trouble locating the gnome's nonresident work permit."

"I have a copy at home. In my sock drawer."

"Not my department," said York. "You'll have to take it up with them. Have you ever seen the persons who abducted Judy Hines before?"

"No."

"And they said their names were Ed and Ferdinand."

"Yes."

"Did Miss Hines seem to know them?"

"No."

Detective York clicked his tongue against his teeth as he read the report again.

"Okay, Mr. Dionysus. I'm going to need you to look at some mug shots, maybe get with a sketch artist."

"Whatever. Can we just hurry this up? I'd really like to get home."

York fixed him with a quiet stare. "I take it you aren't worried about Miss Hines then."

Monster said, "It's not like we were close friends. More like casual acquaintances. Honestly, I didn't even like her."

York took out his pen and wrote something on the report.

"What are you writing?" said Monster.

"Oh, nothing important."

York clicked his pen several times, then scribbled something else. He pushed his chair away from the table and exited.

When he was halfway out the door, Monster blurted, "I never said I wanted her hurt. She's not a bad person. We just don't get along."

"It won't be much longer, Mr. Dionysus." York closed the door, and Monster heard his clicking pen all the way down the hall.

Monster glanced around the small room. The cheap table and uncomfortable chairs, the bars on the tiny windows, the large mirror along one wall. This was an interrogation room.

"Oh, hell."

He closed his eyes and wished he could just stay invisible permanently.

The door opened. It wasn't Detective York coming to arrest him, much to Monster's surprise. It was another cop with a couple of thick mug shot books. She dropped them on the table and they landed with a thud.

"All these?" he asked.

"That's what the detective said."

"Can I at least get some coffee or something?" he asked. "I'm not used to being awake right now. I work nights."

She passed an indifferent glance over him, not bothering to look him in the eye. "I'll check back in about an hour."

As she was leaving, Chester stepped inside the room. "They wanted me to take a look at some mug shots."

She jerked her thumb toward the table and exited. There was

an extra click when she shut the door, as if maybe she'd locked it. He slid one of the books across the table as Chester took a seat.

"How's it going, boss?" he asked.

"Not too good," said Monster. "I think I just incriminated myself." He imagined Detective York sitting behind the glass. Monster tried not to look at the mirror. "Even though I'm completely innocent. It's not against the law to not get along with someone, is it?"

They passed the next twenty minutes flipping through the books. Monster closed his with a slam.

"Well, that was a waste of time. Did you spot them in your book?"

"Sorry."

Monster slumped forward, putting his head on the table. "Now they'll definitely think I had something to do with it."

"You can't blame them for being suspicious," said Chester.

"Sure, I can." Monster stood and put his hands up to the glass. "Are we done here? Can I go home yet?"

"It might not be a great idea to antagonize the cops," said Chester.

Monster was too tired to care.

"Why do you think those women abducted her?" asked Chester.

"I really don't know. Doesn't your spider-sense tell you anything?"

"I'm out of my depth," admitted Chester. "I got nothing."

"This is probably all just a coincidence," said Monster, though even he was beginning to doubt that. He only told himself that because he was trying to stay out of this mess, whatever it was.

"You don't think they'd hurt her, do you?"

"How should I know?"

Monster sat and drummed his fingers on the desk.

"Okay, let's assume there is something going on," he said. "It doesn't really have anything to do with me anymore."

"This isn't just about you."

Monster sighed. "Okay. Point taken. But I can't really do anything about Judy. I'm not a cop or anything."

The door opened and Detective York entered the room. He slid a form in front of Monster and Chester. "Sign these."

Before putting his signature on his, Monster read it just to be sure it wasn't a confession.

"You're free to go, Mr. Dionysus," said York. "I'm afraid they impounded your . . . car."

Monster forced a smile. "Of course."

"And, Mr. Dionysus" — York paused very deliberately as he glanced over the statement with a frown — "please don't leave town. We might have further . . . questions."

Monster's smile dropped. "Yes, sir."

He walked very briskly out of the police station with Chester perched on his shoulder. He found a bus stop bench and sat there, staring at his phone doll, trying to decide if he should call Liz or a cab.

He brushed away the blackened flakes, pieces of Chester's scorched body, clinging to his shirt.

"Excuse me," said a vaguely familiar voice. "Are you Monster?"

He glanced up at Greta. "No, I think you've gotten me confused with someone else."

"Another golden man?" she asked.

"There are more of us out there than most people realize."

A confused look crossed her face. The origami parrot on his shoulder should've been a dead giveaway, but it wasn't hard to throw light cognizants.

"I'm sorry to bother you, sir," she said softly.

"No problem. Happens all the time."

She walked away.

"That's not right," said Chester.

"I don't pay you to be my conscience, Jiminy," said Monster.

"Just consider it a free service. This can't be easy on her. She knows something has happened to her sister, but she doesn't really get it. You know how the Reds are. They don't bother explaining things to incogs. They just give them a plausible cover story and send them on their way."

"Yeah, I know, but I don't see how it's my problem."

"That kind of self-serving attitude is at least partially responsible for getting you into trouble. Who knows? If you'd handled Judy with more delicacy..."

"Karma, huh."

"Karma is just a philosophical construct, a rather simplistic punishment/reward theory that satisfies your egocentric perception of your universe."

"I was just about to say that."

"You can dismiss my observation with levity—"

"I just did."

"—or you can show some basic consideration and human compassion. Notice I join the terms *human* and *compassion* without irony, which isn't always easy."

Greta stood on the corner, waiting for the crosswalk light to change. Monster told himself the best thing he could do was stay away from her, allowing her to settle back into her comfortable obliviousness, but that wasn't really an option. Just like her sister, Greta was obviously a light cognizant. If she'd been a full incog, then she'd be able to rationalize the magic she couldn't accept. And if she'd been a cog, she could've dealt with it at face value. But, being light cog, she was stuck in a rough middle ground.

"Oh, hell."

Monster reluctantly ran after her. He reached her just before the light changed.

"I know your sister. I was there when they took her, and I guess I kind of blew up your house."

"My house," she said distantly. "Oh my God, my house."

"Now, that really wasn't my fault..."

Greta looked through her purse. "I need to call my husband and daughter, let them know about the, uh, the thing."

"Exploding hydra," said Monster.

She paused and tried to absorb the idea.

"Crap. I don't have my cell."

"Here. You can use mine." Monster offered his phone doll but pulled it back just as she reached for it. "It's a local call, right?"

Chester cleared his throat.

"What? The out-of-state charges on this thing are ridiculous."

"Monster—"

"Fine." He handed her the doll. "But I don't see how inflating my phone bill is going to make up for her house. Two wrongs don't make a right."

"Thank you," said Greta.

She stared at the doll a moment.

"I have no idea how to use this."

They found a coffee shop around the corner, and after Greta reluctantly accepted a clarity rune Post-it on her forehead, Monster gave her a rundown of the past two days.

"Wow," said Greta. "It's true, then. All of it."

"Yes, magic is real," said Monster.

"Not that," said Greta. "That's a little odd, but I can deal with it. No, I meant all the weird things in Judy's past."

"What weird things?" asked Chester.

"Just...weirdness in general. She always had strange things happen to her, things that didn't quite make sense, that she couldn't explain. No one in the family talks about it much. We just assumed she was hiding the truth. Turns out all this time, the truth was hiding from her."

"Something like that," said Monster.

"You're telling us this has happened a lot in the past?" asked Chester.

"I don't know," said Greta. "I'm still trying to adjust to the idea, but yes, I think so. Judy has always been the screwup in the family. When she was younger, she was arrested a handful of times. Mostly vandalism, destruction of private property, some minor arson, things like that. Once, the cops were pretty sure she'd smashed a car that belonged to her ex-boyfriend. They couldn't really prove it, though."

"How long have these incidents been happening?" asked Chester.

"They came and went. She'd be fine for a few years, then suddenly there'd be a new round of them for a few months. We were sure she was bipolar or something. Even sent her to a few psychiatrists, but all the doctors agreed that she didn't exhibit any symptoms. Eventually we gave up and tried to ride out the rough times."

Greta sipped her coffee. "Damn. I always gave her a hard time about all her screwups. I never believed her when she said it wasn't her fault."

"You can't blame yourself," said Monster. "It's just how it is.

Even if she had been able to explain, you wouldn't have been able to understand."

"But I still feel bad about it. She must have been having a rough time. One time, we thought she'd dug up the backyard. I mean, dug it all up. There was a hole at least twenty feet wide and fifteen feet deep. And she's standing there, covered head to toe in dirt, and Dad starts yelling at her for doing it. But she couldn't have done it, could she? Not in less than an hour. Not without a backhoe. How could we think she was responsible for that?"

"Because it was easier to believe than the alternative," said Monster.

"I guess." She pressed the Post-it to her forehead. "I think this is giving me a headache. Is that normal?"

"Perfectly," said Monster. "Nothing to worry about."

Greta rubbed her fingers along her temple to soothe the ache. "Does this happen a lot? If magic is real and most of us can't see it, wouldn't this be happening to people all the time?"

"Not really," said Monster. "There's not that much magic around. Not anymore. It's not uncommon for people to run across it once or twice a day, but it usually falls under the category of ignorable incidents. Incogs don't talk about it, don't deal with it, and just work around it when they have no other choice. It's not often a conflict, just a few minutes a day that they conveniently push to the back of their minds and don't think about, writing incidents off as daydreams or something they read in a book or saw in a movie. That's the haze. That's how it works."

"Why does this keep happening to Judy?" asked Greta. "Is she some kind of monster magnet?"

"We don't really know," said Chester. "If there is such a thing, we've never heard of it."

"What do we do?" asked Greta.

Monster shrugged. "We don't do anything. There's nothing to do. We let the Reds handle it."

"That's it?"

"Yep, that's it."

"You don't think they wanted to hurt her, do you?"

"How would I—"

Chester kicked Monster under the table.

Monster offered his most reassuring smile. "I mean, I'm sure it'll be fine. Your sister can take pretty good care of herself. Trust me."

Greta politely smiled back. "Do you know what I find most disturbing about this? It's how unreal it seems, even now. I still can't wrap my head around it. I know I should be really worried about Judy, but it's all too unbelievable."

"I'm afraid the rune can only help you recognize magic," said Chester. "It can't make it more acceptable to your underdeveloped brain. There's really not a way around that."

"What if they never find Judy? What if I never see her again? How will I even remember what happened to her without this stuck to my head?"

Monster and Chester hesitated.

"What will happen?" she asked more insistently.

"You aren't going to like the answer," said Monster.

"Tell me, damn it!"

"Those incidents that are harder to ignore usually result in a sort of autopilot response. At its most extreme, it's called a complete incognizant fugue, and it allows incogs to forget days, years, family, friends. They'll overlook anything that they can't understand and anything related to it as well."

"You're saying I'll forget about her. I'll forget about my own sister."

"It'll be easier for your mind to do that than accept magic," said Chester. "Sorry, miss."

"But I'm sure it won't come down to that," added Monster. "I'm sure everything will be fine. The Reds are pretty good at handling this kind of thing. It's what they're paid for, right?"

"Yes, of course. Thank you, Mr. Dionysus. You've been very kind to take the time to explain this to me."

"No problem." Monster made a show of looking at his watch, tapping it loudly with his fingers. "Is that the time? I really have to get going. There's this...uh...thing I've got to do. Real important, uh, thing. Magic stuff, y'know. You wouldn't understand."

Greta frowned. "No, I guess I wouldn't."

Monster reached over and pulled the posted rune off her forehead before she could react. Almost immediately, the haze fell over Greta. The effect wasn't normally so fast. There were different levels of light cogs, and Greta was more susceptible than her sister. The stressful nature of the memories also made it easier to shuffle them into her subconscious. The irony was that by explaining things to her, Monster had made it even easier for her to forget. Now they were no longer merely mysteries she didn't comprehend. They were secrets she couldn't absorb.

She looked Monster over with a vague recognition. "Don't I know you?"

"I don't think so." Monster pushed away from the table and left before she could think about it.

"You induced a full fugue," said Chester. "And you did it on purpose."

"What else could I do?" said Monster. "It was the only merciful thing. She couldn't help her sister. Now she can move on at least. She would've forgotten anyway. I just helped her forget faster so she could get on with her life. I don't feel good about it either, but I don't hear you coming up with a better idea. It's easy to criticize."

"You're right," said Chester. "I guess it was the only option."

"It'll all work out. I'm sure Judy will show up in a few days and it won't make a damn bit of difference whether her sister worries an extra few hours about her then."

"I said you're right. What more do you want?"

"I just like hearing it. You don't say it nearly enough."

"Be right more often and I would."

"Do you think I'm happy about it? But I'm not a cop. And every time Judy and I meet, one or both of us is almost killed. Greta was just going to forget eventually. From a practical perspective, it might as well be sooner than later. Save her some unnecessary stress. And when Judy shows up again, her sister probably won't even remember any of it."

They crossed the street and watched Greta finish her coffee. She paid the bill, then quietly got up and walked away.

"You could've at least paid for the coffee," said Chester.

"And I could've bought her a new house while I'm at it. Get off my back." Monster brushed Chester aside. "And get off my shoulder. You're shedding all over me."

Chester landed on the sidewalk and tried to fold himself into his gnomish shape. One of his arms snapped off and fluttered to the ground.

"I think this body has had it," he said. "Might be time to get a new one. I have to get going anyway. The wife isn't too happy as it is. Says I spend too much time in this dimension already."

"Get going. I can handle things now."

"Are you sure?"

"This may come as a surprise to you, but I did get along just fine without you for many years."

"Sure, boss, sure." Chester sounded skeptical, though. "Catch you later."

He left his borrowed body. A stiff breeze kicked up and carried it away like the lifeless paper it now was.

"Good riddance," muttered Monster.

16

Without Chester around to question Monster's every decision, he figured he could get back to his life. He checked his wallet. He didn't have enough for a cab. He had his credit card. Liz paid the bill on it, and he didn't use it if he could help it.

He found a space on a nearby bus stop bench to brood. There was a wide-shouldered bodybuilder type taking up most of it, and Monster had to settle for the half a butt cheek's worth of sitting space. It was more exhausting than standing, but there was an old lady eyeing the spot greedily. He wasn't about to give it to her.

He checked his burns. The expired elixir had healed the damage, though they were still tender.

Hot and moist breath blew on his neck. He tried to ignore it. Nothing was going to drive him from his hard-won two and a half inches of bench. Even if his legs were trembling under the strain of claiming it.

The breather snorted and pressed warmly against him.

"Hey, come on! Don't make me—"

He stared into the flaring nostrils of a winged white stallion. The horse pushed its muzzle against his face. Monster pulled away, slipping off the bench and slamming his tailbone against the sidewalk.

"Son of a bitch." He stood, rubbing the base of his spine.

The horse flapped its wings and grabbed Monster's collar in its teeth.

"No, no, no!" He jumped away. The horse tore off a long slash of fabric from his shirt. "Back off!"

Monster turned back to the bench. The old lady had swooped in to claim his space. She smiled at him sinisterly, but he knew her varicose-veined legs couldn't hold up forever. It was just a matter of time.

The horse wrapped its wet lips around his ear. Monster put both hands on its head and pushed it away. "Get lost! Scram!"

The horse moved its head to one side and focused one solid blue eye on Monster. It whipped its head, slapping him in the face with its long mane. It whinnied derisively.

Sputtering, Monster checked the horse for tags or a brand of ownership. It didn't have one. He didn't know where it came from, but winged horses didn't just fall out of the sky. Well, maybe they did sometimes, but a specimen this well bred and friendly had to belong to someone.

The horse stomped its right hoof three times on the sidewalk as it continued to look at Monster with some indefinable expectation.

"Hell, let's get you bagged and worry about the reward later."

Monster pulled out his dictionary. The horse snatched the book. After a brief struggle, a corner of the book and a few scraps of paper came off in Monster's hand. The horse chewed on the rest, then dropped it into a sewer drain.

The stallion reared upward, spread its wings, and whinnied. It settled down and kicked over a garbage can. The nearby incogs glanced over with annoyance as they stubbornly pretended nothing weird was happening.

"Nice horse," said the bench-stealing old lady. "Is it yours?"

He pushed it away. "Does it look like mine?"

"Kind of."

The stallion tried to enfold one of its wings around Monster. He slipped underneath the mass of feathers.

"He sure seems to like you," she observed.

The horse turned around and slapped Monster with its tail.

"I think he wants you to ride him," said the old lady.

The horse snorted and stamped the sidewalk twice.

"Oh, no!" He put his hand on its muzzle and kept it at arm's length. "No way!"

"I've always wanted to ride one of those," said the lady.

"Be my guest." Monster turned his back to the stallion. "I'm not interested. I know Judy sent you. I don't know how she does it, but she did, didn't she?"

The horse's only response was to nibble on its shoulder.

Two street Reds, a doughy human and a stocky dwarf, headed in Monster's direction.

"Sir, is this your animal?" asked the human officer.

"What?" said Monster. "No, it's not mine. I've never even seen it before."

The horse nuzzled Monster's neck.

"Are you sure it's not yours?" asked the dwarf.

"Seems to really like you, sir," said the human cop.

"That's what I said," remarked the lady on the bench.

"You are aware that winged horses aren't allowed on the street, aren't you, sir?" asked the dwarf.

Monster said, "Actually, I'm glad you're here, officers. This horse is looking for some help, and I'm sure you could be of more help than I could."

The stallion bit his arm.

"Ouch! Hey, cut it out." He nearly smacked it across the muzzle, but caught the disapproving expressions on the Reds' faces and eased into a soft pat instead.

Both the Reds pulled out their ticket books and started writing. Monster didn't even bother arguing as they each peeled off a citation for having an unlicensed animal and another for littering.

The dwarf pointed to a steaming pile of horse dung. "And clean that up."

"Sure thing, officer," said Monster with a forced smile.

He did his best to ignore the horse, but it wasn't going away.

Reluctantly, he finally called the only number he could think of. An answering machine picked up.

"Hardy, I know you're there. Pick up. I know you're there. Damn it, pick up the phone, you lazy—" Monster chewed on his tongue as he stumbled for the right phrasing. "Come on, man, you owe me. You're not still mad about that exploding tire thing? That was just a joke. No big deal. I was just screwing with you. That's what we do. We screw with each other. You screw with me. I screw with you. It's all good fun, right? Nothing personal."

The machine cut him off. He dialed again.

"Give me a break, buddy. I've had a really lousy day, and if I had anyone else to call, I would. I just want to go home and I don't want to take the damn bus. It's not like you haven't been an asshole to me in the past, but if you were so desperate that you had to call me for a ride, I'd be a good guy and help you out."

Hardy's gruff voice spoke over the line. "Bullshit, Monster. And I ain't your buddy."

"Okay, I don't like you, and you don't like me. But if you pick me up I'll split the retrieval fee on a winged horse bag."

Hardy snorted into the phone and made an unpleasant hocking sound. "Where the hell did you find a winged horse?"

"Does it matter? It's here with me and if you pick me up, you can score it at the same time."

"Why can't you score it?"

Monster sighed. "Do you want it or not? A winged horse bag is worth a lot of money."

"Sure. I want the whole fee, though."

"No way. I'm only asking for a ride across town."

"In the first place, I don't know if I believe you've got a line on an unclaimed winged horse. Doesn't really add up right that you would. In the second, if you've got one then just score it yourself and let me get some sleep. And in the third place, I really don't give a crap. So take it or leave it. You've got ten seconds before I hang up."

"I'll just keep calling," said Monster.

"I'll just unplug the phone," replied Hardy. "Do we have a deal...buddy?"

"Yeah. Whatever. Just get here soon."

Half an hour and two more dung deposits later (none of which Monster cleaned up), Hardy pulled up in his truck. He didn't park but shouted at Monster through the open window.

"Holy crap—you really do have a winged stallion!"

"Yeah, and it's all yours," said Monster.

Hardy pulled around the block in search of a close parking space.

The stallion fixed Monster with one of its blue eyes.

"Don't look at me like that. You don't expect me to trust you, do you? For all I know, she sent you here to kill me. I'll get on your back. You'll carry me a thousand feet into the clouds then buck me off. You'll excuse me if I don't feel like taking that chance."

The horse nickered and nodded as if it agreed.

Hardy trundled around the corner. He carried a grimoire as thick as a phone book under one arm.

"Don't they have a pocket edition of that?" asked Monster.

"I prefer the large-print edition. Easier to read." Hardy struggled to get the hooks of his glasses under his curved horns and over his ears as he flipped through the book.

Monster settled in. Incantations were Hardy's magic of choice. Monster didn't care for spoken magic. One garbled syllable could have unpredictable and disastrous results. He'd given up on incantations in college when something had gone wrong while he attempted to light a candle with a chant. Instead, he'd melted the table they were sitting on. He knew magic had its own logic, but even he didn't see how a wooden table could melt. From then on, he'd stuck with written magic, convinced that nobody could do anything significant by incantation.

Hardy pulled a large Zip-loc bag from his pocket. He cleared his throat and put his hand on the horse's muzzle. He chanted in strange, unintelligible syllables for a few minutes. A breeze kicked up, and thunder cracked. The winged stallion collapsed into a mound of fine white powder. A miniature tornado swept up the powder and funneled it into the bag.

"What did you do?" asked Monster.

"Dehydrated it for easy storage," said Hardy as he sealed the bag. "Some of us are professionals."

Monster wondered if Judy was really in trouble, but it didn't make a lot of sense for her to ask him for help. He couldn't think of a reason to risk his neck by getting involved. He felt bad for her, sure, but it wasn't his business. He wasn't the kind of guy to jump on a winged stallion and ride to the rescue. She should've known that. He hoped she was okay, but expecting him to get more involved was just dumb.

Monster had Spaghetti-Os for an early dinner, then tried to watch some television. All reruns. He was too weary to pay much attention in any case. Healing magic always had that effect. It wasn't hard to coax the body to quickly recover from wounds, but it still played hell with his metabolism. Combined with his lack of sufficient sleep, Monster was drained. He fell asleep on the couch again, and woke up a couple of minutes later. He'd changed from yellow to a painfully bright orange.

Orange wasn't so bad. He could glow when he was orange. As bright as a spotlight if he put some effort behind it, though prolonged radiance dehydrated him. Not really useful, but it was voluntary and didn't make his life harder.

He sluggishly rose from the couch and trudged toward the bedroom. He was almost too focused on his bed to hear the gentle scratching at the door. Almost.

It wasn't hard to figure that this was probably another crypto sent by Judy. He didn't want to open the door to find out. Maybe if he just didn't answer the door, Judy would get the hint and seek help elsewhere.

Monster flopped into bed and tried to ignore the steady scratching. It grew louder. He remembered the gaborchends, and how that problem had only worsened until he'd confronted Judy. Maybe if he confronted whatever was at the door, he could persuade it to leave.

Worth a shot.

He opened the front door a crack and peeked outside. It wasn't a winged horse this time, but a gryphon. It had clawed away most of the paint on the door, leaving a deep gouge.

"For hell's sake."

The gryphon screeched and pushed against the door. Monster pushed back, but the beast easily shoved its way inside, aside from some difficulty getting its wings through the door.

"No! No! No!" said Monster. "Forget it! I am not going! Do you hear me? I'm not getting involved."

The gryphon screeched. Then tore away swaths of carpet with its claws.

"Why me? Why not someone else?"

The beast tilted its head to one side, then screeched again. But this was just a dumb crypto. It couldn't tell him why Judy had singled him out. It sat on its lion haunches and stared at him with unblinking eyes.

"Fine. Sit there. I don't care. But I'll tell you right now, if you're smart, you won't be here when Liz comes home. See this circle on the coffee table?" He pointed to a barely visible ring marring the wooden surface, and the gryphon focused on it. "That happened because one time"—he held up his finger and waved it at the gryphon for emphasis—"just one time, I forgot to use a coaster. And she nearly chopped my right leg off at the knee for that. I'd hate to think what she'll do to you when she sees this mess."

Gryphons were about as smart as clever parrots, and this one did seem to get nervous for a moment. Its feathers ruffled, and its tail fell limp. But it fixed him with a stare that said, at least as far as Monster could tell, *Buddy, it's not up to me. I'm just following orders.*

Monster considered retreating to the bedroom, shutting the door, and letting the gryphon have the run of the rest of the house. The living room was already a mess after the gaborch-end incident earlier. Any more damage a full-grown gryphon might do was hardly noticeable.

The creature gouged its beak into the couch armrest, tearing upholstery and spilling white foam.

Sighing, Monster found a spare rune dictionary, had the gryphon follow him into the kitchen, then used a dry erase marker to draw the transmogrification circle on the linoleum. He stopped short of drawing the last line.

The gryphon chirped, sounding almost disappointed in him.

"It's not like I don't care," said Monster. "It's just...why should I risk my life for someone I barely know?"

If the gryphon had an answer, it wasn't sharing.

Monster finished the rune and the gryphon transmogrified in a flash. He picked the stone off the floor, placed it on the kitchen table, and stared at it for ten minutes.

He felt bad, and he didn't know why.

Chester would probably know. Monster went to the bedroom and found one of the paper gnome's spare bodies. It was just a long sheet of paper covered with runes. It'd taken Monster a solid week to write them all down correctly. Afterward, he'd just gone to the public library and run off a few dozen copies.

Monster tried activating the new body. The paper folded itself into a face.

"The entity you are trying to reach is currently unavailable. Please try again later. To leave a message, wait until after the—"

Monster smoothed the paper flat. He couldn't blame Chester for blowing him off. The gnome had obligations in his own plane too. Monster stuck the paper in his pocket. He'd try again later.

He went back to the kitchen and grabbed a beer. He sat and stared at the gryphon stone while finishing the beverage.

He couldn't figure out why Judy kept sending cryptos. He was sure their dislike was mutual. She'd even tried to kill him with her subconscious. Sure, she hadn't tried very hard, but it didn't mean that he was over it yet. All they'd done since their first meeting was fight and make messes of each other's lives. Well, bigger messes. She'd even said as much.

So why him?

He decided, guilt or no guilt, he needed some sleep more than anything. Even at his best, he wasn't much good at this without Chester. Maybe in the morning Monster would have a better grasp on things. Maybe he'd wake up and have it all figured out and know exactly what he needed to do to fix everything. Probably not, but right now he was dry. Some sleep couldn't hurt.

The house trembled. Monster grabbed the chair to keep his balance. Maybe it was just an earthquake, he hoped, despite knowing better. He should've seen it coming. First the winged steed. Then the gryphon. Now this. She wasn't taking no for an answer.

The rumbling grew more violent. Pots and pans spilled onto the floor with a clatter. The whole house shook with enough force to cause the furniture to shift and bounce. Monster struggled to stay standing.

"Give me a break!" he shouted at the transmogrified gryphon. "Can't you just find someone else?"

The living room exploded as a giant purple worm burst its way through the floor. The beast unleashed a strangled hissing shriek, splattering Monster with a rain of saliva. A long tongue shot out of its puckering, rounded mouth and snagged Monster by the ankle. He grabbed on to something, anything. But all he found was a kitchen chair, which he ended up dragging along with him as the worm slurped him down.

The creature gurgled. It belched, spitting out the chair, before disappearing into the earth.

Judy sat in Mrs. Lotus's backyard. Ed had been nice enough to go and buy some beers and pretzels, and together they sat under the early-evening sky. They didn't talk. Judy had too much on her mind, although she really wasn't thinking about any of it. Instead, she ate pretzels and studied Ed.

"So what are you?" asked Judy. "I mean, what were you? Before."

"Before?" asked Ed.

Judy hesitated, wondering if it was bad manners to ask this question.

"Y'know..." She let the question hang, but Ed didn't seem to get it. "Before Lotus did the thing to you."

"You mean, the transformation?"

"Yes, that."

"Horse." Ed smiled, sipped her beer. "This is yummy, isn't it?"

Judy examined Ed. It was kind of obvious when you knew

what to look for. Strong legs, thin face with large teeth, big brown eyes.

"I get it," realized Judy aloud.

Ed's blank expression made it obvious she didn't.

"Mr. Ed was a talking horse," said Judy. "On an old TV show."

"Mrs. Lotus doesn't let us watch TV."

Judy had guessed that, since Lotus didn't own a set. It was the only reason Judy was out here in the backyard, watching the evening sky. It was more entertaining than she'd first assumed. The tea was still working its magic, and she noticed things. Like a flock of birds perched on a nearby telephone line. They weren't birds at all but miniature gargoyles. And the garden gnomes in Lotus's garden were really alive. They stood very still, but she caught one of them blinking.

"And Ferdinand used to be a bull — er, cow?" said Judy.

"Yes."

"And all the cats, they used to be other things too, right?"

"Not all of them," said Ed. "But, yes, most. They're the test subjects."

"What is she testing?"

"I don't know."

"Does it have anything to do with preserving the natural order?"

"I really don't know. I can't understand Mrs. Lotus's plans. I don't think anyone can."

"You've never wondered?"

"Mrs. Lotus is very old, you know. Older than anyone. She must know what she's doing."

"Uh-huh," said Judy without commitment.

Several gargoyles swept down to attack Lotus's tomato plants.

The garden gnomes sprang into action, fending off the creatures. The battle was brief, and the gargoyles were repelled.

All they wanted was a single stinking tomato. It wasn't a lot to ask for. Judy went over and picked a couple of juicy red ones from the garden. The gnomes threatened her with their spears, but she brushed them aside. She tossed the tomatoes to the gargoyles. They ate the fruit while crowing with high-pitched glee.

Judy smirked at the garden guardians. She may not have been able to beat her own garden gnomes. Hell, she wasn't even sure what her personal tomato was. But there was something empowering about helping the gargoyles find theirs.

The ground rumbled beneath Judy's feet. She backed away as the garden split open. Gnomes were tossed in the air, much to the cackling delight of the gargoyles. A purple hissing worm rose up. The huge creature convulsed as its round mouth opened. With a horrible retching shriek it spit a Day-Glo orange man before Judy. The worm wiped the drool from its maw with a long tongue, then sank back into the ground, leaving only a seven-foot hole where the garden used to be.

The garden gnomes picked themselves off the ground as the gargoyles chortled at their misfortune. The orange man, covered in slime, groaned.

"Monster?" said Judy. "Is that you?"

He pushed himself to his knees and wiped the slime from his face. "Oh, shit. It's you. I knew it would be you. It's always you."

Ed came over. "Are you all right?"

Monster sputtered and coughed. Slime had gotten up his nostrils, into his mouth, his ears, and just about every other orifice he had. Even the back of his eyeballs felt gooey.

Ed and Judy tried to help him up, but Judy recoiled at the sticky drool that coated him. "Ew, gross."

"I just spent half an hour crammed in a giant worm's esophagus," said Monster. "You'll pardon me if my hygiene isn't up to par."

Ed said, "Didn't I sanitize you?"

"That's a cute word for it," said Monster.

He threw a sucker punch into Ed's gut. He followed with a blow aimed at her face but ended up hitting her in the throat. She choked.

Judy grabbed his arm.

Monster swung out with his other fist and smacked Ed in the jaw. She fell over.

He shook his hand. He didn't have much fighting experience. It hurt like hell.

"Come on!" He yanked Judy toward the gate.

She pulled away. "What's wrong with you?"

"I'm rescuing you."

"Who says I need to be rescued?"

Groaning, Ed stood. Monster grabbed a decorative rock from the lawn and prepared to smash her across the skull with it.

Judy kicked him in the shin and he stumbled. The rock fell on his foot.

"Are you crazy?" he asked between fits of swearing. "I'm trying to help you."

"You're freakin' out!" she said. "You could've killed her with that."

"It would serve her right, considering she tried to kill me. That crazy bitch sicced a goddamn hydra on me." Before Judy could stop him, he kicked Ed. "But I am a professional cryptobiological control agent!" Judy grabbed him in a half-nelson and pulled him back. Legs flailing, he still kept trying to kick Ed. "Bet you didn't know that, didja, you crazy—"

Judy threw him to the grass.

"Are you all right?" she asked Ed.

"Is she all right?" Monster laughed as he sat up. "What about me? I don't believe this. You drag me here, in the belly of a giant purple worm, against my will, and then, when I do try to rescue you, you keep screwing it up. You are seriously messed up, lady."

"I have no idea what you're talking about, Monster, but I'm sure we could work this out if you'd stop being an asshole for a minute."

"I'm the asshole!" he said with mock illumination. "Here I thought I was just some guy, another victim of your lousy subconscious. But it turns out, I was wrong and that somehow I'm the bad guy."

Judy held out her hand, but he made a point of standing without taking it.

"Screw this. Who needs it? I'm going home." He glared at Judy. "And if this is all in your subconscious, please, for the love of gods, let me be. No more Scottish goat men or winged horses or purple worms. You go your way. I go mine."

Judy said, "I still don't know what—"

"Sure you do. In the back of your head you do, anyway. And all I'm asking is for whoever runs things backstage to just let me walk out of this stupidity."

She opened her mouth, but Monster placed a slime-coated hand over her face.

"Don't say anything. Just nod. Please, just nod and let me know that somewhere, deep down inside, you understand and will stop screwing with my life."

Glaring, Judy nodded. He removed his hand, and she gagged.

"Oh my God." She retched and spit the slime from her mouth. "That stuff tastes like freeze-dried dog turds."

He grunted and spat. The area of grass where he'd fallen was already beginning to yellow and die beneath the toxic worm goo.

"Jeepers," said Ed. "I do hope Mrs. Lotus isn't terribly upset when she discovers you're still alive."

"Wait a minute," said Judy. "He's telling the truth? You tried to kill him?"

Ed rubbed her neck, where a small bruise was forming. "Mrs. Lotus called it 'sanitizing.' She said it was . . . Oh, what was that word she used again?"

"Expedient," said Lotus as she stepped onto the porch with a tray of tea and cucumber sandwiches. Ferdinand stood behind her.

Monster studied the gray-haired woman with the wrinkled face, long dancer's legs, and obvious vitality. "I have no idea what is going on here, and I don't really give a crap. If you'll excuse me, I'm going home to take a shower before this slime rots away my skin, then get smacked around by my girlfriend and have some angry sex."

"I'm afraid I can't allow that just yet."

Lotus nodded to Ed, who stepped in Monster's way.

"Don't make me kick your ass again," he said.

She whirled, attempting to land a roundhouse across his chin. The pain of her bruised ribs startled her halfway through the maneuver, and she staggered, clutching her side.

Monster clocked her across the jaw. It wasn't a well-aimed hit, but he put all his weight behind it. So much so that he nearly threw himself to the ground. But Ed was the one who fell.

"Warned you," he said, shaking his bruised fist. "Goddamn, that hurts."

Lotus stood before him. He glanced over his shoulder at the porch where she'd been only seconds ago. She could move fast.

"All right, old lady. You want a piece? There's plenty to go around."

Judy tried to warn Monster, but by the time she opened her mouth, he'd already thrown one of his trademark clumsy strikes. Though the aim was off and it probably wouldn't have done much more than unsteady Lotus, the magic protecting her reacted with brutal power.

It hurled Monster across the lawn. Judy jumped aside just in time to avoid being struck by his flying body. He landed in the grass, sliding several feet before coming to rest at the porch steps.

Judy ran over and checked on him. He wasn't moving, and his eyes were closed. She thought he might even be dead until she noticed he was breathing. His eyes fluttered, and his mouth opened, spilling out unintelligible syllables.

Ferdinand shoved Judy aside and picked up Monster's limp form.

"You still want us to sanitize him?" asked Ferdinand.

Judy hadn't seen Lotus move across the lawn to the table. It seemed impossible that she could run all the way over there without using the porch steps beside Judy, but Lotus was there now, pouring herself some tea as she considered the question.

"Hold on." Judy held up her hands. "You can't seriously be thinking about killing him. Sure, he's an ass, but I thought you said we were going to fix the universe. And I don't see how killing him would fix anything." She paused. "Well, actually..."

Ferdinand wrapped a large hand around Monster's face. He groaned.

"No, no," said Judy. "It doesn't matter. Still doesn't make it right."

"No, I suppose not," agreed Lotus, though she sounded rather disappointed. "I don't see the harm in keeping him safely out of the way until our plan comes to fruition. Won't really matter after that. Ferdinand, show our guest to his new room. The one with the full bath. I'm sure he'll be eager to take a shower once his pain subsides."

Ferdinand dragged Monster, limping along without an ounce of fight left in him, into the house.

Ed wiped some blood from her mouth. "I don't feel very well."

"Oh, dear. That is rather nasty, isn't it? Why don't you go into the kitchen and brew up a pot of my special get-well tea? Second shelf, cabinet on the right, blue tin. You can't miss it. Drink it right up, and you'll feel right as rain in no time at all."

Ed went inside, leaving Judy and Lotus alone on the porch. Lotus sipped her tea. Her smile never wavered, and she looked as warm and friendly as ever, an unlikely cross between a cool grandmother and a gracefully aging Rockette.

But she wasn't either of those things, Judy realized.

"You didn't really try to have him killed, did you?" Judy asked.

"Why all this bother over one insignificant life? I swear, it's as if mortals have no perspective at all. It's not as if their lives amount to much in the end anyway. In my time, I've seen untold billions live and die, and trust me, the world rarely notices or cares. Even kings and gods fade into oblivion, given enough time." Lotus offered Judy a saucer with a teacup. "Care for some sugar?"

"No, thanks." Judy accepted the saucer. "But you can't blame him for being mad about it, can you?"

Lotus shrugged. "I suppose not. Still, he did ruin my garden, so I guess we'll call it even. Have a sandwich, dear."

"He'll be okay, won't he?" asked Judy. "You're not going to hurt him?"

"Perish the thought." Lotus chuckled. "His life means nothing to me, and I bear him no malice. Though I must say I'm a bit perturbed by the garden. The carrots were quite promising this year. Still, if it helps your delicate sensibilities to keep him alive, I'll be happy to indulge you."

Judy opened a beer and took a long drink. She didn't think she could trust Lotus anymore. The woman, if she was even a woman at all, was definitely a little bit loony. But she also seemed so nice, so pleasant, even when issuing death orders.

Lotus had said Judy was free to leave at any time, but somehow Judy doubted that. She didn't trust the old woman, though she kept that to herself and smiled while munching a pretzel.

She felt a bit foggy. The haze was returning.

"You should drink some more tea," said Lotus. "Keeps the head clear."

Judy took a long drink. Within a few minutes, everything came into focus again. It all made perfect sense, really. Lotus was so old and wise. She must have known what she was doing.

"Care for another cup?" asked Lotus, even as she poured Judy's second.

After drinking this, Judy still didn't approve of killing Monster, but she was fairly certain that Lotus had her reasons. And even if Judy didn't understand those reasons, she assumed they were perfectly sensible. Lotus had a point. What was the big deal with one measly life when they were going to make the world a better place in the end?

"I'm thinking about turning your friend into a fish. A koi or possibly a trout," said Lotus. "What do you think about that?"

"Whatever you think is wisest," replied Judy. "You know best."

18

Monster was vaguely aware of being dragged into the house and thrown into a guest room, but it was a few minutes until he regained his senses enough to take note of his surroundings.

He'd been in prison before. When he was eighteen, he'd spent two days and a night in a Mexican jail cell, playing cards with a giant Belgian. The dank cell stank of urine and mold, but the beans had been good and the Belgian knew a lot of knock-knock jokes. He wished he was back there.

His new cell was bedecked in yellow wallpaper. Dinosaur sheets covered the single bed. He went to the window and parted the clown-themed curtains. He was on the second story, but if he broke the glass and climbed down the sloped roof, he could probably make the jump. He picked up a tall, thin floor lamp. It was light but could probably do the trick. He stopped short of smashing it into the glass.

Too easy. They'd probably thought of that. Maybe he was doing something stupid again. Maybe not, but he was getting pretty tired of doing stupid things. It might be smarter to consult an outside opinion. Ferdinand had done a cursory search, but she hadn't found Chester's paper body folded in Monster's pocket. He laid it on the bed.

Nothing happened. Not even the failed connection notice that normally came.

Some kind of nullifying counterspell was interfering. Monster had expected as much. There was no way for Chester to get back into his paper form. Monster was on his own. And if there was a spell keeping Chester at bay, there was also probably another that would bite him on the ass if he tried to escape.

The guest room had a small bathroom with an even smaller shower. But it got the job done. It didn't clean his clothes, though his boxer shorts were relatively slime-free. He lay on the bed in his underwear and tried to come up with a plan that had the least chance of backfiring.

The door opened. Monster didn't even try to make a break for it. He just assumed such an attempt was doomed to failure.

Lotus carried a sterling silver serving tray in her hands and some clothes under her arm.

"Hello, hello," she said. "I thought you might be hungry, so I brought you something to eat." She set it on the end table beside the bed. "And a change of clothes. Thought you might need that too."

She laid the clothes, in neatly folded squares, at his feet. The pants were plaid, and the shirt was striped. The socks were black. Monster held them out at a distance, afraid that if he allowed them to get too close he might spontaneously transform into a grandpa with his pants up to his chest.

She carried something else too under her arm. A flat piece of slate. He noticed some writing on it. Like runes, but unlike any he'd ever seen. Or any he could remember, at any rate. It was hard to pin down without his dictionary.

He didn't bother sitting up, just lay there in his boxers. He turned his head enough to see the food she'd brought: a peanut butter sandwich (the crusts were cut off), some oatmeal cookies, and a beer. He wasn't very hungry, but the beer looked good.

It might as well have had a label on it saying *Perfectly harmless!*

"Now let's see here," said Lotus as she stared intently at her stone slab. "Judy tells me your name is Monster. Monster Dionysus. Is that correct?"

He grunted.

"Is Monster your given name?" she asked. "Or is it, as I presume, a nickname?"

He grunted again.

Her lips puckered into a slight frown. "I can understand your resentment, young man. I truly can. But this will be a lot easier if you drop the attitude."

He looked her in the eye. He grunted but he did so with a smile this time.

"As you wish," she said. "It's no bother to me. You're only making it harder on yourself. In any case, your nickname should work just fine. Whatever you're known best as is usually the easiest cross-referencing tool."

She hummed to herself while running her fingers along the stone. He didn't know what she was doing, but she wasn't paying attention to him. He could've jumped up and kicked her in the head before she knew it. Except he still had that painful reminder that Lotus was under some kind of protection. She wasn't worried about him because there was nothing to be worried about.

She shook her head and clicked her tongue. "This is most puzzling. For some reason, you don't seem to exist."

Monster wasn't interested in arguing with her, but he figured he was too annoyed to be imaginary.

"Most troublesome indeed," she said. "I can't remember the last time I've come across a flaw in the stone's records. In fact, I'm fairly certain I never have."

He didn't know what she was talking about, and he didn't care.

"Lady, I don't know what you're doing here, and I really don't want to know. If you let me go, I promise to keep my mouth shut, go home, and never think about any of this again."

Lotus shrugged. "I wish I could trust you. I really do. But everything is in far too delicate a state at the moment. I think it was twenty thousand years ago, give or take, that I decided the little details weren't worth bothering with. Ended up being thrown in a volcano for my sloppiness. Let me tell you, Mr. Dionysus, there's nothing like having to claw and scrape your way through a sea of molten lava to remind one to keep an eye on the details."

Monster tried to figure out if she was being serious. If she was making a joke, she was very good at keeping a straight face.

"Are you a goddess or something?" he asked.

She chuckled. "Oh, heavens no. Since when do gods bother with mortal affairs? They gave up on this universe a long time ago, once they realized its affections weren't anything worth fighting over. No, I'm just the keeper of the stone, doing what I must to maintain order."

She held the slab toward him and waved it around a bit. Then smacked it several times, held it to her ear and shook it.

"Most puzzling, indeed," she remarked as she left the room, locking the door behind her.

Monster decided Lotus was a nut. A nut with some powerful magic at her disposal, but a nut nonetheless. That only worried him more.

Judy glanced up with glazed eyes as Lotus entered the kitchen. "Hello."

"Hello." Lotus set the stone at its place by the kitchen sink. "How are you feeling, dear?"

"Peachy," said Judy, and she meant it. "This tea is great! It's really, really great!" She took a long drink and poured herself another. "I mean, wow! You should bottle this stuff and sell it. You'd make a fortune."

"Thank you. You're too kind."

Lotus joined Judy at the table and had a cup herself. The pacifying effects of the tea wouldn't affect her in the same way they did Judy, who even now had the mental capacity of a week-old turnip.

"Tell me something, Judy. What's the nature of your relationship with Monster?"

Judy twisted her face in a childish scowl. "He's a dummy. And he's mean."

"You don't like him, then?"

Judy pretended to stick her finger down her throat and made a retching sound. Then she giggled.

Lotus asked the stone, "That man is the anomaly, the thing you kept hiding from me? One little human? You realize how easily I could kill him right now."

She caressed the stone, and it shuddered.

"Oh, fine, play your game, then," said Lotus. "We've done this a thousand times before, and it always turns out the same. But perhaps this variable will spice things up a bit."

"What's that?" asked Judy.

"Nothing, dear. If you'll excuse me, I have some things to take care of."

Judy was too busy staring at her own hand to realize Lotus had left until four minutes after the fact.

Judy continued to drink the tea. Each cup tasted more wonderful than the last, and everything seemed so much more amusing. She spent twenty minutes contemplating a red dot on the tablecloth, wondering if it was part of the pattern or a stain. She failed to notice anything else, including the small furry beast that slipped through the kitchen cat door.

At a casual glance, it could easily be mistaken for another cat. A little plumper than usual, missing a tail. The ears were larger, too. And, if someone noticed the rest of the details, they might also notice that the creature had more of a fox's face and that it stood upright, though it had a tendency to steady itself with its knuckles when it walked. But nobody really would've noticed because nobody was supposed to notice. It was just one more feline in a house crawling with them.

The creature hopped onto the table, finally drawing Judy's attention.

"Hello," said Judy, bobbing her head with each exaggerated syllable. "Hello, hello, hello."

The creature squeaked like a monkey as it pushed the teapot off the table.

"That's not very nice!"

Screeching, it kicked her cup away, sending it shattering onto the floor.

Pendragon and the cats all raised their heads at this strange intruder, but by then it had darted out of the room with incredible swiftness, a fuzzy red blur.

The fox-faced creature slipped into the living room, where

Ferdinand was occupying herself with a crossword puzzle while Ed read a copy of *Animal Farm*.

Ferdinand set down her pen and stared at the puzzle. She wasn't very good at them, but there wasn't much else to do at Mrs. Lotus's.

"What's a five-letter word for 'a skeleton component'?" she finally asked Ed.

"White," suggested Ed.

"That's a color, not a component."

Ed turned a page in her book. "Calcium?" she said absently.

Ferdinand performed a quick calculation. "That's seven letters."

"Is it?" said Ed.

Ferdinand grumbled. She didn't know why she'd asked. Ed was never any help with crossword puzzles. Secretly, she wished Mrs. Lotus would buy a television, but Lotus was quite adamant against the notion. This didn't leave Ferdinand many choices. She couldn't just keep reading and rereading the same book over and over again like Ed.

Ferdinand reached for her pen. It was gone. A glance around the floor turned up nothing. She stood and hefted the recliner over her head.

"What's wrong?" asked Ed.

"Lost my pen," said Ferdinand.

"There are more pens in the kitchen. A whole drawer full of them."

"It was my lucky pen."

"Since when did you have a lucky pen?" asked Ed.

"Since now." Ferdinand dropped the chair and snorted. "I've got a third of this puzzle filled out, and that means that the pen must be lucky."

"Mrs. Lotus says we make our own luck."

"Mrs. Lotus says a lot of things." Ferdinand blew a bubble and sucked it back in.

"Can't you just find a new lucky pen, then?" asked Ed.

Ferdinand spat a wad of gum into the trash basket beside her and crammed several fresher pieces into her cheek. "It doesn't work like that. You don't just find lucky pens. It's not like you can go to the lucky pen store and buy them by the handful."

"I bet Mrs. Lotus could make you one if you asked her," suggested Ed. "She knows how to do that sort of thing."

"I don't want a magic pen."

Ed lowered her book just enough to peer over its cover. "What's the difference?"

"Anybody can have a magic pen," said Ferdinand. "Lucky pens are a lot rarer."

Ed thought about this a moment. She didn't see the logic, but then again, she rarely did. Ed wasn't a logical sort. She made up for it with a sunny disposition.

"I know," she said. "We could go into the kitchen and try out all the other pens. I'm sure one of them will be lucky."

Ferdinand found the idea absurd, but she was intrigued. "How would we find that out?"

"I could think of a number between one and ten," Ed proposed. "One pen at a time, you'll write a number, and the first pen that gets it right must be the lucky one."

Ferdinand nodded. "That's not such a bad idea."

"Goody!" Ed jumped up, throwing her book to the side. "This will be fun! I think I'll go with nine. That's a good number."

"You can't tell me what it is beforehand," said Ferdinand.

"Sorry. Okay, so it won't be nine, then. For sure out of all the numbers it could be, it's not nine. Definitely not."

"It's nine, isn't it?"

"Wow, that's good," said Ed as she followed Ferdinand into the kitchen. "Are you sure you need a lucky pen?"

Meanwhile, the fox-faced creature, Ferdinand's lucky pen firmly in hand, slipped from its hiding place under the couch and darted up the stairs. It was naturally sneaky, so it didn't make a sound. Not that it had to contend with any sentries. Only cats, and they were all too busy with their own concerns (mostly napping and cleaning themselves) to care about one more furry beast roaming the house's halls.

The creature sniffed its way toward its target, guided by its keen sense of smell. One door caught its attention, and a few moments with its nose pressed under the doorjamb confirmed it had found who it was looking for. With one jump, it latched on to the handle. It set its feet apart and twisted its entire body to turn the knob. The protective spell only kept the door locked from the other side, so it opened. The creature jumped off the door, and it slowly began to swing shut again.

Monster was in the middle of putting on his new pants. He jumped toward the door, tripping on the loose pant leg. He still might've made it except that the fox-faced beast dashed under his feet. Monster fell just short, and the door closed with a click.

"Son of a bitch." He turned over on his back and stared at the ceiling, wearing an unbuttoned shirt that was a size too small and trousers only halfway on.

The imp climbed onto his chest and, yipping, held out Ferdinand's lucky pen.

"Thanks." Monster took the pen. "This is just what I needed."

The imp wagged its stubby tail and licked him twice on the chin. It hopped onto the nightstand and tipped the tray, sending the meal flying through the air to land on the bed.

"You didn't have to do that," said Monster. "I wasn't going to eat it."

The creature yipped before making absolutely sure of that by stomping on the sandwich and urinating on the cookies.

Monster sat on the corner of the bed that wasn't soaked with beer or imp piss. The creature, having apparently accomplished its mission, lost all interest in Monster. It amused itself by tearing up the pillow.

Monster studied the pen in his hand. It wasn't hard to figure out what was going on. Judy's subconscious was at work again. She must have summoned the imp and ordered it to bring him a writing utensil as a means of escape.

This still didn't make a bit of sense. One moment, Judy was out to kill him. The next, she was looking to him for rescue. He didn't even see why she needed him at all. She had the power to summon all manner of cryptobiological beasts. There were probably limits, but if she could call up an army of gaborchends, Inuit walrus horrors, winged horses, and purple worms, then she should've easily been able to escape on her own. If she was going to send a crypto to his rescue, why send an imp with a pen when a dragon would work just as well? Why bother with this half-assed approach?

No, there was more to this than just the ineffective planning of Judy's subconscious. There had to be. Too bad he wasn't smart enough to figure it out.

The imp raised its head from the flurry of down around it. It half barked, half purred.

"I don't suppose you have a theory about what's going on here?"

The imp sneezed and went back to gutting the pillow.

"Didn't think so."

One thing at a time. He had to get out of here first, and now that he had a pen, he had a shot. He wasn't great with magic, but he was familiar enough with containment spells to counter them. He assumed the room was sealed with a standard spell that kept the door from being opened from the inside.

He clicked the pen a few times as he recalled basic rune theory. He remembered the symbol that would unlock a door. But its odds of success depended greatly on the kind of magic Lotus used to seal the room. If she'd used an incantation, then this would be no problem. But if she used a rune spell, it would be much harder. Written magic was stronger than spoken magic. And spoken magic lost potency over time, while written magic gained power.

Alchemy would be trickier. He knew enough alchemy to make light beer out of tap water if he happened to have a harpy feather and a bottle cap at his disposal. But he usually just bought his potions and powders, like everybody else these days. Who had the time for all that mixing and brewing?

He remembered his last attempt at serious alchemy. He'd ordered a Make Your Own Homunculus kit through the mail. *So easy a child could do it!* declared the kit. He'd mixed the ingredients together, poured the concoction into the mold, and stuck the thing in the microwave. Just like the instructions said. Instead of a friendly little helper demon, he ended up with a fifty-pound, appliance-smashing beast. Not only did it destroy the microwave, the blender, and most of his plates, but it nearly swallowed his head before dissolving into paste. A month later, he discovered the vial of nightshade powder from the kit that had rolled under the table. After that, he left alchemy to the professionals. Anyway, the asking price for philosopher's stones was outrageous nowadays.

Monster approached the door. A simple neutralizing rune was the easiest thing. It probably wouldn't work, but he might as well start with the basics. He put the pen to the door. A crackle of energy raised the hairs on his arm. A jolt of electricity sent the pen flying out of his hand with enough force to drive it into the wall. Monster's arm went limp.

He backed away. His arm hung at his side. He tried to move it and managed to wiggle his thumb. That was about it.

The imp hopped to the edge of the bed and growled questioningly.

"So much for Plan A," said Monster.

He pulled the pen from the wall. It snapped in half. He grabbed a napkin and used it to wipe the ink off his hand. It didn't really help.

"Don't suppose you have another pen hidden somewhere?"

The imp yipped.

"I didn't think so."

Monster paced the room while waiting for the feeling to return to his arm.

He hadn't expected to escape, but he was disappointed to have been thwarted so easily. Containment spells were part of his job. No spell was foolproof, no matter how good the practitioner. But here he was, trapped like a troll, without any plan. It was too bad Chester wasn't here. It would've been easy enough for him to slip his flattened body under the door and open it from the other side. But Chester couldn't be summoned while in this room, maybe the whole house.

If it was only the room interfering, then maybe Monster had a chance. He didn't figure he had anything to lose. He went to the door, getting as close as he dared without actually touching it, and listened. The imp trotted over and listened with him.

It was quiet.

There probably wasn't a guard posted. He listened for a few more minutes to be safe. He also watched for any passing shadows blocking the light coming under the door. It appeared all clear.

Monster flattened Chester's body out and very carefully slid it under the door.

"Chester," he whispered. "Come on, Chester. Come on."

The imp hopped close and licked Monster's ear. He brushed it away.

"Chester, this is important." He hadn't received the "away" message yet, so either the spell keeping Chester at bay was still working or the gnome was considering it. Or he'd just turned off the connection altogether.

Monster risked raising his voice. "Chester! Damn it, I need you. Okay, okay. I admit it! I need you! I'm screwed without you, and this wouldn't be the first time. You're my secret weapon, my partner. Hell, you're smarter than I am, and we both know it. So come on and—"

The door opened. Chester stuck in his head. "Monster, is that you? I thought I heard your—"

Monster checked the hall before pulling Chester into the room and almost shutting the door. He kept it open with his foot. As long as it was open, the containment spell was inactive.

"Are you wearing plaid with stripes?" asked Chester.

"Never mind that," said Monster.

"What the heck is going on?" asked Chester. "Where are we? And what were you saying? I didn't quite catch any of it."

"Nothing," said Monster. "It was nothing."

19

The imp sniffed at Chester's fingertips. It licked a paper digit.

"Careful there. This is a fresh body. I don't need it getting all soggy right away." Chester rolled his arm up and smacked the creature across the nose. "Why is there an imp here?"

"Judy sent it," replied Monster.

"Why would she send an imp?"

"You'll have to ask her. I tried asking the imp, but it didn't feel like sharing. There will be time to figure things out after we get out of here."

"Shouldn't we find Judy first?" asked Chester.

"She wants to be here," said Monster.

"Does she? The way I see it, she brought you here to help her escape, even if she didn't know it consciously at the time."

"Yes, and then she smacked me around when I tried to help. So screw that. If she doesn't want to be rescued, I'm not going to waste my time trying."

"I don't know. I'm not sure you have a choice. Even if you

manage to escape without her, what would prevent her from sending another giant purple worm or some other cryptobiological to retrieve you again?"

"Because I told her not to."

"Because that's worked like gangbusters so far."

Monster heard someone coming down the hall. He put his finger to his lips as he closed the door but kept the handle turned so that the latch didn't catch. The person walked past and kept going.

Chester stuck his head under the door to check if the person had truly gone before they dared to speak.

"Okay, damn it," said Monster. "You're right. It probably is smarter to grab Judy when we go."

His original plan was for Chester to run a quick recon and then for the two of them to make a dash for the front door. Having to take Judy along meant more risk. Without his runes, Monster didn't stand much of a chance. He sent Chester to scout the place and find some supplies. Monster sat by the door, scratching the imp on its head. Just when he was sure Chester must have been caught, the paper gnome returned. He handed Monster a notepad and two black pens.

"What took so long?" Monster took a quick inventory. "There are only six sheets left on this pad. And I wanted a green pen."

"This is all I could find," said Chester. "You're welcome."

"Yeah, yeah. Thanks. Hold the doorknob while I get this ready."

"Live to serve," said Chester with blatant insincerity.

Monster scribbled a few runes from memory. Nothing complicated. Without his dictionary, anything beyond the most basic spell was bound to backfire. He had enough problems without adding the embarrassment of blowing off his own hand. The practical joke runes he'd learned were the only ones he could remember. It'd been years since he'd used them, but they were still strongest in his mind. Simple magic, meant to annoy more than anything. But without his dictionary, they were the extent of his arsenal.

"There are a lot of cats," said Chester. "The two women are in the study. It's at the bottom of the stairs, just to the left."

"And the old lady?"

"Didn't see her."

"Did you look everywhere?"

"I didn't check the basement," said Chester. "Maybe she's there. Or maybe she's out of the house."

Monster hoped so. The old lady was a loony, but she had a lot of power. He would rather not tangle with her.

"Judy is in the kitchen," said Chester. "I think we can get her and leave by the back door. If you're quiet, you could probably sneak past the women too."

Monster scrawled out the runes and folded them carefully into his pockets, putting one in his shirt pocket and one more in each pant pocket. A third he crumpled up into a ball and held in his fist. He took a few minutes to commit each location to memory. There wouldn't be much time to remember in the heat of escape.

"I think Judy's been drugged," said Chester. "She's acting dopey."

"She's always acting dopey."

"What's the plan?"

"We run downstairs, grab Judy, and make a run for it," said Monster.

"You do realize that your detailed plan has three steps and two of those steps hinge on running?"

"It's easy to criticize," said Monster. "I don't see you coming up with the plan."

"Good point," agreed Chester. "Let's do it."

Monster and Chester stepped out into the hall and moved as quickly to the stairs as they could without making a lot of noise. The imp trailed behind silently. Monster leaned over the banister and scanned the bottom of the staircase. There was no one there, and the front door was standing unguarded. It would've been easy to bolt for it, but he had to find Judy. He sized up the archway to the den. It was about eight feet wide. If he was lucky, he could slink past it without being seen.

Something meowed behind him.

There were many cats in the house. They lined the hallways and steps but were so quiet and unobtrusive that it was easy to forget they were there. Hearing a feline sound caught him by surprise.

Monster turned to face Pendragon. The cat mewed again.

"Shhhhh, kitty." Monster scratched the cat's head.

The imp growled at Pendragon. The cat arched his back, and Pendragon and the imp circled each other, making too much noise. Monster tried shushing them. He went to grab the imp before a fight broke, and ended up nearly getting roasted by a blast of flame from Pendragon. Monster jumped back as he beat out his smoking sleeve. He stepped on another cat's tail and it roared like a lion. He stumbled and kicked another feline. This one honked like a goose. His foot caught the edge of a step and he tumbled down the stairs, sending cats screeching and howling in all directions. His fall came to an end as he collided with a small table, tipping over a flower vase, causing it to shatter.

The clamor of an imp wrestling with a fire-breathing cat,

along with the fireballs and shrieking at the top of the stairs, destroyed any chances of being sneaky.

Monster's vision cleared just in time to see a giant hand wrapping around his throat. It squeezed his windpipe closed and lifted him off the floor.

"You aren't supposed to be here, are you?" said Ferdinand.

He beat her with his fists, without noticeable effect.

"I forget," said Ferdinand to Ed. "Are we allowed to kill him?"

"I don't think so."

Ferdinand blew a bubble. "I guess I'll just choke him out."

Monster slammed the rune spell in his right hand onto her arm. She released him and staggered backwards, knocking Ed aside.

"What did you do to me?" Ferdinand asked.

"Instant vertigo," he replied.

"You son of a —" She swung at him, but he easily dodged. She collapsed on the floor and struggled to get up.

Ed kicked his knee, and Monster fell. She raised her leg above her head and prepared to bring it down with skull-crushing force.

Chester, in the form of a paper octopus, flung himself at Ed, wrapping his tentacles around her head. Her foot came down an inch from Monster's face as she whirled around the room.

Monster pulled another spell from his pocket and crumpled it into a ball.

"Get clear, Chester!"

The gnome folded himself into a bird and flew away as Monster hurled the rune. It bounced off Ed's chest. She swung out with her right foot and narrowly missed striking him across the ribs. He pressed closer to the wall as she tried to follow up the attack, only to discover that her left foot was stuck to the floor.

"That's not fair!" she said.

Monster dug in his pocket and found another spell. He rolled it into a ball and hit her with it. Instantly, Ed started croaking like a toad. It didn't really do anything to further impede her, but it cheered him.

Monster worked his way around the edge of the room to stay out of her reach as Ed continued to croak and Ferdinand flopped around on the floor. Ed would remain stuck to the floor until she touched her nose. Or a handsome prince came along and kissed her. He figured the nose thing was more likely. Either way, she was out of the way for a while.

The imp, its mouth full of red fur, hopped before Monster. "Did you win?"

It barked and wagged its tiny tail.

"The kitchen's this way," said Chester.

"That wasn't so hard," said Monster.

"Don't count your eggs yet," said Chester. "You've been lucky."

He couldn't argue. Ferdinand and Ed were dangerous, but he'd been prepared. If Lotus was still in the house, then she'd probably make short work of Monster and his weak magic. All the more reason to get out of here.

Judy was in the kitchen. She raised her head at Monster's arrival. "Hi, how are you? Want some tea?"

She held out a saucer and cup. He knocked it away.

"A 'No, thank you' would've been sufficient," she said.

"Come on." He tried to pull her out of the chair, but she resisted.

"What's your rush?" she asked. "Sit down. Have some tea."

"I don't want any tea." He pushed the cup off the table.

"Why do people keep doing that?" Judy stood. "Now I'll have to get another cup."

The imp scrambled up onto the kitchen counter. It yapped and howled as it struggled to lift the stone beside the sink.

"I don't think Mrs. Lotus would want you touching that," said Judy.

Monster pressed a rune spell across Judy's forehead. She went limp and fell into Monster's arms. The paper wasn't sticky, so he had to hold it in place. He lowered her the rest of the way to the floor, keeping the spell pressed to her forehead.

"Chester, find some tape or something."

"You didn't have to keep the rune pressed on the others," said Chester as he rifled through the drawers.

"This is a different spell," said Monster. "They don't all follow the same rules."

"I don't know how you keep track of it all."

"I don't. That's why I need my dictionary. I only remembered this one from my college days."

Grinning, Judy giggled.

"Cheaper than weed," said Monster.

"I'd heard getting high on magic can be dangerous," said Chester.

"I handled it fine," replied Monster. "Until the freakout. Now I never touch the stuff."

"Never?"

"Okay, so maybe I'm getting a bit of a contact high, but there's no way around that."

"She's already pretty buzzed from that tea," said Chester. "Is it a good idea to mix the effects?"

"Not really." Monster glanced down the hall and checked on Ferdinand's progress. She was on her knees, taking in deep breaths and regaining her equilibrium. "How's that tape coming?"

"No dice."

"I can't keep holding this..." Monster snapped his fingers to get Judy's attention. "Hey, how you feeling there? Pretty good, right?"

"Peachy." Her eyes crossed as she giggled.

"If you want to keep feeling peachy you'll have to hold this in place. Can you do that?"

Judy nodded, and Monster lifted her hand to her forehead and let go. She kept the rune in contact. She didn't resist as he helped her rise.

"We're leaving now. How's that sound?" asked Monster.

Judy nodded as her eyes nearly rolled back in her head. He slapped her lightly on the cheeks.

"Come on now. Stick with me. I can't carry you out of here."

The imp barked and continued its struggle with the stone slab.

"I think he wants us to take this with us," said Chester.

"So take it. I don't care."

Chester grabbed the stone. He yelped as his paper body wilted and fell flat, floating to the floor. He slowly folded himself back into gnomish shape.

"Geez, that packed a punch."

"What happened?"

"I don't know. Touching it disrupted my interface with this body. Must be some some kind of hard-form interdimensional sink."

"Must be," said Monster, as if he understood any of what Chester had just said. "Leave it, then."

The imp grabbed Monster by the pant leg and yanked while yipping and barking.

"Okay, okay."

He released Judy. She managed to stand on her wobbly legs.

"We really don't have time for this." He took the stone and tucked it under his arm. "That crazy old broad could show up any—"

"That does not belong to you, young man," said Lotus. She'd freed Ferdinand and Ed from their spells. They stood behind her in the doorway, but Lotus was the real threat.

Monster pulled another rune spell from his pockets and crumpled it. "Stay back. I'll use this if I have to."

Lotus smiled. "And what will this spell do? Make us all terribly itchy?"

"It's my last resort. It'll start a raging fire."

"I'd be careful, ma'am," said Chester. "He isn't very good with magic, but he does excel at burning things to the ground."

Judy spun around, laughing. "To the ground!"

Ferdinand and Ed moved forward, but Lotus held them back.

"I pride myself on my patience, but you have nearly exhausted it, Mr. Dionysus. Now if you would put down the stone."

"Wait a second, boss," said Chester. "I wouldn't do that if I were—"

Lotus flicked her fingers at him. Invisible blades sliced him to shreds.

"The stone, if you please, Mr. Dionysus."

Monster studied the pile of confetti.

"Wait a second. You're afraid of me because I have this, aren't you?" He tightened his grip on the stone.

"Why on earth would I ever be afraid of someone as ineffective as you?" said Lotus.

"He's a dumb-face," said Judy with a snort.

"Go on then," said Monster. "Take me out. I'm waiting."

Lotus smiled humorlessly. "You're brighter than I gave you credit for."

"That's right. I am."

"Ferdinand, Ed, would you please remove the stone from Mr. Dionysus's possession?"

They advanced.

Monster shut his eyes and let loose with a burst of bright light. Ed and Ferdinand recoiled, turning their faces away. They rubbed their eyes. Judy was blinded too, but her senses were already playing tricks on her, so she didn't think it odd that everything went white and spots danced in her vision.

Lotus had been looking straight at Monster when he'd flashed. She wasn't bothered. She did not appear pleased, but she didn't make a move toward him. The stone kept her at bay. He clutched it close to him and tightened his grip.

He still had to worry about Ferdinand and Ed. Once they recovered, it wouldn't be hard for them to kick his ass and take the stone.

His only choice was to make a run for it. He grabbed Judy's hand and bolted out the door leading to the backyard. He dashed down the steps, toward the picket fence. He'd leap that and then he'd...

He wasn't sure. He hadn't worked out his plan much beyond that.

A trio of Lotus's garden gnomes, spears at the ready, sprang between him and escape. Screaming, they charged. The imp leaped on the lead gnome. Monster used the stone to deflect the second gnome's spear, but the third gnome cut him on the thigh.

"Ow! You little son of a—"

He kicked one gnome and smacked another with the stone. Both went flying across the lawn. The imp and the lead gnome rolled around, locked in combat.

Monster glanced back at the house. Ferdinand and Ed came stumbling onto the porch. They were halfway down the steps when Monster flashed again. Ferdinand had had the foresight not to be looking directly at him, but Ed hadn't. Her blindness made her miss the third step on the short flight. She fell onto the lawn, tripping Ferdinand.

He didn't waste any time congratulating himself on his luck. He turned back toward the fence.

Lotus and a legion of cats stood in his way.

He could try blinding them again, but he was beginning to feel weak. He swallowed, reminded of the absence of even an ounce of saliva. At most, he had another two bright bursts in him before he risked collapsing from dehydration. Ferdinand, Ed, Lotus, the gnomes, and the army of cats surrounded Monster and Judy.

"Though I do admire your resourcefulness," said Lotus, "it's time to end this farce. Don't you agree, Mr. Dionysus?"

He shook Judy to get her attention. "Why don't you do something? Call up a dragon or something. C'mon!"

Judy gaped at him. "Whaaa...?"

Even if Judy had any conscious control over her crypto-summoning powers, she was blitzed out of her mind. There'd be no help there.

"Oooh, pretty." Judy touched the stone. It changed color, from black to bright red. The tingle in Monster's hand became a stinging bite. He released the stone. Or he tried to.

He couldn't let go.

Time slowed. It was so slow, it almost appeared to stop. But Monster noticed the slight ripple in the grass. He and Judy were unaffected, but the rest of the world had ground to a halt.

"What did you do now?" he asked.

Judy pointed to a bird hanging in the air and made a cooing sound.

"Give me the stone now!" shouted Lotus, unaffected by the time slip. Monster yelped in terror of the old lady (he would deny that later) and struck her with the stone in his hand. Three things happened. Not exactly at the same time, but close enough that most wouldn't have noticed.

In the instant that the stone made contact with Lotus, the force of Monster's glancing blow was amplified ten thousand times. With a thunderous boom, she was hurled upward, a luminescent comet burning through the night sky. She passed through the atmosphere before gravity slowed her enough to begin her descent. The earth had rotated beneath her by then, and she came down somewhere in the Pacific Ocean.

The second effect was a twist in the fragile framework of time and space. Judy and Monster disappeared.

The third and final effect was the restoration of the normal flow of time.

The triumphant imp howled over the defeated gnome, then scampered away, disappearing into the bushes.

"What just happened?" asked Ed.

"Beats me."

"They escaped," said Lotus from behind them.

Ed and Ferdinand jumped. It wasn't Lotus's sudden appearance. Both of them were used to that by now. It was something in her voice, a quality they'd never before heard. She was angry.

She was also soaking wet, and a strand of gray hair fell across her face. It was a small thing, seemingly insignificant. But Ed and Ferdinand had never seen a single hair out of place on Lotus's head.

Ed asked, "But how—"

"I don't know," replied Lotus.

Ferdinand and Ed exchanged glances.

"You don't?" said Ferdinand.

"No, I don't." Lotus smoothed an errant strand of hair out of her face. "But believe me, I do intend to find out."

20

Monster had never teleported, but he'd heard it was a lousy way to travel. It wasn't difficult, magically speaking, to cut loose from the fabric of space and time. The hard part was the reconnection. The body wanted to remain part of the universe — so much so that it'd fall back into place just about anywhere. Without proper aim, a teleport spell could transport someone anywhere in the universe, and anywhere was a very big place, so big that the odds of actually ending up somewhere where you didn't die instantly qualified as a miracle. Not to mention the extreme gut-wrenching strain on every cell of the body, not so much painful as unpleasant, like riding in a centrifuge for six hours straight. Or so Monster had heard.

This teleportation was so gentle that he didn't notice until it was done — like rolling across the surface of the universe before plopping comfortably into a Monster-shaped hole that was already there and waiting, warm and inviting.

He cursed, realizing the stone in his hand had become white

hot. He released it. It bounced off his foot, and when he hopped around, he tripped over someone.

It was Judy, out cold. She was breathing. He put his ear to her chest, and her heartbeat seemed okay. Not that he knew enough to be sure. He slapped her lightly on the face, but she wouldn't wake up. He opened her eyelids and checked her pupils. He wasn't sure what he was looking for, but they usually did that on TV, so he gave it a shot. She looked okay, he guessed. Just unconscious.

He took stock of his surroundings. Wherever this was, it looked like someone had let a minotaur loose in the room. The furniture was upended and broken. A fern in a broken pot lay beside him. There was a huge hole in the middle of the floor.

It was his house.

"Son of a . . ."

Monster limped over to the refrigerator and found a beer to soothe his dry throat. The clock on the wall read half past nine. He sized up his situation. Or he tried. But he didn't get any of it. None of the pieces made much sense. There was a woman who could summon and control cryptos (but only in a half-assed subconscious manner), an enchanted stone tablet, a crazy old lady with awesome magical powers. And he was stuck in the middle of it.

He checked Judy again. She was snoring. He prodded her with his foot. She didn't respond.

The weird tea she'd been drinking and the inebriation rune had taken their toll. The teleport might not have helped either. Nothing to do but let her sleep it off.

He didn't know if the house would be safe. Lotus would be looking for them. And the stone. He hadn't forgotten about the stone. It'd gone from white to black. He left it on the spot of burnt carpet where it'd fallen.

Liz would be home soon, and at the moment an angry demon girlfriend ranked higher on his concerns than some crazy sorceress. But the stone or Judy or both had drawn him here, and he couldn't think of any better place to go.

He considered leaving her on the floor. Not like it made any difference to her right now.

"Aw, screw it."

He would've thrown her on the couch, but it teetered on the edge of the hole. He dragged her into the other room and laid her on his side of the bed. She didn't stir, just snored louder. Her half-open eyes fluttered, but she wasn't conscious. Maybe all the mind-altering magic she'd been subjected to had given her brain damage. Although he was pretty sure most coma victims didn't snore loud enough to scare away dragons.

Where did her power come from? If there was some spell or curse, there had to be a mark on her body. He lifted her up and pulled back her collar to check for one. Then he lifted up her T-shirt. Just up to her belly button. He turned her over and checked her back.

Nothing.

Monster lifted her shirt another inch to the bottom of her bra. Still no sign. It could be anywhere. He might have to strip her naked to find it.

He went to the drawer and activated one of Chester's spare bodies. "This is getting monotonous, boss." The gnome unfolded himself in a stretch. "You escaped. I'm impressed. How'd you do it?"

"Beats the hell out of me. I think Judy and that stone did it. I was just along for the ride." Monster pointed to Judy. "I need you to check her. If she's human, then there has to be some kind of mark on her body."

"Will do."

Monster exited the room, leaving the door open a crack so they could talk while Chester searched Judy.

"What did you call that stone again?"

"A hard-form interdimensional sink," shouted Chester. "It's difficult to explain to a purely physical entity such as yourself."

Monster stared at the stone, still lying where he dropped it. "Try me."

"A hard-form sink is an object that resonates at a variable actuality rhythm."

"You know what? Never mind." Monster had taken only one course in interdimensional theory in college, and he'd failed it miserably.

"All you really need to know is that it's an anomalous object of tremendous power."

"And that's how it teleported us?"

"Could be. It's not difficult for a hard-form sink to slip around the edges of reality. Though it would have been directed. Unless it was self-aware." Chester opened the door. "I checked. There's nothing."

"There has to be something."

Monster went into the bedroom. Judy was draped in an awkward pose, still dead to the world. She was also half naked. Her pants were barely to her hips, and her torso was exposed. Monster noticed her breasts, but he quickly turned his eyes.

"Damn it, Chester! Why didn't you put her clothes back on?"

"I did. All the important ones, anyway."

"Her tits. You didn't cover her tits."

"Sorry. I forgot those were considered naughty." Chester shrugged. "How am I supposed to keep track of all these arbitrary distinctions?"

"Tits aren't arbitrary." His gaze averted, Monster sidled up to the bed and threw the blanket over her. "They're one of the big differences between men and women."

"So is an Adam's apple. But I don't see you walking around with a turtleneck all the time. I don't know what the big deal is. You keep saying how much you don't like her. So what if you see her breasts?"

"Because they're breasts," said Monster. "You wouldn't understand, but we lower biological entities have certain lower biological responses, even if we don't want them. Seeing naked boobs will trigger those responses, whether I like them or not. And Liz can sense these things. She'll know I've seen foreign breasts now, and she's not going to like it."

"It was an accident," said Chester. "Blame me."

"I'm planning on it."

Judy stirred. She rolled over onto her stomach and smacked her lips before resuming snoring. Monster took this as a good sign. She wasn't awake, but she was getting there.

"There has to be a mark," said Monster. "Did you check her back?"

"Yes."

"There are only two options here, Chester. If she's human, then any magical condition that would give her the power to summon and control cryptos would require some kind of permanent mark on her body."

"What if she's parahuman?" said Chester. "Could be wearing a disguise."

"If she's wearing a disguise, then odds are that magic would leave a mark as well. Unless it came from some kind of charm or potion. She wasn't wearing any jewelry, was she?"

"No."

"I guess we'll have to do a more thorough check."

Monster found one of his giant drawing pads and a selection of markers. He also dug out his unabridged rune dictionary. The big one that weighed twenty-five pounds. A layer of dust had settled on it since last it'd been opened. He wanted to do this right.

Chester asked Monster about the stone. "Are you going to just leave that there?"

"Sure. Why not?"

"You do realize that this stone tablet may be among the most dangerous objects in this universe."

"Uh-huh," said Monster, half listening. "That means it's probably better to leave it alone. I'm not going to be the guy who blows up the earth." He thought about it a second. "Well, I'm not going to be the guy who blows up the earth *by accident.*"

"Guess you have a point there. I wonder how that crazy lady got a hold of it. And what she was planning on doing with it. And why she needed Judy."

"You wonder too much," said Monster, a red marker clenched in his teeth as he flipped through his dictionary.

"I think this is probably important enough to wonder about," said Chester. "This is big stuff here. This could be a singular object in your universe, the Rosetta stone for most, perhaps all, of its secrets."

"I'd just be happy if it could tell me how to keep Liz from gouging out my eyes when she gets home."

"This is a big deal, Monster."

"I get it, but that stone and Judy are somehow connected. Maybe if I figure out what's happening with her, I'll be able to make sense of this."

He completed the rune and laid it next to the bed.

"Help me put her on this."

Monster took her shoulders. Chester handled her feet. The blanket fell away, revealing her naked chest. Monster averted his eyes, not that it mattered now.

"You'll have to take off her pants," he said.

Monster turned his back as Chester did so.

"What about the underwear, boss?"

"That can stay."

Monster felt kind of bad about this, almost as though he were taking advantage of Judy. If she were awake, it wouldn't seem so inappropriate. But if she were awake, she probably wouldn't cooperate. He kept his back to her and asked, "Is anything happening?"

"No."

"Any strange symbols forming on the body?"

"No."

Monster glanced over his shoulder. Her naked, sleeping form was a hazy outline in the corner of his eye. "There has to be something. That's a revelation rune. Even if it doesn't give the whole answer, it should show something."

"Maybe you did it wrong."

Monster, keeping his back to Judy, moved around the room and flipped through his dictionary once more.

He heard the front door open.

"Stay here and watch Judy," he told Chester. "I'll have to keep Liz from freaking out."

Monster dashed into the living room and shut the bedroom door. Liz stood perfectly still, her hand still holding the front doorknob as she stared quietly at the gaping hole in the ruined living room.

"Hey, baby." He smiled his widest. "You won't believe the day I've had."

Though the air around her shimmered with heat, Liz remained calm. She set down her briefcase, walked around the hole and into the kitchen. She grabbed a beer from the refrigerator. Her hand caused the liquid inside to boil, and the bottle cap popped off the top as warm foam ran down the edges.

"How was your day?" he asked.

Liz took a drink of her beer but said nothing.

"I can explain this. I really can—"

"Don't bother."

"But you have to hear this. It's completely unbelievable."

"I'm sure it is, and I couldn't care less. Because I'm through with this, Monster. I'm through with you."

"What?"

"I've been talking to Gary about this, and—"

"Whoa, whoa. Who is Gary?"

"Nobody. Just some guy at work. You met him at the company picnic a couple of years ago, but of course you don't remember."

"What the hell does he have to do with anything?"

"Gary gets me. He understands and supports me in a way that you never did."

Monster struggled to wrap his head around this. "Wait a minute. You're dumping me?"

"*Dump* is such an ugly word," said Liz with a forced smile. "But in this case, it's entirely appropriate."

"But what about last night? I thought we were back on track. Y'know, with the sex and all that."

"It was nice," she admitted. "And I was thinking maybe I was wrong about you. But one good night doesn't make up for the rest of it. For crap like this. Life is too short."

"But you can't dump me. We have a contract!"

"I'm exercising my escape clause."

Monster said, "Wait, wait, wait. If you dump me, you go back to the underworld."

"That's right."

"You'd rather go back to the Pits than stay with me?"

"It wasn't an easy choice to make," she said, "but Gary and I agree that it's the healthiest choice. You're not good for me, Monster. I have enough to deal with. I don't need to add your irresponsibility to the list."

"I am not irresponsible."

She finished her beer and tossed the empty bottle into the giant hole in the living room.

"That isn't fair. It's not my fault. I was nearly killed today. A couple of times." He stopped. "Wait a minute. Wait a goddamn minute. I can't believe you want to drop this on me today, not after the day I've had."

"Gary said you would try to make this about you."

"You're screwing him, aren't you?"

"Oh, how immature." Liz shook her head. "This isn't about sex."

"You're a succubus. It's always about sex."

"See? Gary told me you never got me. You never tried to understand what was important—"

"Screw Gary. The guy sounds like a real asshole."

Liz flared and incinerated her chair. She fell on her butt.

Monster smiled. "Did Gary see that coming?"

Standing, she dusted herself off. "I know what you're trying to do. You're trying to bring me down to your level. But I'm better than that. I'm better than you." The heat radiating from her body lessened, allowing him to step closer as he tried to come up with a rebuttal.

"You know what? I just realized I don't give a crap either," he said. "Actually, I'm kind of relieved. This scene was getting old. You're so happy with Gary, then go back to Hell. I don't..."

She squinted at him.

"What?" he asked. "What is it?"

"You were looking at boobs, weren't you?"

"What if I was? You're dumping me, aren't you?"

Liz scowled. "You asshole. You cheating asshole. And to think, I felt bad when I decided to kill you."

"I didn't cheat. I just saw some tits. Completely by accident." He stopped. "Wait. You can't kill me. That's against the rules."

"Oh, yes, but what happens when I break the rules, baby?" She smiled sweetly. "Do you remember what happens then . . . baby?"

"You go straight back to . . ." Monster slouched. "Oh, hell."

Chester stuck his head into the room. "Something is going on in here."

"Something is going on out here," said Monster.

Liz sucked in a deep breath and spit a fireball. Monster ducked, avoiding getting his head blown off. Standing over him, her cheeks bulged as she prepared to spit again. Monster flared, throwing off her aim. The fireball exploded a few inches to his left, singeing his arm.

"Stop being a jerk." She covered her eyes. "You're just making this harder on both of us."

Monster crawled across the floor, keeping his head down as Liz spit a barrage of flame in the direction of his glow.

"Can't we talk about this?" he asked. "I can change."

"Gary said you'd try to talk me out of it, but that I have to be strong. For my sake."

He crawled in a serpentine pattern, thwarting her attempts to draw a bead as flames burst all around him. His throat tightened. It was a miracle she hadn't blasted him yet.

Liz's burning hand seized his ankle. The heat scorched his socks and blistered his skin. His concentration broke, along with his glow.

"You don't have to do this!" he said. "I'll release you from our contract, if you really want it so bad."

"Oh, I know I don't have to do it," she said with a grin. "But I want to do it. Gary agrees that it'll be good for my self-esteem."

Monster kicked wildly with his free leg. His foot caught her square in the face, and she fell back, letting him go. He scrambled away, but a fireball exploded in the carpet ahead of him, stopping his flight. He rolled over onto his back. He searched around for something to defend himself with. His hands fell in potting soil and smoldering carpet scraps.

"You don't want to do this, baby," he said. "This is a mistake."

Liz sighed. "Maybe we had some good times. But things change. If you were being honest with yourself, you'd realize that this is best for the both of us." She shrugged. "Okay, maybe not you, but I have to do this. For me. If you really cared, you'd stop making this so difficult. It's not like I don't feel bad about this. But I think it's the only way to be sure I've moved past our relationship. That way, when Gary and I start our contract, it'll be—"

"Wait a minute. A contract with Gary? He's not a demon?"

Liz winced. "Uh...well, no."

"I thought you worked with him."

"I do. He works in the mail room. He's human." She shrugged. "Affirmative action."

"You're not going back to the Pits!"

"Sure, I am," she said. "For a few days at least, until Gary and I hammer out the details."

Monster sat up. "So living with me isn't worse than the Pits."

"Don't be absurd. Of course not."

"So if it wasn't for"—he scowled as he spat out the

name—"if it wasn't for Gary, you wouldn't be breaking up with me," he said. "Admit it."

"Okay, I admit it. Does that make you feel better?"

He wasn't sure how he felt about it. Their relationship had its low points, but he'd gotten used to having her around.

"This is it?" he asked. "This is how it ends? Just like that?"

"I guess so. You know, Monster, I don't want you to think this is all about you. You're not such a bad guy. A bit of a loser—"

"Well, you can be a bit of a bitch."

The tips of her long black hair turned bright red. He edged toward the stone. If it truly was the most powerful object in the universe, maybe it would save his ass again. It'd already done it once.

Liz cooled. "I'll give you that, Monster, because there's no point in fighting at this stage."

Chester opened the bedroom door and dared to stick his head into the room. "Are you through with your...talk? Because there's something you probably want to see going on in here."

"In a minute," said Monster. "Listen, Liz. There's nobody to blame here. We had a few laughs, had some good times. But I think you're right. It's time to call it quits. If you want to end it and move in with this new asshole—"

"Gary. His name is Gary."

"Sorry." He held up his hands. "If you want to move in with...Gary, then go right ahead. That's cool with me. And I'm happy for you and...Gary. Really, I am."

She smiled. "Thanks, Monster. That's awfully big of you."

"Yeah, well...there's no reason we can't be civil about this."

"You weren't such a bad guy either. I'm sorry it didn't work out."

"Thanks."

"No problem." Liz cracked her knuckles. "I'll try to make this as painless as possible."

"You're still going to kill me? But I thought we were parting on good terms."

"Oh, we are, but I'm still kind of mad that you never did the dishes."

"But you never asked me to."

Liz said, "I shouldn't have had to."

She exhaled a cone of fire. Monster shielded himself with the stone. It absorbed the flames, becoming bright white.

The stone spat the flame back at Liz. It funneled down her throat. Her crimson skin turned a dull copper. Glowing fire spread in a spider-web pattern under her skin. Her inflammable hair sizzled and burned away at the tips, and her eyes burst from their sockets, replaced by orbs of seething flames.

She put her hands on her hips and scowled. "Monster, you always were a blessed son of a—"

Liz exploded in a shower of ash and bones.

He stood, wiping the ashes from his face and hair. He covered his mouth, trying not to breathe in too much of the soot.

"Sorry, baby." He nudged her cracked and blackened skull with his toe. "I don't do dishes."

It was a bittersweet moment. Liz hadn't been a great girlfriend, but she'd been the best he'd ever had.

Chester threw open the bedroom door and came running out. Intense light poured from the other room, but Monster didn't have trouble seeing. It must've been the stone. If it could repel hellfire and bend the laws of space, it probably didn't have any problem protecting his eyes from bright lights.

Chester ducked behind Monster. "I think you screwed up somewhere."

Monster moved toward the light.

"Shouldn't we be heading the other way?" asked Chester.

"It's okay," said Monster. "Nothing can hurt me while I have the stone."

Chester stayed back, but Monster entered the bedroom.

Judy hovered in the air. She was still asleep, snoring louder than ever. He looked away from her radiant naked body, but then he remembered that he'd just killed his girlfriend, so it wasn't a problem anymore. Her nudity wasn't what drew his attention anyway.

Golden lines of power spiraled and whirled all over her body. They slipped off her skin and floated around her. The revelation rune spell beneath lifted off the paper and orbited her. This was rune magic way beyond his community college education.

The golden runes joined with the revelation spell. The stone trembled violently in Monster's grip. His hands sizzled. There wasn't any pain, but he tried to drop it. The stone was stuck in his hand. Strange letters carved themselves into the tablet. They held his gaze, filling his mind with information.

Monster knew.

He knew...everything, and that was a lot to know. Too much. He didn't so much lose his mind then as close up shop and go running, screaming, into the dark and welcoming alleyways of his unconscious.

The storm brewed overhead—a maelstrom of colors and shapes, ancient secrets written in the dark clouds.

Monster stood on an expanse of dusty, cracked earth. There was nothing else around him. Not a tree, bush, or rock. Just the rumbling storm above and the ground beneath.

A drop of rain struck Monster in the eye, and he knew that the universe began on a Tuesday. Another drop fell on his shoulder, and he realized that the most recent beer he had drunk had three atoms that had passed through the bladder of Confucius. A bigger drop splattered on his neck. He knew the name of every pharaoh of ancient Egypt.

The light sprinkle of information continued. Most of the rain passed right through him, sizzling away on the dry earth. But a few drops, here and there, fell into Monster, filling his head with trivia without rhyme or reason. The history of a single hydrogen molecule, the flight pattern of migrating geese, Nero's exact height and weight, Bashō's six least-popular haiku poems, the current record for the number of angels dancing on the head of a needle, and the true inventor of the cotton gin.

It was overwhelming. And the storm was only beginning. Lightning crackled in its dark interior. Thunder rumbled, and every distant boom carried hints of knowledge that would drive Monster mad. He scanned the landscape for some form of shelter.

A yawning black cave appeared behind him. He wasn't surprised by it. He was too eager to get out of the rain. He stepped into the edge of it. A rocky overhang sheltered him from the increasing downpour.

"I wouldn't go in there, if I were you," said Lotus as she stepped into view. She stood in the middle of the downpour but remained dry.

"How did you get here?"

"I've been here from the beginning."

He edged away from her.

"I'm not your enemy here, Monster. The only thing you have to fear here is...fear itself. A bit corny, I know, but very true. And that's all you'll find in there."

He looked into the cave's inky darkness, an impenetrable void. A cold wind blasted out, but instead of pushing him away, it yanked him into it. He fell shrieking into the abyss.

Lotus seized him, pulling from the edge. She set him down on solid ground and offered him an umbrella.

"Use this. The symbolism is rather blunt, but that will probably work in your favor, given your rather limited imagination."

He opened the umbrella. He glanced over his shoulder, back at the cave. Something was breathing in there.

"Ignore it," she said. "It's only the assembled fears of the collective unconscious. No one has the power to conquer them, so unless you want to be devoured by them, you're better off pretending they're not there. Of course, that feeds them too, but there's no way around that."

"Where are we?" Monster asked.

"It's difficult to explain. You are not exactly in the stone, not exactly in your own mind, not exactly in the collective unconscious. You're in a temporary astral landscape cobbled together from bits of all three."

The wind picked up. The rain fell harder.

"I suppose we'll have to find some cover if we're to keep you from going mad until the storm passes."

The clouds formed shapes older than Monster's universe. He glimpsed secrets of other places that made no sense in the reality he understood. Realms where gravity worked in reverse, where life-forms reproduced by traveling through time to have sex with their future selves. Realities composed of lonely, singular intelligences who passed eternity humming and wishing they had thumbs to twiddle. All manner of possibilities, most of them colossal failures as universes went, falling into various forms of terminal entropy within a few billion years.

"You should stop looking up there," said Lotus. "You can't handle it."

He lowered his eyes to the ground.

"We'll have to find shelter." She pointed to a house in the distance. "That should work. A mind can only take so much, and that umbrella won't protect you when the heart of the storm hits."

A burning ball of hail landed at Monster's feet.

"I'd hurry if I were you," said Lotus, disappearing like a ghost.

He ran for the house as lightning bolts and miniature meteorites exploded around him. A shard sliced him across the cheek, and Monster learned that Elvis's downfall was engineered by vampires, that a dairy farm in Iowa had several superintelligent cows plotting the overthrow of the human race, and the mathematical equation for cold fusion, which he forgot almost immediately.

The storm grew worse the next few steps. His umbrella burst into flame. He was drenched in knowledge, flooded in bits and pieces of information. It passed through his mind without taking hold, eroding his own knowledge like a rushing flood against crumbling soil.

He was getting stupider, and if he didn't get inside, he'd probably forget his own name.

The sky opened up and revealed the Big Secret. Not the meaning of life, something not even the ancient and all-knowing stone knew, but something almost as important and twice as unknowable. Something that, had Monster glimpsed it for even a moment, would've reduced him to a quivering, gibbering mass. Fortunately, he kept his head down and his eyes shut. He didn't open them until he ran into the house, cracking his head on its door. His eyes still closed, Monster threw open the door and rushed inside and out of the rain.

The ground rumbled. A tsunami of facts and data raged around the house. The force of the storm rattled the entire structure, threatening to tear it to pieces and sweep it away. The house couldn't hold out long.

"Shut the door," said Lotus.

He did. Instantly, the storm died down. The house became quiet.

Monster cracked the door. The house trembled and groaned under the storm's fury. He quickly shut it again, and the storm faded.

He was in a den. There was the usual furniture. Some chairs, a couch, a coffee table. A little overdecorated with knickknacks and framed photographs, but dry and inviting. Lotus sat in a recliner, reading a *Life* magazine from the 1950s.

He went to the window and looked outside. Everything was calm and sunny. No sign of the storm.

"Where is this?" he asked.

"It's a happy place, most likely a remnant of a comforting memory," she replied.

He surveyed the room. All around were photographs of people he didn't know wearing clothes that placed them a few decades before he had been born. "I don't remember any of this."

"It's not your happy place," she said. "It's just one that happened to be convenient."

Though soaking wet, he wasn't dripping. He tried ringing out his shirt, but the water refused to fall away from him. He didn't even leave soggy footprints on the rug. He brushed his wet hair from his eyes and sat in a chair.

He wished for a beer, and one appeared. But it wasn't a twist top, and he didn't have a bottle opener. He tried wishing for one, but nothing happened. He went the manly route and tried to twist it off. The cap bit into his fingers and drew blood. More annoying, the cap didn't come off.

"If you don't expect it to open, it never will," said Lotus.

Monster smashed the bottle against the end table. The table broke. The bottle didn't.

"I get it," he said. "This beer, cold and refreshing, is a symbol of my own personal happiness. And I can't open it because I never expect to be happy, right? I always expect it to be just out of reach."

"Something like that. You're brighter than I imagined. Your exposure to the storm must've made you smarter."

He tossed the beer over his shoulder. It shattered, spilling his metaphorical happiness in a puddle on the hardwood floor. "Lady, I'm stupider than ever."

"Very good," she said. "The wisest man knows he knows nothing."

"Yeah, yeah. One hand clapping." Another beer appeared on the table beside him, but he didn't take the bait. "Why are you helping me?"

"I have my reasons."

"Oooh, mysterious," said Monster with every bit of sarcasm he could muster. "What now?"

"Now you wait for the storm to pass."

"And then?"

"And then your mind rejoins with your body and you remain as ignorant as ever."

"How long will that take?"

"In the world of flesh and blood, a few hours. Here, in this random astral scrapyard, who can say?"

He leaned back in his chair and made himself comfortable. After a few minutes of silence, he wished for something to pass the time. A television appeared, but it only played documentaries on the history of knitting. A deck of cards presented itself, but every card was the seven of spades. A game of Monopoly materialized, but it was missing the dice and the race car. He picked up one of the old magazines but found that the writing was in Japanese.

He didn't know what was more frustrating, being bored or knowing that he was boring himself through his own subconscious expectations.

The grandfather clock by the door ticked away the moments. Its pendulum swung, but its hands didn't move. Time didn't move. Monster opened the front door, and the storm rattled the house's timbers. He sat in the chair for ten minutes. He counted every tick, just to be sure. Then he opened the door and checked the storm again.

Still there, still threatening to sweep up the house in its merciless tide.

Monster decided he didn't like astral planes, and that the collective unconscious could kiss his ass too.

For the first time, he noticed that the room had other doors. Or maybe the doors had materialized on their own. A flight of stairs appeared too.

"What's behind those doors?" he asked. "What's up there?"

Lotus said, "I don't know. Secrets, I suppose."

"Whose secrets?"

"If I knew that much, I'd probably know what was behind the door."

Monster stared out the window at the lovely spring day that he could see but not touch.

"Why did you want Judy?" he asked.

"No reason," she replied quietly.

"Come on now. You can't lie to me here. This place is all about information, isn't it?"

"I'm not here to share my secrets with you. I'm merely keeping you sane and connected to the stone so that I can better locate you in the real world. I have a connection with the stone, so I could track it down in time. But while you commune with it, the resonance is stronger, so it speeds things up considerably."

"Aha! You aren't helping me! You're just using me! I knew you'd slip up."

"I didn't let it slip. I just didn't care if you knew. It's not as if that knowledge will help you any. Look at you, Monster. Here you are, at one with all there is to know in the cosmos, and you're hiding in someone else's happy memory. If I hadn't saved you, you'd either be swallowed by humanity's fears or driven mad with knowledge." She set down her magazine and picked up another. "Do yourself a favor and wait it out. This will all be over soon enough."

He thought about arguing with her, but she wasn't wrong.

"How long before you find me?" he asked. "In the real world?"

"A complicated question. What is the real world, after all?"

Monster realized he wasn't cut out for this metaphysical bullshit.

"Come on," he said. "Tell me the truth. What's the big deal about Judy? How can she summon cryptos? What's it matter if I know? I'm useless, aren't I?"

"Perhaps," she agreed. "But even fools can be dangerous. You've already complicated my plans. I don't know how exactly, but—"

"You don't know?"

"No, I don't." She snarled. It was very slight, but it was there.

Monster laughed. "Ha! And I thought you were supposed to be so damn smart. Here we are in the repository of all knowledge in the universe. Why don't you ask? Because you can't! Because your connection to the stone is fading while mine is growing. Because I have the stone in the real world, and you don't. And as long as I do, that'll continue to happen."

"You won't have it long," said Lotus softly.

"But no one else has ever bonded with the stone the way I have," he said. "And that scares you, doesn't it?"

She chuckled, but it was a little forced. "Don't be absurd."

"After hundreds of millions of years, you're finally scared that someone is going to take your..." Monster stopped. "Hey, how do I know all this?"

He was dry now. All that information, that metaphorical rain, had soaked into his skin. And unlike the downpour, it'd worked its way into his mind without overwhelming him, without his even realizing it. And the balance of knowledge gained exceeded the amount lost. He couldn't remember his phone number, but he did know that the omniverse was a series of fifty dimensional spheres and that they rested upon one another like a bunch of rubber balls in an infinitely large box.

Almost all of it was useless information. Like knowing the exact temperature on Mars. Somebody might benefit from it, but not him. His problems were more immediate than the nature of reality itself.

He sat and pondered. What did he need to know? The stone could tell him anything, but if he didn't make a conscious effort to choose what he learned, he was going to learn too much and too little at the same time. He was only mortal. His mind could only hold so much, needed time to assimilate whatever fell into it. The universe was filled with secrets, and he understood now that one of the biggest was that no one needed to know them all.

This was a realm of imagination and symbolism. He needed to think in those terms.

He picked up the beer and stared at it. He focused on the positive. His demon girlfriend had tried to kill him but hadn't succeeded. He was a free man now. His house was ruined, but really, it wasn't his house. The lease had been in Liz's name. He was broke, but so what? He wasn't dead yet. He was one with the universe, and he had managed not to go insane in the process. Overall, things were actually looking up.

The cap fell off the bottle.

"Take that, collective unconscious."

Monster took an experimental sip of the beverage. It wasn't

as cold as he liked, and it was a little flat. But he wasn't expecting miracles. He finished the beer and approached one of the doors at random. There were no markings on it, so he had no clue what lurked behind it. Secrets. His secrets.

He touched the handle. A clap of thunder rattled the house. It was his fear. He got that now. Fear of knowing and fear of not knowing.

"You don't want to go in there," said Lotus. "You won't be able to handle it."

He glanced back at her, and he glimpsed the fear in her eyes. She was afraid too. Afraid of what was behind the door. Afraid of what he'd learn.

She stood. "You won't be able to handle it."

"Maybe you're right." Monster chugged the last of his beer and tossed the bottle aside. "But maybe not."

A crackle of electricity ran through him as he opened the door leading to his innermost mysteries and entered the darkness within.

Monster lacked imagination. So the anthropomorphic personification of the universe appeared as a miniature sun orbited by a tiny earth. The sun wore sunglasses, even though that made absolutely no sense to Monster.

He shielded his eyes. "Hello?"

The sun glanced down at him. A giant smile spread across its bright yellow face. Monster braced himself for the divine wisdom.

"Judy."

"What about her?"

"Judy," repeated the sun in its slow, neutral cadence.

"Yeah?"

The sun frowned.

"Judy."

"I got that, but what—"

The sun darkened in frustration.

"I know you're trying to tell me something," said Monster, "but I don't get it. I don't understand."

The sun snarled as it struggled to express itself. Monster decided the universe was an idiot. It would certainly explain a lot of things.

"Help. Judy."

"Okay."

The universe sneered at him.

"What? You want me to help Judy. I figured that out. Am I allowed to ask why?"

The sun beamed a bright light down on Monster, and a series of images flooded into him as the universe tried to answer his question in relatable terms. He didn't get most of it, but he gleaned enough, filtered through his subconscious and offered up in the form of spontaneous knowledge.

There was a plan, all right. A cosmic struggle reaching the endgame. Judy was a central part of it, the most important piece in the game.

"Really?" he asked incredulously, thinking the universe was playing a joke on him.

The sun nodded.

Monster would've been okay with that except for his own part in this. He was part of the cosmic plan too. A random pawn, an unknown variable thrown in at the very last minute. One chance encounter in a supermarket with some yetis and another with some trolls in an apartment had put him on this path. Dumb luck had made him Judy's guardian. The universe hadn't given a damn about him before that, and it didn't even bother lying to him about it. Just as it didn't bother lying to him about his chances of survival.

"Really?" he asked. "That's it? That's what this is all about?"

The universe laughed in a lighthearted, childish way. With a hand of cosmic flame it reached down and patted Monster on the head.

It changed him.

"Help. Judy."

Then the world fell out beneath him.

Chester tried to wake Monster. First by shouting at him. Then by shaking him. But physical contact disrupted Chester's paper body. The sink effect had become part of Monster himself, and that could've meant any number of things, all of them bad. A human body was too fragile to exist like that outside of a few seconds, but the only effect seemed to be that Monster changed color every few seconds.

Chester tossed a throw pillow at Monster. Then a magazine. Then the twenty-five-pound rune dictionary. It bounced off Monster without any effect, not even causing him to sway.

Out of ideas, Chester sat and waited. Five hours later, Monster remained locked in his trance. The only movement at all was a subtle twitch of his eyes.

Judy stirred, sitting up. "Christ, what the hell did I do last night?"

"Judy, you're awake. That's a relief."

She put her hands to her head and retched. The painful dry

heave reminded Chester how grateful he was not to be a bio-logical entity.

She tried to stand but failed. Chester helped her with her second attempt. She could only manage to get halfway up and had to sit on the bed.

"Why am I naked?"

"There's a logical explanation, Miss Hines."

"Forget it. Not the first time I went on a bender and woke up naked in a weird place. Although it is the first time I've ever met a paper man."

"We've met before," said Chester. "Several times. Nothing untoward happened, I promise. We were just checking your body for marks." He scooped her shirt off the floor and handed it to her.

"Makes sense," she said as she slipped on the T-shirt and noticed Monster. "What's with him?"

"Do you remember him?"

"Sort of. He's kind of an asshole, right?"

"He has his moments, but he did rescue you. Right now he's defying every known law of interdimensional physics by some-how not having his atoms spread across the universe."

"What did he rescue me from?"

"I don't know. I was hoping you might. Maybe once we fix your memory problem."

She pulled on her pants and stood. The sudden light-headed sensation made her groan. "I could use some aspirin and a cigarette."

Chester folded into a bird, flew into the bathroom, and returned with a bottle pilfered from the medicine cabinet. While Judy struggled with the childproof cap, he opened Mon-ster's rune dictionary.

"I don't have much practice at this, but hopefully this'll

restore your memory, giving us an insight into what is happening. According to this, I'll have to draw on your forehead. I hope that's okay."

"No, thanks," she said. "Just point me to the exit and I'll be on my way. Whatever weird kink you guys are into—and I'm not judging, mind you—I'm just not interested. Not my scene." She found a crushed pack of cigarettes and a lighter in her pocket and lit up. "It's been swell, but I have to..."

She sifted through her mental playback of the past few days but couldn't find any clear memory. Part of this was the haze. The other was the aftereffects of too many cognition-enhancing magics that rendered her mind as intractable as quicksand. She might've panicked, except she didn't have the energy for that.

"Don't bother showing me the door. I'll find my way out." She slipped around Monster's immobile body. "You might want to drape a tarp over him to keep him from getting dusty. Just a suggestion."

"I don't think going outside is such a great idea," Chester said. "There are people looking for you. It could be dangerous."

She gaped at the ruined living room. She stumbled over Liz's blackened femur and kicked the demon's skull into the pit.

"Uh, yeah, I'm sure I'll be much safer here."

The front door burst off its hinges as Ferdinand and Ed smashed their way into the room.

"Run, Miss Hines! Run!"

Chester folded himself into a falcon shape and flew at Ferdinand. He inflicted a few shallow paper cuts to her cheeks, drawing blood. She seized him, crumpled him into a ball, and threw him to the floor. Before he could unfold, Ed stepped on him, pinning him to the carpet.

A legion of cats filtered into the house and surrounded Judy.

Pendragon hissed, spitting out fire and roasting the carpet at her feet. Judy retched at the burning smell.

Ed surveyed the demolished room. "What happened here?"

"Who cares?" said Ferdinand.

The giant woman went over to Monster. She circled him, waving her hands in front of his face and prodding him. He didn't react. She tried pushing him over. He didn't budge. She tried taking the stone from him. He wouldn't release it. She punched him in the head and wound up with bruised knuckles. He was unharmed.

Lotus entered. "You're wasting your time. Leave him to me."

Judy said, "I don't know what's going on here, but I know it has nothing to do with me, so —"

The cats parted and Lotus glided forward. "It has everything to do with you. Though I'll admit I still haven't figured out his place in all this." She waved toward Monster. "But it isn't his destiny to take my power, and neither is it yours."

She performed a sweeping gesture and pressed two fingers against Judy's forehead. Judy's body went absolutely straight and rigid. She fell.

"What do you want with her?" asked Chester, still trying to squirm his way from under Ed's heel. "She's only a light incog."

"She's so much more than that," replied Lotus. "She's a pretender to the throne, a usurper of the natural order."

Ferdinand picked up Judy's frozen body and propped it over her shoulder like a piece of lumber.

"Rest assured, I bear you no malice." Lotus stroked Judy's cheek. "Take her to the house."

"What about the stone?" asked Ferdinand. "Don't you need it?"

"I'll take care of that. Now do as I say. This could get... unpleasant."

"And the paper man?" asked Ed, grinding her heel into Chester.

"Leave him. He's nothing to be concerned about."

Ferdinand and Ed left with Judy, leaving Lotus and her army of cats. Chester smoothed his crumpled body, but he didn't make a move against Lotus. She'd already proven she could destroy him in an instant once before. Not that she would have to bother this time. The cats would tear him to shreds at her command.

Lotus paced several full circles around Monster, speaking as she did.

"I know you think you can stop this, but you really should abandon that foolish notion. We've been together for far too long. You should know that we are bound in a way that will never be broken. Your power is my power, and that is the way it will always be."

"I don't think he can hear you."

Lotus chuckled. "What makes you think I'm talking to him?"

She touched the stone, and it trembled. The world rumbled just enough to knock every loose book off a shelf, tip over every row of dominoes under construction, and collapse every house of cards on the planet.

She pulled, but the stone refused to come loose from Monster.

"You're beginning to make me angry," she said. "You don't want that, now, do you?"

The stone hopped from Monster into Lotus's hand.

"There we are. I knew you'd come to your senses."

Monster snapped to life. "Wait. You can't—"

She backhanded him, sending him sprawling.

"I still don't know why you are here, but I've decided I don't really care either. You've proven more troublesome than I imagined, but rest assured, you've done nothing to disrupt my plans. The order will be restored, and everything will be as it should be. I hope that brings you some small comfort in your last moments."

She disappeared.

The cats advanced. Monster and Chester stood at the edge of the hole in the floor with no means of escape. Pendragon licked his lips and snorted a pair of flames from his nostrils.

"I hope you have a plan," said Chester.

"Actually," said Monster, "I do."

Pendragon pounced. Monster slapped the cat aside, but the force of his charge pushed Monster's foot over the ledge and he fell into the pit with a yelp, disappearing into the darkness below. Chester didn't hear Monster hit bottom.

"Hang on! I'm coming!"

Chester folded himself into a bird, but the writhing and yowling red cat distracted him. The other felines backed away as Pendragon's fur fell off in clumps, exposing golden-red scales underneath. His tail grew to tremendous size and whipped wildly. Cats were knocked every which way.

Monster, now a burning goldenrod color, floated out of the black pit and hovered beside Chester.

"How...?" asked Chester.

"I can fly when I'm goldenrod."

Pendragon screeched, spitting a torrent of fire in the air, setting the room ablaze. The cats scattered. Several were squashed beneath the giant reptile's feet and flailing tail. Wings burst from the dragon's shoulders.

"Since when can you do that?" asked Chester.

"Since about five minutes ago," replied Monster.

The dragon's wings and spikes along his back ripped through the roof.

"How did this make our situation any better?" asked Chester as flaming pieces of ceiling pelted them.

Pendragon, the size of a bus in his true form, turned his shiny red eyes on Monster. The dragon snorted but made no attempt to swallow them in his cavernous maw or roast them alive. A thankful purr rolled from his throat.

Monster put a hand on Pendragon's snout. "Don't mention it."

Pendragon's lips pulled away to reveal a toothy grin. He reared up, smashing his way through the ceiling. With a flap of his powerful wings, he soared into the night sky, but not before an accidental swish of his tail brought the whole house crashing down. The good news was that the rubble smothered the fire.

Ten minutes later, Chester crawled his way to the surface. The climb left him ripped and ragged, but his body was still holding together.

"Boss! Boss!" He started clearing away debris. "Monster, are you in there?"

A blue hand pushed its way free and waved. It took fifteen minutes of hard work to dig Monster free.

"You had me worried for a second there," said Chester.

"I'm fine. I'm invulnerable when I'm blue."

Monster slipped in his effort to climb down the small mountain of debris, tumbled and fell onto his front lawn.

"It's all right." Monster dusted himself off and sneezed. "Blue. Invulnerable."

"Since when can you change colors at will?"

"A guy can't help but pick up a few things when he's one with the universe." Monster stood on the lawn and surveyed the rubble that used to be his home. "Man, am I glad my name isn't on that lease."

"An apartment and two houses in two days," said Chester. "That has to be a record."

"The apartment really wasn't my fault." Monster shifted to goldenrod and took off.

Chester folded into bird and soared after him on tattered wings. "Slow down."

"No time." Monster doubled back and scooped up Chester.

The paper gnome folded into a monkey and wrapped his arms around Monster's neck. "What's the rush?"

"We have to save Judy."

"I thought you didn't care about her."

"She's okay, but if we don't stop Lotus, she'll use Judy to destroy the human race."

"Hmm," said Chester. "That is bad. I guess."

"If she succeeds, I won't be around anymore, and you'll be out of a job."

Chester tucked himself into Monster's shirt to avoid the wind shear. "Pick up the pace."

23

"It's all about Lotus and Judy," shouted Monster above the rush of wind.

"What? Judy? The cryptos?"

"Everything," replied Monster. "The entire universe is just a reaction by the stone to Lotus's parasitic presence. Because that's what the old hag is. She's a leech. And the stone created the universe in order to get rid of her. The whole thing is like a giant immune system. It's a billions-year-old struggle between the stone and Lotus. Older than this universe. Lotus isn't as powerful, and all the power she does have is borrowed. But she's smarter in the short run. That is her advantage. But the stone thinks long term. It's slow to adapt, a little dumb if you get right down to it. But it moves in ways too large for anyone, even her, to grasp."

"You're losing me."

"Sorry. It's not easy to explain. The stone was first, but until Lotus came along, it didn't do anything. It wasn't even a stone.

It was all potential, but without motivation. Then Lotus found it, was drawn to it. She's not human or parahuman. She's not anything like that. And as long as she draws power from the stone, there's no way to stop her."

"Then why are we trying?"

"Because it was what Judy was made to do. It's like in bio-chemistry when an antibody defeats a virus by preventing its ability to bond with other cells."

"Since when did you know anything about——?"

"Universe bond," said Monster.

"Right. I keep forgetting about that. Let me see if I understand this. Your entire universe is merely a by-product of a battle of wills between a negligibly intelligent primeval power source and an ancient cosmic parasite."

"Yes."

"And Judy is the ultimate goal of this process."

"Yes."

"You do realize how crazy that sounds, right?" asked Chester.

"Yes."

"I mean, I'm a sixth-dimensional non-corporeal entity who has witnessed some pretty bizarre and inexplicable events in the last few days, and even I don't believe it."

Monster said, "I know. It's insane. But it's the truth. It's a cycle that's been going on for ages. Every million years or so, the universe creates a being intended to become one with the stone. That being will have absolute power for a few moments, but that's just a side effect. The ultimate goal is to sever Lotus from her power. And that's Judy's role."

"But what about all the crypto attacks Judy has been going through her whole life?"

"Misfires. The stone doesn't think in human scale. It doesn't always *get* it. And until Judy matures, the communication isn't perfect. So if she thinks too long and too hard about how much she hates her apartment or her job or her life in general, the universe sometimes responds. But it's not a perfect process. The stone isn't smart in a practical way. It's like an idiot savant. It can subtly guide generations of breeding and even steer events. But it doesn't really grasp the fragility of life. Most of the time, the avatar is accidentally killed by the stone itself. Or eliminated by Lotus. She's been working against the universe from the beginning.

"She's destroyed a hundred worlds before this one. She killed the dinosaurs. She sank Atlantis. Her manipulations led to the Dark Ages and the fall of Chinese dynasties. She invented the cell phone and created reality TV. All with only one purpose: to hold back the development of the life in the universe. She's the reason magic is disappearing, because she's strangled nearly all of it out of the stone.

"She doesn't even want to do anything with it. By now she should have the power to shape the universe. But she never really learned how to use it properly. Because all she cares about is having it, not using it. She just wants to have it because she doesn't want anyone else to have it. And every bit she uses is less for her."

"So if Judy's such a threat, why hasn't Lotus killed her?"

"Because Lotus doesn't just kill the avatar. She uses them first."

"For what?"

Monster tried to remember, but the information escaped him. Since he had never been intended to be one with the universe, he'd had two choices. He could either go mad or forget. If this was the way the haze worked for light cogs, no wonder they were always so grouchy and frustrated.

"Use her for what?" asked Chester again.

"I don't know. But I do know we have to stop it."

"Any idea how you stop an invincible parasitic entity older than the universe?"

"I can't. She's unstoppable. Her only weakness is the stone, and she's had that under her thumb since the dawn of the universe."

Monster came to a stop, hovering over Lotus's house. There were more than three dimensions, though the others weren't much use for anything. But they let him peek around its walls. Just another trick he'd learned from his brief hours of enlightenment, along with the instinct that let him know where Lotus, the stone, and Judy were at all times.

"They're in there. Waiting."

"Do we have a plan?"

"It's all about the stone. When the time is right, when things line up the way they're supposed to, it'll all come down to who is holding it. Best-case scenario: Judy is holding the stone at the time of alignment. Worst case: Lotus is holding both the stone and Judy."

"What happens then?"

"I don't know, but I'm willing to bet it isn't going to be good for anyone."

"So, get the stone, give it to Judy. Or at least keep it and Judy away from Lotus."

"Yeah. Now hang on."

Monster shifted from flying goldenrod to invulnerable blue and plummeted from the sky.

As the time of alignment approached, the haze fell away. Judy realized that magic was real. Again. And she also realized she was getting tired of realizing that over and over again.

She sat on Lotus's floral print couch with Ed and Ferdinand crowded on either side of her while two dozen cats milled restlessly. Lotus entered with a pot of her enchanted tea.

"Care for a cup, dear?" asked Lotus. "It'll make this easier."

"No, thanks," replied Judy.

Lotus poured a cup and went to the window. "Suit yourself. Such a lovely night." She picked up the stone. Smiling, she ran her fingers across it. "It won't be long now."

"What are you going to do to me?"

"Why, I'm doing exactly what I promised. You wouldn't understand, but you will. For one brief moment, when things are aligned, you will understand everything. It won't last long, but it should be some consolation. And once it's all over, I promise to give you a nice saucer of milk." Lotus sipped her tea and smiled. "Won't that be lovely?"

"You're going to make me into a cat?"

"Oh, yes. You and everyone else."

"But...why would you do that?"

Lotus said, "Consider it a reboot. Just something that must be done from time to time in order to preserve the order of things. Every so often the universe develops something, some species or world, that just shouldn't be. I usually allow things to carry on for a while, but sometimes I must intervene."

"By turning them into cats?" asked Judy.

"This time." Lotus laughed. "It's not always the same. Depends on the situation. But I think this will work out wonderfully for everyone."

"How does it —"

"Tell me, Judy, are you happy?"

"What?"

"It's a simple question." Lotus sat in the recliner across from Judy. The silver-haired woman picked a piece of lint off her skirt, crossed her dancer's legs, and folded her hands in her lap. "Are you happy?"

"That's not a simple question."

Ferdinand snorted.

Judy said, "You can't just expect someone to quantify something as hard to define as—"

"Ed, are you happy?" asked Lotus.

"Yes, ma'am," replied Ed.

Judy glared. "You can't count her. She's always happy."

"Ferdinand, are you happy?"

Ferdinand took a moment to answer, but only because she had to tuck her huge wad of gum in her cheek. "Sure."

"They don't count," said Judy. "They're not human. Not exactly."

"You're right. They're not. Not exactly. I didn't change them all the way, because I'm not that cruel."

Judy glanced at the guards posted on either side of her. Ed batted her big brown eyes. She took a bite of her apple and grinned. Ferdinand snorted, chewing her gum. She half smiled. There was a blank quality in her stare. And Ed's too.

"Do you know what separates humanity from the other beasts of this world?" asked Lotus. "It's not the ability to make tools or complex language or any of that other nonsense you tell yourselves. No, humans are unique in all this world because they're the only creatures that can make themselves miserable. And do you know how you do that? You do it by expecting to be happy. You're so busy thinking about happiness, obsessing about finding it and why it isn't where you expect it to be, that you completely miss the point.

"The other creatures of this universe don't go looking for happiness. They don't even expect to be happy. They just expect to be, and that's good enough."

"You're crazy," said Judy.

"Am I? How about your friend Monster? Was he happy? Or anyone else in your life? Can you name anyone who you think is satisfied with their lot in life?"

"My sister isn't doing too bad."

Lotus shrugged. "Fair enough. I'm sure there are one or two genuinely happy souls out there. But can you honestly say that you think it's more than three or four percent? And that's being generous."

Judy tried to come up with another example. She thought of Paulie, but he wasn't much more complicated than an animal. As long as he had a roof over his head and some weed, he was in solid shape. He had no aspirations beyond that.

No one else came to mind.

"Admit it," said Lotus. "Admit that if tomorrow all of humanity disappeared to be replaced by cats that this would only be an improvement. No traffic jams or pollution, no wars or television shows. Every ridiculous, time-wasting, misery-inducing preoccupation of your species . . . gone. Just like that. Doesn't it sound lovely?"

"Oh, very lovely," agreed Ed.

"But what about the logistics of a world suddenly full of so many cats at once?" asked Judy. "What happens when the cities start crumbling and all the mice are eaten?"

"Trifles," said Lotus. "Oh, there will be some growing pains, I'm sure, but it'll all work itself out in the end, and when it does, the world will be a much better place for it."

Judy thought about it, and it didn't seem so bad to become a cat. Her life hadn't been going very well, and it wasn't as if she had much of a future. But things like that didn't bother cats. She wasn't sure how she felt about having a tail, but she did like tuna salad and sleeping in. She wanted to argue with Lotus, wanted to come up with some brilliant reply that countered everything she had just said.

Nothing came to mind.

A blue meteor smashed through the ceiling, colliding with Lotus, who was knocked through the floor and into the basement. The stone flew out of her hands and landed in Judy's lap. She grabbed it and was struck by a flash of insight.

The stone needed her, and she needed the stone. Her whole life had been leading to this. Things hadn't been going wrong in her life. She wasn't a screwup. She just hadn't known her purpose.

The stone throbbed with a bright blue light.

Ferdinand wrapped her hand around Judy's neck and yanked the stone from her hands. Ferdinand's powerful muscles strained and she wrenched it free, taking a layer of Judy's skin with it. Judy yelped.

"You're not supposed to touch this." Ferdinand tossed the stone to Ed. "Keep it away from her."

"Okeydokey," said Ed.

The stone called Judy. Lotus was right. The time was near. Nearer than she'd imagined. The culmination of her life, of every life. But the window of opportunity would close as suddenly as it opened, and she needed to be holding the stone before that happened.

Ferdinand dragged Judy to the edge of the hole. They peered into the dim basement.

"Bet Lotus didn't see that one coming," said Judy with a smile.

"Is she okay?" asked Ed.

There was no doubt that Lotus was only inconvenienced. But Ferdinand and Ed were right to be worried. Under normal circumstances, one invulnerable blue guy plummeting from the sky would've bounced off Lotus like a single drop of light rain. But the balance had shifted. The stone, though still too afraid of Lotus to leave her completely vulnerable, had withdrawn some of its protection. But Judy knew Lotus wasn't harmed, merely stunned. And that wouldn't last long.

A paper hummingbird flitted out of the hole. Ferdinand swatted at Chester, who nimbly darted out of reach.

"Judy, you're here! And the stone!"

Chester folded himself into a mini-pterodactyl and dive-bombed Ferdinand. She grabbed him by the ankle and threw him to the floor.

Chester refolded in such a rush that he ended up tearing off a few pieces of himself. He became a full-size bear, putting the extra effort into folding himself some jaws with a full set of teeth, which he flashed in a grin.

"Roar."

He wrapped Ferdinand in a powerful embrace.

"Hurry. I can't hold her for long." His paper body was stretched to its limits, and his arms were already half torn from the strain.

Judy turned toward Ed.

"Give me that." Judy took a step forward. The cats intercepted her. They hissed, honked, growled, and screeched at her.

"Get lost."

A ripple ran through the universe, and suddenly the room was full of fox-faced imps. They filtered from all the unseen corners and shadowy nooks and crannies, from under the couch and smashing through the windows. The army of imps and the legion of cats turned the den into a deafening war zone.

Judy walked through the middle of the battle. "Give me that stone."

Ed turned and ran.

A sasquatch stomped its way out of the kitchen, and a manticore roared at the top of the stairs. Ed dashed out the front door and was confronted by a full-grown lake horse on the lawn. The crypto wasn't happy. Not surprising, considering that it was a twenty-five-ton sea creature stuck on dry land. It flapped its flippers and whipped its tail, with little effect. Its head turned in Ed's direction and growled.

"Give me that stone!" shouted Judy.

Ed's horse nature took over, and she bolted in a panic down the street.

It turned out that Monster wasn't completely invulnerable when blue. His kamikaze attack against an unstoppable godlike being resulted in several lost teeth, a broken arm, and maybe some internal injuries.

The only light filtering into the basement came from the hole in the ceiling. He could see in the dark when chalk white, but he was stuck in regenerative turquoise. His broken arm mended and several new teeth pushed their way out of his gums. The pain lessened.

Monster felt around for Lotus. There was a hole in the foundation in a vaguely human shape, but she wasn't there.

Someone hoisted him by his collar and flung him across the basement. He crashed into a pyramid of cardboard boxes and was buried under a mound of moldy clothes, trilobite fossils, and discontinued soda bottles Lotus had collected over her many millennia.

Lotus grabbed him by the throat. Invulnerable blue didn't seem capable of stopping her from crushing shut his windpipe. Monster's vision blurred. He could still be only one color at a time. Shifting to anything else would risk having her tear off his head. But if he didn't do something soon, she'd strangle him.

Monster turned lightning bolt gray and put both hands on Lotus's head. He pumped a few thousand volts through his fingers. The electricity surged through the both of them, sending them hurtling in opposite directions.

A few moments of turquoise allowed his throat to repair itself. Lotus was already on her feet, unharmed except for a few strands of sizzling hair and some cracks along her skin, exposing a sickly yellow flesh beneath.

"Who are you?" she asked. "You seem human, more or less. A few tricks at your disposal, true, but I just don't see your place in this, other than to cause me a few moments of inconvenience."

"I'm just some guy." He turned laser-vision peach and unleashed a blast of pure destructive power. The lasers sizzled against her chest. The smell of burning flesh and vanilla incense filled the air as Lotus advanced. He tried to think of something else, but he was pumping out enough force to disintegrate a tank.

Monster stopped, rubbing his burning eyes.

Lotus said, "You can't stop me. You can't even hurt me. So why do you keep trying?"

He became superstrong green and threw a punch. She caught his fist and twisted his wrist. He fell to his knees.

"You're like a bug I can't squash. It would almost be intriguing under normal circumstances, but..." She offered a bemused smile. "You're not important. You're just an inconvenience, a puzzle to keep me distracted."

She cocked her head to one side and addressed the universe directly.

"How very clever. Taking advantage of my curiosity, I see. You're getting smarter, aren't you? But not smart enough. Not by a long shot."

She vanished.

Monster rose. "Damn it."

He flew through the hole and into the den above. Chester and Ferdinand, surrounded by clashing cats and imps, were locked in battle. Chester was ragged and torn, barely recognizable in his bear form. Ferdinand punched a hole in his chest and ripped off his head.

Monster came up behind her and put his hand on her back. The sharp shock of magic, like a sting of static electricity, passed between them. Ferdinand gasped as a tail burst out of her pants, and her face lengthened. Fur sprouted on her face.

"What did you...moooo?"

She ripped out of her clothes and fell to all fours as her body twisted and grew.

Monster checked on Chester, who folded himself back into his gnome shape. He went slowly, but bits and pieces still tore off in the process.

"Are you okay?" asked Monster.

"Been better." Chester stood, but his movements were slow. "Ouch."

"Does it hurt?"

"It's not so bad." Chester shrugged, and a rip split his back. "The pain I feel is more of a static feedback. More irritating than crippling." He winced as his paper leg crumpled. "Ow. How do you material entities deal with this on a daily basis?"

"You get used to it."

The brown cow in the den blew a huge bubble that popped and covered her nose.

"That's a nice trick, boss."

A cat shrieked like a banshee as several imps descended on it. A large gray feline trumpeted as it batted aside several attackers. Monster and Chester tiptoed their way through the melee and stepped out into the other room. The clatter of a sasquatch smashing plates in the kitchen and the hungry eyes of the manticore at the top of the steps suggested that the house might not be the safest place.

Outside was safer. The marooned water horse had given up on trying to move and grazed on the lawn. It used its jaws like a steam shovel to scoop out a flower box.

A glittering phoenix picked through some nearby garbage cans. A hairy purple primate with two heads leaped at the bird. The bird responded by self-immolating in a golden flash, sending the ape scurrying away, yelping.

"This can't be good," said Monster.

All around the neighborhood, cryptos of every size and classification roamed. A giant feathered serpent coiled on a chimney across the street. At the house beside that one, an eight-foot anthill was spewing raccoon-size insectoids. An amorphous blob with a single huge eye slithered its way over an automobile, consuming it with a satisfied slurp.

A kracken sat in a driveway. A turtle beast, nearly as big as a house, lumbered its way down the street at the breakneck pace of four feet per minute. And a dragon and a drake engaged in an aerial dispute with plenty of hissing and howling.

"It's the stone. It's confused," said Monster.

A flock of pixies flew down to sprinkle sparkling dust on a cat. The feline turned to glass.

"You don't say," replied Chester.

"Where's Judy?" asked Monster.

"I lost her in all the confusion. I thought you had a homing sense."

"Whatever the stone did to me, it's fading."

"Kind of a shoddy enhancement magic, isn't it?" Chester leaned against Monster to take the weight off his crumpled leg. "I don't suppose you have the power to mend paper now, do you?"

"Maybe. I'm not really sure. I'm mostly functioning on reflex here." A slight tingle at the base of his skull told him Judy was near, and a knot in his stomach let him know that Lotus was close by too. But he wasn't getting directions.

"All the cryptos seem to be coming from that one direction."

A giant winged caterpillar with a lion's head dived at Monster. He turned green and smashed it across the jaws. It crumpled to the ground, struggling to clear its head.

"Good enough for me," said Monster as he ran against the tide of the great crypto migration.

24

Ed could run farther and faster than any human being, and panic pushed her beyond her ordinary limits. A jellyfish nearly scooped her up in its tentacles. An albino alligator man tried to grab her from a sewer drain. And a small pack of goblins tried to pounce and devour her, only to be left behind in her mad panicky dash. She ran down the street without ever looking back, oblivious to most of the cryptos appearing spontaneously around her, never giving a second thought to them once she was past them.

She just ran.

Somehow, Judy got ahead of her. Ed stopped so abruptly, she fell off-balance and skidded across the street. A speeding car being attacked by a purple people-eater nearly drove over her. It swerved at the last minute to plow through a fence and into a car parked in a driveway.

The neighborhood was in chaos. Cryptobiologicals of myth and legend, many forgotten even by those with the power to remember, were everywhere now. Hairy and scaly creatures of all shapes and sizes were busy fighting each other, chasing humans, or just engaging in general destruction. A two-hundred-pound saber-toothed woodchuck toppled a utility pole with one bite. The power went out, and only the half-moon and aura of the city lit the neighborhood.

"Golly."

A voice spoke in the dimness.

"Give me the stone."

Ed thought it was Lotus at first. It sounded a lot like her. Not the voice itself, but the tone, the quiet, assured quality that went with it. But it was Judy, who materialized before Ed. Judy hadn't changed in any real way. She still looked the same, but an aura of power covered her.

"Give me the stone," she repeated.

Lotus had trained Ed well, but Judy reminded Ed so much of Lotus that she tried to hand over the stone. It didn't budge, remaining suspended in space.

"That doesn't belong to you," said Lotus, who appeared opposite Judy.

Ed tried to give it to Lotus, but the stone refused to move. Ed released it, and it hovered in place, exactly between Lotus and Judy. Static electricity put a tingle in Ed's skin and made her hair frizz. Lotus and Judy moved in unison, matching each other step for step, gesture for gesture. They held out their hands. Green and white lightning surged from the stone and into their palms.

The earth rumbled. Terror seized the nearby cryptos. Ed was nearly trampled by a fleeing minotaur. A raging whirlwind swirled around Lotus, Judy, and the stone. Gravity went weird and Ed was drawn toward the storm. A three-headed hellhound dug its claws into the street, but the force ripped it free. The cyclone snatched up the crypto and disintegrated the helpless hound. Chunks of asphalt, fence planks, clumps of grass and dirt, and unfortunate cryptos were swallowed by the storm. Debris was flung in all directions, and what didn't get thrown out of the storm was consumed by it. Ed grabbed ahold of an SUV door handle as she was lifted off her feet.

The last few inches between the two women and the stone were the hardest. The stone went through a rainbow of colors. Golden lines, hidden runes of ancient power, formed on the women's flesh.

Monster and Chester stopped at the edge of the gravity anomaly. Monster leaned back and braced himself to avoid being swept up into the void. Chester clung to Monster's leg.

The world trembled as if it might shake apart. Car alarms blared. Every house and streetlight came on spontaneously and burned bright enough to turn the night into day for a few seconds before exploding.

"So what do we do now, boss?" shouted Chester over the howling winds and grumbling earth.

Monster didn't have an answer.

Judy and Lotus touched the stone at the same moment. The whirlwind instantly vanished. The ground ceased rumbling, and the stone went black as the runes faded from its face. The force Monster had been resisting faded, and he fell over.

Judy and Lotus stared into each other's eyes in the eerie quiet. The runes rose off their skin and whirled around them, struggling for dominance.

"Is this a good thing or a bad thing?" asked Chester.

"Bad," said Monster.

A residual connection to the stone remained with him, and he could sense the struggle raging beneath the surface of the universe as Lotus and Judy fought for control. Under the right circumstances, this could be a battle of equals, a stalemate lasting until the end of time. But they weren't equals. Not quite.

Lotus had the edge. She wasn't so easily shed. The stone still feared her, couldn't stop feeding her. Judy had interrupted that flow of power, but it was only a temporary disruption. The balance would shift. Lotus would take control, and she would hijack Judy's momentary oneness with the universe to fulfill her agenda.

"If we can separate Lotus, we might be able to break the stalemate," said Monster.

The wind kicked up, and a slight tremor churned the broken asphalt. Judy and Lotus glowed, but Lotus shone just a little brighter. Monster picked his way across the uneven ground.

Ed stepped in the way. "I'm awfully sorry, but I can't let you interfere. Mrs. Lotus wouldn't—"

He put his hand on her shoulder. The spark passed between them. Ed whinnied as she ripped out of her clothes and reverted to her equine form. She reared up and bolted down the street.

Transforming Ed had used up the last of the magic the stone had given Monster. He retreated as the gathering power caused the sky to burn while the asphalt glowed beneath Judy and Lotus's feet. Monster was scarlet now, immune to heat. Either a parting gift from the stone or a lucky break.

"What's wrong?" asked Chester.

"What am I doing? I gotta be crazy."

Monster backed away.

"But what about Judy?" said Chester.

"What about me?" replied Monster. "This is her destiny. I'm just some dumbass who got swept up in it."

"You can't just run away."

"Sure I can."

He turned, but Chester jumped in his path. "Damn it, Monster. You have to stop doing this."

Monster glanced over his shoulder. Judy and Lotus boiled with power. Nearby fences and lawns caught fire. Chester withered and crinkled at the edges.

"Is this how you want to keep living your life?" asked Chester. "Always making the same mistake, always listening to the instinct of the moment?"

Monster tried to speak, but Chester held up his tattered and smoking hand.

"Let me finish. I don't know how much longer this body will hold out.

"I've been coming to this universe for a long time now, and in all this time, I've seen some very stupid behavior. But then I reminded myself that you're just bags of meat doing the best you can with what you've got. And from that perspective I guess you're doing all right, even if mostly driven by the same selfish instincts that compel all blobs of marginally sentient protoplasm. It's just what you are, and I try not to judge you for it."

The fingers on Chester's right hand started burning. He tore off the limb, tossing it away before the fire could spread.

"You are the most shortsighted, impulsive, and self-centered blob of protoplasm I have ever met. But here's your chance, Monster. It's time to prove that you aren't just one bad decision after another, that you can do what needs to be done when it comes right down to it. It's time to be more than just a human being looking out for himself. Or you can be just another blob of protoplasm. It's your call."

Chester burst into flame. "Damn it, that stings." He burned away.

Judy and Lotus were ablaze now. White fire danced along their bodies. They weren't burning, but nothing else could get close without being overwhelmed by the heat.

Though immune to normal heat, Monster was sweating. Every sensible instinct told him to run, even though there was nowhere to go. Chester could abandon his body and retreat to a safe other-dimensional distance. But Monster wasn't a parahuman immigrant. He was stuck here in this universe, and whatever happened between Lotus and Judy would affect the whole thing.

He wasn't important. He knew that. He was just some guy caught in a battle between titans. He didn't see how he could affect that battle either way. It would be smarter to just ride it out and hope for the best.

The fire erupted in a tower of white hot flame. Monster wasn't blinded by the light, but he shielded his eyes by reflex. In the heart of the column of fire, the silhouettes of Judy and Lotus stood locked in their standoff.

Monster hesitated, unable to either flee or go forward.

He ran through his choices. He could throw himself into the flames and do something. He wasn't sure what, but he didn't have time to think that far ahead. Or he could just hide and ride it out.

Chester had been right. That was what Monster always did. He just went with the flow, let life and circumstances push him around. It hadn't been working out very well, but in this case, going against that instinct probably meant being incinerated in the magical pyre that sealed Judy and Lotus away from the rest of the universe.

He stuck his hand into the pyre. His scarlet skin darkened but didn't burn. He pulled it out and inspected the limb. Still solid. Moist with sweat, but otherwise not a blackened stump.

"Man or protoplasm," he mumbled. "Which is it, Monster?"

In the heart of the fire, Judy's knees wobbled, and a ripple ran through the universe as reality was rewritten. Whiskers sprouted on his face, and fur grew along his arms. He ran his fingers across his pointed ears.

He lowered his head and plunged into the flames before he could talk himself out of it. Though the unnatural heat was stifling, he wasn't blasted into ashes. He kept his eyes on his goal. Every step was harder than the last as his feet sank into the street, a sea of boiling tar. He had to keep moving or else he'd sink up to his knees. Halfway there, his shoes got stuck, but his shrinking feet slipped loose. His suddenly large clothes fell off as he became a scarlet cat. Lighter and faster, he danced across the sticky tar even as his mind became foggy. But he kept reminding himself that he had to reach Lotus. Even after every other human thought disappeared, he managed to hold on to that one. Claws extended, he hurled himself onto Lotus's leg just as the tar threatened to drag him under.

Lotus was unaccustomed to pain, having not experienced it in several millennia. But the stone's protection was gone, and the scratching, biting, hissing feline climbing up her leg took her completely by surprise. Shrieking, she released the stone and whirled, beating at Monster as he sank his fangs into her rump.

The tower of flame disappeared and the sea of tar instantly cooled into an uneven black plain. Judy and the stone burned brighter.

Lotus finally succeeded in detaching the Monster, who was a cat in mind and body now. He hissed and spat, arching his back and raising his hackles. She pointed at him, blasting a stream of fire. It disintegrated before reaching him.

She tried again, but nothing happened. A chill breeze swept over her, and Lotus shivered.

Judy held the stone under her arm.

"That's mine!" shouted Lotus. "How dare you!"

She charged like a slathering beast. Judy made a small gesture. Barely a flick of the wrist. The tar liquefied under Lotus and sucked her under. She was up to her waist before it turned solid again.

Lotus leaned forward and continued to claw at the air with her hands.

"You can't have it! You can't control it! Give it to me before the power drives you mad and you ruin everything!"

Purring, Monster rubbed against Judy's leg.

"It's over," said Judy to Lotus. "Can't you see that?"

"No! It's never over! There is a way to things, a natural order! The stone and I are one. We always have been."

"Not anymore."

Lotus went limp. She struggled to hold herself together, but she was a parasite without a host. She raised a trembling arm as she stared with burning eyes at the stone. Then the fire fizzled and Lotus disappeared, back to the formless nothingness from which she had been spawned.

Judy felt the universe all around her. A surge of revitalizing power flooded into it as everything that Lotus had been holding on to returned to the stone. There wasn't much time. Only a few seconds before the alignment would fail and Judy's perfect communion with the stone would end.

She willed the destruction gone, and the neighborhood was restored. There was no flash, no divine thunder. It was just fixed.

Monster mewed at her feet. Judy scratched him on the head, and she willed him to become whatever he wanted. Human or cat—it was his choice.

Naked, scarlet, and furless, he squatted beside her. He stood and didn't bother to cover himself. He was just happy to be human again.

"Did we win?"

"We won," she replied. "Though it isn't quite over."

She held the stone before her. Even without the perfect attunement, she would become the most powerful being in the universe if she held on to it. She felt the stone object to this arrangement, but it couldn't stop her. Nothing could. This power was hers now, and it would take at least another billion years before the stone could try to take it away. And even that wasn't guaranteed to work.

It was only fair. Her life had been a mess because of what the stone had made her into. She didn't need to hold the power forever. Just a few years to make up for the annoyances she'd suffered in the name of the greater good. Wasn't she owed at least a decade of near omnipotence? Maybe two. Was a century really that big a deal in the grand scale of time? She could give it back after she'd indulged herself for a millennium or two, and everything would work out fine in the end.

The stone filled Judy's mind with a billion years' worth of memories, of the long, long life of the last creature to covet its power above all else. The power the stone offered wasn't really good for anything. It could transform every person into a cat, move planets, create universes. But for a human being, it was worthless, a glittering bauble that granted immortality and awesome power but nothing of practical value.

Lotus had lived for ages, but she hadn't really lived at all. A life span of billions of years, existing for no other reason than to keep existing. That wasn't living, and Judy should know. That had been Judy's life for as long as she could remember. Because until today, that was the best she could hope for.

But now it was time for things to change.

Judy threw the stone in the air. It hurtled upward and onward. Now that Lotus was gone, the stone was free to return to its original unformed state. It disappeared in a flash.

She felt human again. And maybe really alive for the first time.

"Is it over?" asked Monster as he slipped into his pants.

"No," she replied. "It's only just beginning."

The next four weeks were busy for CCRS. A surplus of cryptobiologicals had been released during Judy's ascendancy, and they didn't just disappear after it was over. Monster scored four times the bags of even his busiest weeks, and he wasn't the only one. Every freelance agent was working fourteen hours a day in an effort to keep things under control. Monster was no exception, and though he was initially grateful for the extra income, he was beginning to wear down.

It was probably how the kobold got the jump on him. At least, that was what he told himself afterward.

The hairy crypto leaped out of the doghouse and snapped at him. Monster fell in the grass, still wet from the sprinklers. The kobold chuckled at Monster before scrambling over the fence and disappearing.

"I got it!" said Chester.

Monster stood. "Let it go. It's been a long night, and I'm tired."

Chester shrugged. "Whatever you say."

The homeowners stuck their heads out of the house. "Did you get it?" asked the wife. "The thing."

Monster tugged at his wet pants clinging to his ass and thighs. "It ran off."

"It wasn't a dog, was it?"

"No, but it won't be back."

"But what was it?" she asked.

"Just a kobold, ma'am," said Chester, "but there's nothing to worry about."

The couple looked at Chester and smiled awkwardly. The response was becoming more common. Neither full incognizant haze nor light incog passing acceptance nor cognizant awareness. But something else.

People were starting to notice magic.

It wasn't as if all the incogs just opened their eyes and acknowledged it. But Monster caught more of them looking at the cryptos in their midst with a vague acknowledgment that this was unusual, that the sea serpent in their bathtub was more than just a "big snake" and that the vampiric, disembodied heads floating in their attics weren't just a "bat problem."

Things were changing.

Magic was getting easier to remember. Even for cogs. It'd been at least a week since he'd had to consult his dictionary. The runes just came to him when he needed them. The cognizant community was abuzz with the discovery that they too had been laboring under their own haze—not as powerful or obvious as the haze on incogs, but still there and still dulling their senses. A fog unperceived by anyone and everyone until it mysteriously lifted. Advanced theoretical thaumaturgists were still speculating about what caused the so-called New Enlightenment.

No one had bothered to ask Monster.

Chester and Monster climbed into his new van. It was new in the sense that he'd just bought it. Otherwise, it was the same white model he'd lost to the kojin attack. There were actually a few more dents, but the air-conditioning worked, so as far as he was concerned it was a step up.

The radio crackled to life. "Monster, I've got a call for you."

He stifled a yawn as he lifted the mouthpiece. "Count me out, Charlene."

"It's just a pickup," replied Charlene. "The caller said the crypto is already contained."

"So send someone else."

"They asked for you specifically."

Monster suspected. He didn't suspect anything specific, but he hesitated.

"If you don't want it, I could always let Hardy have it," said Charlene.

Monster snarled. "Screw that. I'll take it."

"The Oak Pines apartments. Do you need the address?"

"No, I got it."

"Isn't that kind of a contradiction?" asked Charlene. "I don't think trees can be both oaks and pines."

Chester folded his arms and cleared his throat.

"Do you think it's Judy?" he asked.

"Don't know. Don't care."

"Come on. You can't tell me you aren't curious. You haven't talked to her since that night, right?"

"Nope."

"The two of you restored balance to the universe," said Chester, "vanquished an ancient cosmic parasite. You don't wonder what's happened to her since then?"

"Nope."

"You'd think that there'd be some kind of special bond between the two of you. Like old army buddies who have been under fire together."

"Nope."

Chester said, "Your universe has just gotten a fresh start, a chance to finally grow into something more. It seems to me that a person with any sense at all would take that opportunity to grow with it."

"Mmm-hmm," said Monster as he sipped a cup of coffee.

They arrived at Oak Pines. Paulie was sitting outside his apartment.

"Hey, dudes!" said Paulie.

Monster mumbled a reply and nodded, but kept walking. Judy's old apartment was still in ruins. Construction had just started.

He found the second-floor apartment Charlene had given him and knocked on the door. A young girl answered.

"You must be the blue guy and the paper guy." She looked Monster over. "Why aren't you blue?"

"Sorry to disappoint," replied Monster.

"We're here for the cryptobiological," said Chester.

"Yeah, sure." Shouting, she retreated into the apartment. "Aunt Judy, the blue guy's here! But he's burgundy! Maybe radish-colored!" She plopped onto a couch, stuck in some earphones, and flipped through a video game magazine.

Judy stuck her head out of the kitchenette. "Hey, guys. Come on in."

Monster stepped inside. "So you moved back here?"

"Eh, the rent is good. And the new manager is actually a decent guy."

"Who's the kid?"

"My niece," said Judy. "She's staying with me for a while

until my sister and her husband settle with the insurance company for the house."

"Yeah," said Monster. "Sorry about that."

"Forget it. You did what you had to. It's kind of a good thing. Gave me a chance to get to know Nancy." She walked over and gave Nancy a hug. Nancy half smiled, though she quickly masked it under some artificial annoyance.

"She's actually a pretty cool kid," said Judy. "Don't let the reception fool you."

"Uh-huh," said Monster. "So where's the crypto?"

Judy went to the bedroom and returned with a transmogrified crypto in rock form.

"Thanks. What is it?"

"Naga," she said. "Just a little one."

"Are you still having crypto trouble?" asked Chester.

"No, that problem is over. No more subconscious manipulation of the fabric of the universe for me anymore, thank God. I just found this one outside and thought you might like it."

"Who transmogrified it?"

"I did. I've been studying up." She pointed to a few used magical textbooks on a shelf.

"You're cognizant now?" asked Chester.

"I guess so, but then again, I'm not the only one, am I?"

"That's wonderful news."

"Wonderful," agreed Monster halfheartedly. "So if that's all you need—"

"How long have you been studying?" said Chester.

"About two weeks," she replied.

"And you can already accomplish a full-fledged transmogrification? That's amazing."

"Amazing." Monster reached for the doorknob. "So I really have to be going—"

"Are you thinking about a career change, Judy?" said Chester.

"I'm considering a few things." She smiled. "If I can bring myself to leave the glamorous world of stacking canned goods into decorative pyramids."

"Tell you what, Chester," said Monster. "I'll meet you in the van when you two are done catching up."

"Monster, wait."

He stopped halfway out the door. "What?"

"I just thought that maybe we were friends now or something."

"Why?"

"I don't know. It's just something you see in the movies all the time. Two people meet and at first they don't get along. Then they go through some big crisis, help each other out, develop a begrudging level of respect."

"Movies, huh?" He laughed. "Sounds like bullshit to me."

"Guess so, but you helped me get on with my life. I'm free. For the first time in my life, I'm living for me. No destiny or cryptos screwing with my life anymore. You didn't have to do that. You could've run away and left me to Lotus."

"No, I couldn't." He grimaced. "I hate cats."

They shared a laugh.

"Monster, you're not as big a jerk as you give in your first impression. Just wanted to let you know that."

"Thanks."

"No matter what else," she said, "we did do something special, didn't we? Something important."

"I guess we did."

She offered her hand, and they shook. "Take care of yourself, Monster."

"You too."

After they left Judy's apartment, Chester asked, "Something bothering you?"

"It's nothing."

"Come on. I know you. You've been down these last couple of weeks. Even by your standards. Don't deny it."

Monster didn't respond.

"Later, dudes!" shouted Paulie.

Monster climbed into his van and started it up. He stared out the window with a slight frown.

"Do you want to know what's bothering me?"

"I asked, didn't I?" said Chester.

"Magic is making a comeback."

"Isn't that a good thing?"

"It's a good thing for most people."

"You've lost me."

"It's simple. Everyone is starting to figure it out. The one thing that gave me any edge in this world at all is changing. And it's all my fault."

He dropped his head against the steering wheel.

"And to top it off, I lost my girlfriend and my job is more work than I ever wanted now."

Chester patted Monster on the back. "I hadn't thought of it like that. I guess that is kind of a lousy turn of events for you. Although, your girlfriend was a demon."

"Still the best relationship I ever had," mumbled Monster. "I should've stayed a cat."

Someone knocked on the window. He turned his head very slowly and looked into the smiling face of an angel.

He rolled down the window.

"You're Monster, right?" asked Gracie.

He nodded without raising his head off the wheel.

"Can you give me a lift?"

"What about that guy?" He pointed vaguely in Paulie's direction without turning to look at him.

"Don't get me started on him," she said. "If you haven't anything nice to say, don't say anything at all. That's my credo."

"You and Thumper," said Monster.

"So can you give me a lift or not?"

He sighed. "Hop in."

Gracie jumped into the passenger side. She pulled her wings close, but they still brushed up against Monster.

"If you don't need anything else, I'll be clocking out, boss."

"Knock yourself out."

Chester folded into a square and tucked himself into Monster's pocket.

"Where to?" Monster asked Gracie.

She frowned. "You look sad. Why so down?"

"It's nothing," he said.

She wrinkled her nose and noticed his fresh, brimstone-free scent. "Well, I'm glad to see that you ditched your demon girlfriend, at least."

"I killed her," said Monster.

"Good for you. I know that you're not perfect, but a cute guy like you can do better than that."

"You think I'm cute?"

"Sure. Who doesn't like a red guy?"

She smiled.

"I'm not always red," he said.

Gracie winked. "Even better." She struggled with her seatbelt, but her wings made it difficult. "After I'm done with this errand, do you want to maybe grab a cup of coffee or something?"

"Are you asking me out?"

"Maybe. I just figured we could hang out, have some laughs, see what happens. You look like you could use some cheering up, and that's my job, isn't it?"

"I thought you didn't help people like me," said Monster. "Not-nice people."

"I don't know what you've been doing lately, but there's some positive energy in your aura that is just gosh darn sexy."

"I helped fix the universe. At least, I think I helped fix it. I'm not really sure. I did something with the universe, anyway. So, angels can date humans?"

"Fiddlesticks." She gave up on the belt, tossing it aside. "Sure. Your imperfect souls are amusing but tend to make long-term relationships difficult. Most angel-human relationships are all about sex. Is that all right with you?"

Smiling, Monster pulled his van into the street.